The Flowers

The Flowers

Dagoberto Gilb

GROVE PRESS/NEW YORK

Published simultaneously in Canada
Printed in the United States of America

FIRST EDITION

ISBN-10: 0-8021-1859-3
ISBN-13: 978-0-8021-1859-2

Grove Press
an imprint of Grove/Atlantic, Inc.
841 Broadway
New York, NY 10003

Distributed by Publishers Group West

www.groveatlantic.com

08 09 10 11 12   10 9 8 7 6 5 4 3 2 1

The Flowers

Not that many years ago I would go to a house in the neighborhood, not always someone's I knew, one I'd never been inside of, where I'd only have to maybe hop a fence, nothing complicated, and from the backyard I'd crawl through an open window. People always latch the ones in the front but never in the back, and especially not the bathroom one, you know, and it wasn't so small I couldn't get in quick. I could've stole lots of shit in those houses, except that's not what I was going in there for. I wasn't like that. Maybe I don't know exactly what I was doing except I was doing it. I never took nothing, nothing much if I did, because I didn't want to. I was more watching how the people lived, imagining how it would be in their house. I stared at the framed pictures they had of their family. Husbands in suits and wives with necklaces and old grandparents from the other times way before. Unsmiling dudes, glaring at you, in tilted military hats and coats with medals and ribbons. Full-body shots of happy daughters in white veils and lacy crunchy wedding dresses that poured all over into the bottom of the picture. Shocked little babies on blue backgrounds squinting like What's going on here, what's all this light shit? Dopey-dumb I'm-so-proud high schoolers graduating and making a face like they were department store managers. If I felt like it, if I had the mood, I sprawled out on their couches or lay down on their beds. Go, How would I be if I lived here? I'd let that come into me, I'd let my mind go to the show it liked. Maybe you could say I would go off to my own world. To me it wasn't mine, nothing like mine, because it would go to black. I loved that color. It was like when the eyes aren't open but try to see. What would finally come were colors and lines busting through, flying out and off and cutting in, crazy fires and sparks, and it'd come out speeding, and I'd be like a doggie out the window, those lane dividers whiffing by on the freeway straight below an open car window. I'd start to see shapes floating and straightening and wiggling and see it like it was a music that didn't make sound but was making a story. Not a regular story and I don't mean one you would hear some loco nut tell you, one that didn't have nothing to do with people or places you've ever seen. It's that I can't describe it better. Just, I have to watch, I have to listen. It was always good too. Say like when you hear music and it gets inside your brain and goes and goes, sticking there. And so I guess it got in mine like that. I listened and watched until I stopped getting too stupid because, you know, I had to leave and get out of there fast. And once I got up, shook it off and remembered where I really was, even if I opened their refrigerator, when I looked inside, wasn't like I didn't think of eating or drinking, I didn't take even a soda, thirsty as I might have been. I didn't want them to know I'd been there. Though I kind of opened the fridge door because maybe I do think of—well, like orange juice. It's that I like orange juice. So maybe when there was some orange juice I might have taken a gulp or two. But see, even then, nobody'd really know. One time I was in this one house, and I was looking inside a drawer in this girl's bedroom. I knew about her because she was this dude's older sister, and she was in junior college. It was that there were a bunch of bras, and I picked

them up and looked at them, touched them because I was holding them. Wasn't like I never seen my mom's and my sister's,
it wasn't like I didn't know the difference. And it was the only
time there was something like that, swear, and I did stop and
yeah I still got jumpy about it and felt like it was fucked up,
real bad of me and afterward I only snuck into one more house.
Like I said, I didn't know what I was doing it for, and it wasn't
like I liked doing it.

I heard this shit because she was on the phone and I listened to
her. It was her sound, a white ripply line right into the black.
Not above. Black was everywhere and the white came from the
front, above, maybe below. I don't know. I think it was Nely
she was talking to, probably. That was who she talked to. That's
who I thought. My mom was going like *What can he do?* and *So
what he screamed. Listen to me,* she said. *No, listen to me. No, listen,
listen.* And I listened to what I could. I saw the white ribbon
curling and swirling. *Men.* She kind of laughed. *He will never know,*
she said. *Ay, ay, no!* She laughed. She said, *He is a man, and I
didn't ask for that.* She was laughing but not laughing happy and
I'm listening and I'm like going to that somewhere else inside
my head, all by myself.

I got worried I was getting sent to juvie when I did have to go
to the court because of nothing, for so much less. That was this
time when the police scraped the tires of their black-and-white
against the curb ahead of me. I was walking by myself. At first
I didn't believe it was about me, but that policeman kept wanting to know what I was doing. I was not wanting to say. Okay,
maybe, even really I was scared like anybody and I didn't want
to show it but probably I did. How was I supposed to answer
because what'd I do? I was just walking, you know? Maybe a
couple days earlier I pocketed a chocolate bar and I folded a baby

comic book down my pants. It wasn't like the first time I did that, and when I did get caught this one and only time, when a drug-store man yelled something, I ran, and I never made it back to that store again and that was the worst of it and that already was back then, and no way anyone could still care or remember. So the passenger policeman who came up to me first, he goes, *So what're you doing?* and I'm like, *Walking on the street, mister,* which is when the driver policeman comes around to stand next to his partner, and he frowns at me too, like I'm stinky. Until a second or so later, he gets this expression on his face. His eyes go a little up to the sky, and his body gets kind of stiff, and he blows this fat old pedo. And so, like anybody would, I laughed. I did because it was funny, right? And so yeah I'm all guilty of laughing. But that's when they both get all blowed up mad—I'm disrespectful, and I got attitude, and who did I think I am? They got so close into my face I thought they were gonna kick the crap outta me. And so that's why I had to go to the juvie court, to hear a commercial about disrespecting the police and authority and to hear about all the potential trouble I was going to be in if I didn't go right and goodboy, straighten out and care about school and my education and get good grades. My mom had to be there with me too. She had to take off from work and listen and act like she was all worked up about me too, which she wasn't, I knew it, because I heard her talking all the time on the phone about what she was up with, but the lady judge wasn't going to notice nothing. Once I told my mom how the police dude threw a fart, she cracked up just like me, because it was funny, right? But I knew not to say nothing to a judge about what really happened. I'm not stupid. That judge, she wouldn't have laughed, and then I don't think my mom would've laughed no more, and she never laughed as much as me. She was tired, and she didn't like to waste time because she was already way too busy.

It was that my mom, if she wasn't at her job, was out on dates and whatever. And sometimes she'd get in so late I wouldn't be awake. That was better for me than when she was home, because when she was home, though I lived there and slept there, it was better to be inside a neighbor's house than pissing her off. She could get all mad and complaining about me and go how I messed up this and that and she could yell at me how she couldn't afford a maid to clean up after me, though once in a while a lady named Marta, a sister of a friend, would come to pick up the house and scrub the floors and wash windows and dishes and vacuum even under the torn couch cushions. That Marta thought I was all right because I made my own dinner and lunch and did my shit without nobody. She told me whenever she came too. That didn't mean much to me except when I was getting yelled at and I knew it really wasn't about none of what the yelling was about. Probably my mom's screaming at me was that it used to be my sister, Ceci, she would yell at. Then it got to be me. I didn't ever believe it was because I was a man or made bigger messes, like she said. My mom used to fight loud with my sister. She would get so she'd go after Ceci with belts or wooden hangers or whatever was near. One time it was a soda bottle. I remember that time good. I was eating banana after banana during the fight and my mom turned on me for one second too— maybe why was I eating all the bananas the minute she bought them—and my sister screamed right back so much it jumped back over to them and they called each other out, like they would go at it for real. Sometimes both of them would cry for a while during and after, though mostly it was my sister, once she got old enough, and meaner, until she finally stopped being at home much. Ceci wasn't talking to me very much then either. Then they were both gone mostly. It was just, without my sister there, I was starting to have the whole house, like it was mine. I never got hit or yelled at like Ceci. My mom would be around for maybe an hour or two, and she'd either change clothes and leave or be so tired she went into her bedroom and went to sleep.

This one night I was watching the TV. I already ate a cheese enchilada frozen dinner, which was crap, and the fried chicken, which I loved but my mom said cost too much. My dog, who I named Goofy because of her floppy black ears even though she was a girl dog, was with me on the couch after she licked the tin containers all clean, dragging them all around with her tongue, then scratching and biting at her pulgas back near my lap, when all the sudden she heard something and she was digging her claws against my legs because she was on it before a human ear could, running so fast she was barely able to make a corner turn to the straight-ahead for the front door, barking all excited like it was somebody she hadn't seen all day. I didn't hear nothing, probably because I had that TV on and nobody ever knocked on the door unless it was a Mormon or Jehovah or one of those ex-tecatos who love Jesus like their heroin, and I learned to stop opening the door for any of them. Usually I wouldn't even look if I did hear but because Goofy's barking so crazy I go, and before I even get near the door I could feel the pounding on it through the floor and I heard some man yelling at it loud and he's beating on it, so hard that it's shaking and rattling. I ain't going to answer but he keeps hitting on the door so much I can't help myself, the words pop out of me that my mom's not here. It was that he was screaming about her. He was screaming like *You bitch, open the fucking door right now, you goddamn thief, you slut, you bitch, open this door, Silvia, right now, or I'll fucking bust it in.*

I was standing there not sure what to say or do next, Goofy all barking and wagging like it was something fun.

"Open the door," he says. "Open the fucking door."

And without thinking first, now I'm talking too. I'm saying no. I'm saying that my mom's not home. I go reach over and check that it's still locked, and I hook the chain thing, backing away from it as quickly as I got close.

"Open the door," he says. He was beating on it so that the door was wanting to give in. "Open it!" I felt like the whole house was shaking.

Finally I can think for a second. It was hard because Goofy was going all crazy. "She's not home!" I shouted. I can think finally, and what I'm thinking is that I know who it is. I'm thinking it's the man I heard her talking on the phone about. That once he'd shot a man. That he got drunk a lot. This man's voice sounded drunk.

"You open the door," he says, "or do you want me to bust it in?"

I swear he was slugging the door with his fist, and there was like a crackling wood sound.

"Do you hear me, kid? Do you fucking hear me?"

I'm whispering to Goofy to stop barking, *Come on, Goof,* trying to make her calm, but she's on automatic. It got like she was barking at another dog and wanting to bite.

"Where is the bitch? You tell that fucking mother of yours to open the door or I'm busting it in right now! You hear me?"

I ran to the kitchen. I had to open a bunch of drawers because my mom never put things in the same ones or maybe I didn't because I didn't know which drawer either. I found that big knife. It was as long as my wrist, a wood handle. As soon as I grip it in my hand, I don't feel as scared. I didn't care if he carried a gun. He comes in, I cut the dude. Goofy was still wailing at the door and he was still hitting on it and saying shit but it seemed quieter to me. I walked back a little slow, and I didn't go near the door but to one side of it. I held the big knife in my hand and I'm gripping it so hard I didn't feel like it was a knife but me.

The man started kicking the door. Then he was throwing his body against it, and you could hear wood cracking. I'm just standing there and I didn't hear Goofy no more, if she was even barking. When the door blasts, splintering the side it opened on, it swung so hard and wild that Goofy didn't move away and she made a loud crying yelp, getting thrown against the wall, crushed between it and the door. The man was standing outside on the front porch and breathing fast. He rolled up the sleeves of his white business shirt and tucked it into his black slacks and there was some tattoo on his right forearm muscle and he had on a slippery tie loose around an unbuttoned collar and he was big. His face all purple. Real quick Goofy went back to her barking again and the man couldn't figure out which of us to look at first until I see him see my knife. His eyes were slits but I could feel heat and breathing out of them too and I was standing there maybe ten feet away, one hand with the big knife loaded in it, the other hand clenched and a little up, looking ready to jab in a left-right combination.

"Watch yourself now, kid," he says, stepping inside toward me.

I stepped back, though not like I was backing off.

"You have to put that down right now," he says to me. "You just drop it, okay kid?"

I didn't say nothing. I stepped back once more, keeping the same distance between us. He stepped toward me again and I backed up once more, thinking where a knife should go. . . .

Then he went at me. He was so fast he took me down even before I saw him come and his hand locked my hand with the knife in it to the floor. He pushed the air out of me because his body on me was so heavy I couldn't breathe. Goofy was growling and biting him and I was trying to at least kick his nuts but I didn't do a thing to him and when I made him roll a little, it made the knife dig into my own stomach.

He got me onto my back and pinned me, both my hands pressed to the floor, his knees into my chest, hurting my ribs, the knife not cutting me or him.

"Stop," he says, too close to my face. "You gonna stop?" Goofy was back to biting him and that was when he let go of me, ripping the knife away from me as he stood up. Goofy kept going for his leg until his hard black shoe lifted her jaw and head when he kicked her there really hard, and she whimpered, hurt. I got up once he got off me, and I was crying, and I saw how I was bleeding at my stomach. It didn't hurt or nothing yet. He was standing there watching me for what might not have been such a long time, and then he just turned around and took off out the broken front door.

And so all the time it seemed like I was hearing her on the phone when I didn't want to. I probably wanted to know, but I didn't want to hear. Wondered who it was when I heard her going, *Whatever I have to do,* or, *No, I won't, no.* The phone was nothing good. It was like waiting on a school bell, jumping at how loud and always expecting. When I can't not listen in on her, I want to smash that quiet between. When it was her voice I was following, when there was silence it meant that some shit would hit. So I tried to never listen. I made it go black inside my head, and then words, when she'd make them, were these shapes that wormed around, spraying light that would disappear into a hole that was bigger than any room I been in.

It was like right then, even if it was really days or something, that my mom introduced me to Cloyd Longpre. He was wearing a fake blue suit and tie. I never saw him in one ever again. Also, his hair was all pomade oil. That also would be the only time it was so neat that you could see the comb lines. I was sitting on our couch in the living room, and he sat in a chair—it was Goofy's favorite unless she was sitting with me on the couch watching the TV—across from me, a kind of stupid but really happy stupid smile on his face. He had a silver tooth on one side, showing at the edge of his mouth. Between us was the floor where I'd been taken down. I was still feeling mad about it, so there was that. Not the cut. I didn't care about that. It didn't hurt no more. It didn't really hurt even when it was supposed to, right after. My mom was sitting next to me. She was wearing a flower dress—I think roses, though I call all flowers roses—a new one, and shiny red shoes that matched. She was being too pretty like always. I loved my mom, and sometimes it scared me because I thought maybe I wasn't supposed to say that even to myself. Maybe I wouldn't have thought about it except that I was always seeing how men looked at her. When I did too, just to think about what it was about, I knew what it was about. How pretty she was in the way men are flipping through pages of dirty magazines. My mom sometimes would go around in her bra and panties in the house. You know, especially in her bedroom and bathroom and between. Nothing fucked up, she just wasn't embarrassed. So seeing her, I really started knowing what it was about her. It made me sick when I did too. I even had some bad dreams a couple of times. One that made me the most upset was that I was going up some stairs and then I opened a door and went to the bed there to—well, you know, and when I was getting in and shit like that I saw how it was my mom and I jumped right out of that dream. It woke me up feeling messed up.

Cloyd Longpre had questions. He was trying to show he was, you know, interested in me. That I mattered to him. It was a show for my mom. He thought it would matter to her. It was hard for me to pretend back. There was nothing I could do about who my mom went out with, and mostly I didn't say or think shit about it. But there was something else I couldn't point to about him, and it made it even longer to sit there.

"You look a lot bigger for your age," he said.

I should say no? I should say right?

"Built," he went on. "Strong." He looked at my mom, stupid smiling. "I could maybe even put him to work now."

I looked at my mom too. She had an expression that this Cloyd was supposed to see as proud and that for me was to feel proud too. He was only flirting with her, and she was only going along with him.

"You gonna play football?"

I played street and schoolyard football a lot. My side usually won. I played for the junior high team for two games and stopped. I made more touchdowns on kickoffs than anyone, more on interceptions too, and we won, but then I stopped going. I didn't like coaches telling me nothing, yelling. They screamed and shit and so fuck them. I didn't like nobody getting on me, never. Pissed me off bad. I didn't watch sports on TV, college or pro. Sports was in my head, it was just for me to play, a game to keep the brain in shape. I could play but didn't and didn't say any of this to him though, because I could play this game too and already I thought maybe I had to.

"Dile, tell him," my mom said. "He's an athlete, always the fastest runner."

She didn't know that. It wasn't even true no more. It hadn't been true since elementary, since sixth grade, when I finally got beat by a black dude who was four legs and I never could beat, hard as I tried and I tried. That other time, hundreds of years ago, was probably the last time I told her about anything that made me happy—or that she heard from me anyways.

"But you like sports?" he asked.

"Sure," I said, my first sound in front of him. That was because I wanted to make my mom happy, not him.

"I like sports," Cloyd Longpre said. "Though I can't say I get to follow it much these days."

"Maybe he likes baseball," my mom told him. "I think that's his favorite." She came over and sat on the armrest of the couch, next to me. She touched my hair like she did her skirt when she first sat there. "Don't you, m'ijo?" She had no idea. We never talked nothing about me.

He didn't wait to hear an answer from me. "What about huntin'?" he said. "You like huntin'? You ever been?"

"No sir, " I said.

He smiled and it came out dumb. This was when I saw it that way for the first time. It was that he meant it, it was a real and honest smile, and it came out looking stupid. "No sir you never been, or no sir you don't like it?" When he said *no sir,* I could tell he was making fun of how I said it.

"He's never been," my mom told him for me fast, defensively.

"That I never been," I told him. I don't know which I would have answered if my mom hadn't jumped in for me. The truth is, I didn't want to go hunting and especially not with this hillbilly.

"You'd love it," he said. "Wait till you eat fresh venison or fresh duck. Nothing better."

I was back to not knowing what to say, or wanting to say something, and it was way quiet.

"I can get you a rifle," he said.

My mom looked at him sideways, then away from him, then moved like she wanted to stand up.

"Not a big one, Sil. Just a twenty-two. To get the boy used to it."

"No guns. I don't want him to shoot anybody," she said.

I didn't say. It didn't seem to be about the gun anyways.

"Well then, what would you like?" he asked me. "What would make you happy?"

My mom stood up, a little nervous, like she didn't know which way to go.

He noticed and spoke to her. "Okay. What say I promise any one big thing? How's that sound?" He ran his fingers through that greased-back hair of his and messed it some. Then to me— "You pick it."

My mom, for a second or two, made her mad look. Then, like that, she changed, and she went over to Cloyd Longpre and sat on the armrest of that chair. When she was next to him, and she put her hand on his shoulder, scratching him with her polished nails, he looked up at her like he was the luckiest man because her warm body was next to him, thank you, and thank you Lord. She made her eyes go like she's so flattered, and you're welcome. What he didn't know, and I did, was that she went like that lots of times. It was nothing special.

At the same time I watched this, while it seemed like he might have forgot, I thought of something to ask for.

"One thing?" I said.

He had his finger rubbing the belt of my mom's dress, above her butt.

"You name it, partner." That smile all stupid.

It's that I picked up on what was really going on here, and now I wanted to play too. I wanted to mess with him. "I wanna go to Notre Dame," I told him. Not that I did, because I didn't. I didn't care. It's what I thought of and I wanted to think of something. It's that I just saw a movie on TV, and people in it were at Notre Dame.

He made a laugh that went along with his smile. My mom was surprised too.

"You gotta get good grades to go there," he said, "and, son, that has all to do with you and nothing to do with me."

"No—" I started.

"Oh, I hear you! But I thought you weren't interested in football!" he said. "He wants to see a football game. Are they coming to town soon?"

It took me a couple of seconds. "No, that's not what I mean." I almost gave it up right there. Then I didn't. "I mean Notre Dame the church. The one in Paris. In France."

My mom and Cloyd Longpre both laughed like it was the wildest thing they'd ever heard. They didn't think I meant it. That I could possibly mean it.

"Oh, *that* Notre Dame game!" he said.

"Well, you said anything!" my mom said, laughing just like him.

"I did, I did," he said. "Wouldn't that cost a fortune!" he told her. "The boy don't think cheap, I give that to him."

His body leaned toward me from the chair.

"You keep your eyes open and you watch me surprise you," he told me. A couple of times in the sentence, he made fast winks, kind of crooked, like that was to let me know how this was a special communication between us only.

That he didn't believe me, or he did? I say that at first he didn't, but as he looked longer, he snagged something. Didn't catch what I was up to, because there was no way. I was good at not being seen inside, even if I wasn't sure yet how I would hold him to this promise or whatever you call it, or how I was going to make it into a big dream I was counting on. And so yeah he was on to something behind my eyes, because when we looked at each other again, him kind of rechecking, maybe he saw more, and he backed off wondering what I was up to.

I got one of the bedrooms in Cloyd Longpre's two-bedroom apartment. I never really thought about the bedroom I'd been in before that. For a while I'd shared it with my sister, until she made herself one out of the dining room to be alone, which had been where we watched TV, ate dinner, and I'd played with toys. That old bedroom wasn't mine no more than the kitchen or the bathroom or the whole house, but this new bedroom was in a land far

away from my home. It wasn't only because it'd been Cloyd
Longpre's son's, who'd left it like this hundreds of years ago with
all his junk still in it. For example, a really ugly red checkered
bedspread. I never even had a bedspread before. Only my mom
put one on her bed back in her room, and she only made it sometimes, when she was in a mood. In my home, I slept with a blanket, once in a while two when I got cold. When you pulled back
this bedspread deal here, there was a blanket and it also had one of
those sheets under it. I had a pillow for my old bed too, and it was
on the side where my head would go when I got in to go to sleep.
Here, the pillow was folded into the bedspread at the top, all show,
and above it was a headboard, one with a shelf cut to go inside it.
That was the only thing I got used to and even liked. It also wasn't
because I hated baseball pennants on the wall, but I did hate the
one about National Parks in Utah, and the one from Carlsbad
Caverns, and the one from the Grand Canyon—I wanted to yank
them down without asking. What did that have to do with where
I lived? Except why bother when I wasn't going to be here that
long, so I liked them there for proof I wasn't staying. Didn't ever
move the fishing rods in the corner, or the globe, which I sort of
liked really but I didn't spin around or even touch anyways because it wasn't mine, or the bookcase with a bunch of boyscout
camping books—which why would I fucking want and so I left
exactly there too. But no, I didn't sit down on the bed there thinking how I missed my old bedroom. I didn't have feelings nothing
like that. This just wasn't the bedroom back in my home and
wouldn't ever be and that's it.

"Whadaya think?" Cloyd Longpre asked me. He was standing at the door, grinning dumb, wearing his work uniform,
matching gray pants and shirt, laced high-top work boots. His
hair was messed up because he also wore a gray work cap, which
he was holding in his hand.

"It's okay," I said.

"I can get you a studying desk too," he said, looking at an empty space. "I got the one that was in here out back in the storage unit." He was trying to be nice, but really it was more have-to-be-nice than nice. It was to make my mom happy, probably.

"It's okay," I told him, shaking my head no.

"It's not a problem," he said. "It fits right there. I don't even remember why I took it out."

"I don't need it."

"I must have taken it out because it was broken, not just small. Yeah, I think that was what it was. But I can glue it up, make it work for you, and then I'm sure I can find you a chair for it."

"I don't need nothing, man." I was sounding nice, I swear.

He looked around and paused, but he was thinking about me. "You gotta study. That's what the Notre Dames want."

"I can probably just lay on the bed if I have to," I said, trying, honestly. Still, a few seconds later, I couldn't stop. "Notre Dame, France."

"Always good to have a desk," he said, copping attitude.

I was hoping not to talk much more. I didn't like the way it felt, me sitting there on the bed he owned, and him standing above me. "Yeah, thanks, but I don't want it." I looked up at him for less than a second, which was hard for me to do. "I like it here the way it is now."

"Have it your way," he said. Now he sounded ticked at me.

"Thanks though." I don't know why I didn't want to say it to him directly, but I said it looking away.

"You need anything. . . ." he said.

"A French book," I said.

It was almost like he was hearing me talk in French. "Wha'd you say?"

"A French book. I probably need a French book. To study it, you know?"

"O-kay," he said, making two words.

He almost closed the door behind him, but my mom was next, already pushing it back open. She'd had her nails done. It was how she was holding her hands.

"Is everything fine, m'ijo?"

I nodded.

"Then what's wrong?"

"Nothing."

"Nada nada?" She used a mami voice to me.

"Yeah. Nothing."

"It'll be good living here," she said. "Don't you think?"

I nodded like I was trying to really mean it.

"You'll see."

My mom was dressed too pretty to take serious, shampoo in her hair and body lotion smell, and she was trying too hard to sound happy. Nobody'd believe her except her.

"I won't have to work, so I'll even get to cook for you."

That made me smile because it was almost funny to imagine.

"I can too cook! Don't you laugh at me!"

Sometimes she'd cooked at home. She made enchiladas and tacos fast. What I loved was this deal made with noodles and beef and green chile and cheese and canned creamed corn. She would make one or the other of them for birthdays, although she usually bought our food someplace. I couldn't imagine her in the kitchen more than like once a month. First off, she didn't have the clothes for it. She'd have to buy special clothes. Second, moms who cooked were fat and slobby. And third, they wore their hair like for being home, for vacuuming and watching daytime TV. She never even watched TV. She wasn't any fat, and it seemed like she was always going to a

beauty parlor to try a new hairstyle, which everyone complimented her on because it would like "fit her face so well"—
what she'd say the girls said, no matter what style—and she had
to wear lots of shining jewelry. Nobody cooks meals wearing
hoop earrings and silver bracelets.

She came over and sat next to me on the bed, putting her
arm around me like she might make out with me. "Todavía
you're my baby boy, you know, and now I'm going to get to be
a mother for you. I know I haven't been. I haven't had any time
for you, have I?"

I shrugged. This whole scene was beginning to make me
pretty much think about, I don't know, studying French, just to
mess with everybody.

"I'm so sorry, m'ijito. I really am." She kissed me right on
the lips.

I couldn't remember the last time she kissed me anywhere,
unless it was for show when she'd also be drinking. You know,
one of those *Qué guapo es my little man!,* and then a hard smooch
like she couldn't resist me, leaving her audience, her fans, usually her girlfriends, giggling and aahing. But this was softening
me, enough to almost straight out ask her, *So why this Cloyd dude?
It ain't funny. What are you thinking?* I already knew her answers,
once I took a second. I was older than her in a way that isn't
about years, and she even expected me to tell her practical shit.
But I still wanted her to tell me herself. I didn't want to only
listen in, overhear her talking on the phone. I loved my mom
even when I wondered why everyone was supposed to love their
mom. Maybe because, if she wasn't drunk, it was so easy to
understand her. Simple. Except the part about these men. Especially except the part about this Cloyd man. How could she? I
don't mean the practical part. I meant, How was she planning to
live here with him every day? How was she gonna get out of
here clean? She did not like him. So I wanted her to tell me in

words, to describe it to me kind of, well, so it'd be a story that
made sense, and I'd see it that way.

All you had to do was look around the apartment to know this
Cloyd wasn't right for either of us. That big dinner table which
he called the supper table, with the heavy wooden chairs all
around it—I don't think I'd ever seen so much wood, even in a
picture of a forest. And we never ate dinner at no table before,
unless it was at a restaurant. My mom told me the furniture was
maple. That was the same wood as all around the house, the end
tables and the coffee table, the little knickknack shelves, and a
china cabinet. I figured it was that maple went with the color of
a dead deer's head. Those were in the living room—that room
next to where the dinner table was—hanging from a wall. Okay,
all the others were in his office, and there was only one deer head
in the living room. A buck, he explained. Another body on the
wall was a prize-winning rainbow trout, he said—it was a fish,
to me, before he said it—and another was an owl, which took
over the top of the maple cabinet, its claws gripping a branch
which shot off a thicker branch which was in a varnished slice of
a tree trunk. He didn't shoot this owl, Cloyd told us. His son
just gave it to him as a present. Not on a birthday or Christmas,
no holiday whatever, just plain gave it to him to be his kind of
cool. His son was a taxidermist and did the work himself. All of
it, in fact, was his own professional work. The lamps, wood with
flying birds—mallard ducks, he said—painted on them, he bought
those at a store for decoration.

He asked if I wanted to hear about the day he shot that buck.
I was supposed to say yes. I couldn't stand there nice and listen,
could not. No, not even if I sat on that ugly red sofa or that big
leather chair, the one that was his favorite chair, he said, more
reliable than any woman—his Sil here excluded, of course! I was
welcome to sit in it too, he said, but if I got used to it, I better

not be surprised if he just landed on my lap. He was so funny, huh? I wanted to laugh. Yeah, he'd been sitting in it for so many years it was like a bed to him. He liked to fall asleep in it after work. He'd get so comfy and cozy he'd get mad at himself when he woke up past his bedtime. A couple few beers, he said, a couple few sips of Old Grand Dad, and, well, that chair was the one to make Zzs in. But no anyways, not even if I could sit in that chair of his, did I want to hear about the buck that was up above, across from it. Maybe later, I told him, as polite as I could make myself.

I was slouching against that red sofa, waiting for the end. "So when is Goofy gonna be able to come here?"

"We're working on that," Cloyd said. "We're trying to figure that one out."

My mom was pretending not to hear my question, and I did not want to talk about it with him. But I didn't want her to say some lie to me either. She was always lying.

"What happened to her?" I was asking my mom.

"She's with my son," he said.

"You mean the dude who stuffs dead animals?"

"That's not what's happening," he said. "Be smart."

"He is smart," my mom said.

"Let's not get in a fight over this," he said.

"I just don't think you need to say anything like that about Sonny," she said.

"I only wanna know what happened to Goofy," I said.

"And all I meant to say, all I said was, she's fine," he said.

My mom got pissed off eyes for him, so didn't look at him. "She can't live here with us, m'ijo, I'm sorry. I know it's hard. I'm sorry."

"The dog's fine," Cloyd said. "The dog's happy."

I would have to learn to talk in French. I wanted a sentence. It made me smile, thinking how I would learn French.

* ★ ★

"Why don't you ask where she is?" Joe or Mike said, the first dudes around here I met. I couldn't get which name went to which yet. We were walking home from the new to me school.

"At least you could ask to go over and see her," said his brother Mike or Joe. "I'd be so mad."

"Me too," said Joe or Mike. "I'm pretty sure they really gassed her in the dog pound ovens. I'd be pissed."

One of them slanted an eye at his brother. "You shouldn't say that," he told him.

"Okay, yeah," said the other. "Sorry."

"So lots of people have those sheets on their bed?" I asked. I wanted to change the subject.

"Yeah, dude," one of them said, though either could have. "You raised up allá el rancho grande or what? Everybody gets sheets in the big city."

I'd seen these twins, José and Miguel Hernández, after the first day, and when I saw them going my direction I made them my walking-home friends. They told me they lived a block farther than I did, which, they explained, meant I lived the second farthest away than anybody else. That was a fact, one of them said in these words, a quantifiable, measurable fact. My fact was that I not only couldn't tell them apart, I was never sure which one of them was the one talking unless I was staring because they sounded exactly the same too. And since I hadn't ever known twins before, I wasn't sure how to bring it up. They parted their black hair on the side the same way, the cut too short, waxed hairs still popping out, and they both wore the exact same black-framed glasses, and they both dragged the soles and heels of their black wingtip shoes. They were strange, you could tell. And not the science-and-math kind of strange, and not the hanging-out-too-much-at-the-library type either.

I had a feeling that, before I came along, they didn't have lots
of other friends. Or any. I didn't have any here either, and I
decided I didn't want any while I was living here because I was
convinced it was just for a few months until my mom busted
us out. I was so mad at everything that nobody knew I was mad,
only that I snapped like a backyard German shepherd. I was
not gonna let no new kid fuck with me, and I walked the
schoolyard that way. The twins were so harmless I didn't even
have to think about anything with them, which was like world
peace, and they were funny, so I liked them and I walked home
with them.

We were stopped at a malts-and-dipped-cones stand another
day and were drinking tall shakes at a wobbly picnic table near
the sidewalk. The street beside us seemed wider than four lanes.
All kinds of cars cruised it, from the best low ones, with glittery
spokes, to the finest-looking rods with pipes gurgling and wide
slicks, and older Caddies all customized or streeted out, and newer
Lincolns that were stock and wet-glossed, and sick, sputtering,
wheezy coupes with duct-taped windows, and dried-up station
wagons with new various-sized retreads and no hubcaps ever.
And always lots of shouting huge loud radio stations floating by,
lots of broken tunes and words.

"What's he do?" one of the twins asked me.

"A plumber, I think," I said. "For like new homes and
businesses, you know."

"He must be rich if he owns your apartment building," said
the other. "How many apartments?"

"Six or maybe seven. I can't remember."

"Any hot ruquitas live there?" one asked.

That was the first time one of them made me laugh out loud
and not just to myself. It's because I couldn't imagine either of
them even standing near a girl, so it was crazy hilarious to hear
the word like they were on it. "You mean girls?"

"Hell yeah, chicks, what else?"

"What else." I laughed. "I think so," I said.

"You don't know?" said the other. "How can you not know?"

"I think there's this one," I said. "She's in an apartment above."

"Oh yeah." It could've been either of them who said that. He said it in an all-hip tone, like she was already a sure thing. "What's she like?"

"What's she got?" the other jumped in. "Jugaluggas, buenas nalgas, o todo el paquetote?"

They made me laugh! It was like, did they think I thought they were experts on the subject? They were both serious, like we were talking cars that passed. "I dunno, man," I said. "Big chichis, it seemed like, and a nice butt. I only caught a glance. Both were good, I'd say."

They nodded at each other scientifically, and then a distant look away, like to God, like pretty soon they'd make a move to check out my crib.

These black dudes with too much bass in their ride pulled up to the curb and were looking at us like that was why they pulled over. I looked back, and then away, keeping them so far at the corner of my eye that it wouldn't seem like at all. One of them got out, gold chains slapping his chest while he walked, and he bobbed and weaved like right to where I was sitting, jamming me with his eyes on the way, then went past, not saying shit else until he got to the order window. Another dude had turned off the engine but not the sound system, which took everything like a headache. Our straws were sucking the bottom of our cups and it seemed healthy to get going.

"Wouldn't you hate to have a name like that?" one of the twins said, getting up.

They were still talking about Cloyd Longpre. It was as though he didn't see what was maybe happening. He tossed his empty cup in the barrel, which was near the dude at the window. He was watching but not straight on.

"Wouldn't you hate telling people that your dad was named *Cloyd?*" the other said.

The brother watched the other twin toss his in the barrel near him too, ready for a wrong move. I held on to mine even though it was empty. Once we started walking, and the music got quieter and behind our back, I threw my empty in front of the door of a closed-down store. It was more like they didn't know those dudes wanted to get us into some kind of roll.

The twins had started woofing on names. They were competing on who could come up with more of what Cloyd's brothers would be named: Hoss, Elmer, Jethro, Wilbur, Honker, Gomer, Horatio, Horace, and so on.

I wished I could make myself joke more about Cloyd Longpre.

"Lots of Mexican names are howlers too," one of them said. "You gotta admit it."

"Yeah, lots of names just like that in Spanish, even crazier," said the other. "Think of it. Like say your name is Ramiro Ramirez. Or maybe Gonzalo Gonzalez. Or maybe Rodrigo Rodriguez."

"You know what I hate?" said his brother. "Beto. I know it's muy common, pero to me it sounds como like saying butthole, with an accent."

"But *Cloyd!*"

"Ay, yeah, that is a really, really, really bad name, even for a white person! And, hijole, a stepdad!"

Laughing, they both looked at me, wanting me to agree. When I didn't do nothing, they slowed it down.

"Pero nothing like Skip. Or Tad. Tad. Hey, man, you wanna tad? Or like saying Jack. How can that be a real name,

you know? Besides, no Mexican can say Jack, you know? It's
'cause it's hard to say when you try to say it: Yack, hey yack."

"What about the name Dick."

"Dick!" His brother cracked up.

They were both bent over dying over those names. I guess
I didn't really care about it as much as they did. "Hey, I don't
want you guys telling nobody his name," I warned them. "Don't
be talking about it, funny or not funny, nothing."

"We wouldn't," one said, a big old grin still there.

"I'm not fucking around," I told him.

They both shut down and got a little afraid of me, I could
tell.

"You don't have to get pissed off," one said. "We're not
laughing at you."

I'd probably sounded worse than I meant, but, you know,
it was probably better so they wouldn't dare make the mistake.
"I just don't want you telling nobody at that school," I said.

"We won't," one said. "Swear to God."

"Yeah, swear to Quetzalcoatl y la Lupe," the other said.
"Sorry, okay?"

I don't know what I was up to at first, spending so much time in
that bedroom my mom was calling mine, sometimes watching a
TV alone there, avoiding the other rooms and people like Cloyd.
If I were to go out there, they'd want to sit at the maple dinner
table and eat supper. I hated that word, but I would've hated the
deal no matter. I'd say junk like *I'm not hungry, but thanks,* or *I
already ate too much after school, I'm so full.* The first couple of times
my mom made me sit there anyways. Once it was deer meat,
which I could barely chew or swallow—ugly!—so much I didn't
even want to eat mashed potatoes, which I love. Which made
my mom feel hurt because she said she made them from real potatoes, not a box. I hated deer meat and will always hate deer meat.

Cloyd food. Another time was fish. I pretended to get sick on that, which in a way wasn't hard because this fish had an eye staring up at me from the plate. Like the deer, he killed it, it was *his*—he was proud of that kind of shit. I just went to the bathroom and came out and told them I threw up. I knew Cloyd didn't buy any of that or like it or both, and probably my mom didn't really either— she didn't eat that fish either—but she backed me.

I had my own little stash but for right then she also started giving me a few dollars, passing a few to me kind of sideways so he wouldn't know. I rounded the corner onto the boulevard, passing the World Motel and Mercado Tires and La Copa de Oro, and I bought burritos off Manny's lunch truck or hot dogs at a stand, Lucy's Tacos, until I found this six-lane bowling alley and diner, Alley Cats, where I really liked eating, though I had to get used to going there because the lady there kept asking me questions. I liked the bowling. If I didn't have enough money or want to spend my own, I'd just stay hungry until the Cloyd went to sleep, when I could sneak out and make sandwiches. I never liked watching TV so much and finally I turned it off, even if I'd never had one in my bedroom before. I listened to radio. When I listened to music it was Fourth of July, colors and explosions of colors and lights and shapes, the singers' voices spinning like planets and moons, getting bigger, and smaller, and farther away, and closer, and closer, then over there, and up. I loved this world. When my mom this one time wondered how I could listen to a radio so much, I told her, or I tried to, and she stood there with this somewhere-else look on her face, and she didn't understand, or maybe she didn't listen to me, and she didn't ever wonder again, so I didn't have to try to explain. That's how she usually was. She had other things in her ears, she saw other things. Yeah, we were kind of alike, I know. But it wasn't the same, it wasn't.

★   ★   ★

I didn't like being inside #1 at Los Flores. You know, hearing new shit: *No. I know. No. I know. I know. I can't be louder. I said I know. Don't. Because I'm not. I'm not going to. I'm not, no. Stop. I'm telling you. No. No.* All that kind of movida. It would make me see these words like curving and turning, up fast and too sharp, down without looking. Bad music, wild light.

I took walking cruises on the boulevard and turned pages of comics in stores because comics weren't good no more, they were gone from me. I looked at other mags, even men's ones, until I got told I had to stop or leave. One thing that was also true was that I didn't want to be in my old neighborhood. So here it was all the black streets and white sidewalks. Walking and walking and walking until the night and late would come. Glass and mirrors, beer and cars and dirty girls inside La Copa de Oro. The night might start watching me. I didn't like that. I wanted to know who and what the fuck? I started thinking how I could go bowling, right? I went to Alley Cats. I could eat there.

Right before a sunset I stuck closer, did the good. The exact answer to the twins' apartment question was: Five upstairs, #3 through #7. Downstairs, we were in #1, and along the driveway, which went around to six other carports, was #2, an apartment next to Cloyd's office, which otherwise would have been a third bedroom. There was a carport for two cars on the same side the apartment doors faced, where Cloyd parked his work truck, as gray and stiff as his starched uniform, metal tool compartments welded all around it. Lots of pipe and some two-by-fours stuck out from the bed and were piled on the rack above. He had his luxury Mercury sedan next to that, which was what my mom got to drive. Beyond the carport was the laundry room—only two quarters to wash and two quarters to dry. One of the jobs Cloyd had made mine was to make sure the laundry room was cleaned up. Check the lint filter in the dryer. Check the trash can and empty it. I mopped the floor, and I sprayed and wiped glass cleaner on both machines so they shined. He said this was to keep my end of the deal up. To learn responsibility. I didn't shake my head to that out loud. I was thinking it was about him paying me too. I didn't mind working. I wanted something to do. It was about how I first met Cindy. She lived directly upstairs, in #3.

"Sonny," I told her.

"You're the boy I've seen," she said.

Cindy was in a paisley bikini top and black stretch pants and flip-flop chanclas and all ten fingernails were painted cherry and she had the blondest hair above dark roots. Her skin made curves, from a lot below her belly button way up, and it was hard not to pay attention to there because it came so close to those places you weren't supposed to stare at but couldn't not at the same time. If the clothes seemed too small, also everything fit her good. Still, she didn't dress right for her, or something. I mean, she was wearing the clothes, yeah, but it was like the blond hair.

"What's your mom's name?" she asked.

"Silvia Bravo," I said, forgetting that her last name now was Longpre. One of the first things she did was get a driver's license with Longpre on it. She wanted that last name, didn't want her old last name. I think that was the story she had. "He keeps calling her Sil." I don't know why I hated that he did and that she let him.

She was nodding, smiling. "If you're still in high school, you need to graduate," Cindy said.

I made a face away from her. Not only because of school, but because she said that right outta nowhere.

"I miss high school," she said. "That's why I say so."

"Really?"

"I need to finish." She was folding, and stacking, then pulling a few hot things from the cylinder and piling them on top of

the dryer to fold them. "It's important." The clothes that I as-
sumed belonged to her seemed more small, in comparison to how
large she seemed to me, standing near.

"You're gonna need your diploma." She was being all older
and wiser.

I still wasn't sure she wasn't messing around. "Thanks, miss."
Though I wasn't planning to drop out, the more I hear commercials, the more I want to rip shit off.

She shook her head smiling. "It is important, you know."
She meant this. Except not really, because she was trying so hard.

"Didn't you say you didn't finish?"

"I'm certainly no example!" she said. Then she slugged me
in the arm. "Smart-ass." She stopped to look at me. "I had to
get married." She was facing me, holding herself steady, long
enough to get me fidgety. "You're a cute boy, aren't you?"

I could've said something to her, I just didn't.

"So, do you have a girl yet?"

"Of course."

She showed off some really white teeth when she smiled.
She was folding underwear, men's boxers and women's panties.
"I'll bet you do," she said. "You will, anyway."

As she was putting her stuff into the plastic laundry basket,
I decided to wet the mop in the washbasin, like the floor's what
I was going to get to next.

"See you later, Junior."

"Bye," I said, not correcting her. I grabbed the trash can to
carry it to the barrels in the back. I wanted to watch her go to
her apartment all the way, but I only peeked for a few seconds as
her chanclas flip-flopped up the stairs. If I watched too long, I
bet she'd turn around and catch me.

"It's in my blood," Cloyd told me. His office was right next to
the kitchen, and he looped around from his swivel chair, attached

to that gray uniform, catching me looking down, wordless. If at eye level it was more gray—gray desk and gray chair and gray cabinets, even gray machines on it—above was a woodsy forest of laquered construction licenses and plaques, and above it all were the mountings of dead animal heads. The walls were pulled by the weight of petrified horns and marble eyes and those black noses that reminded me too much of Goofy's. There were at least two on the side walls, three facing the door. It's that when I walked in, it was like one of the horns had poked my eye. I was just thinking about that possibility, and probably Cindy, so long that he must have decided I was finally interested. "My family descends from mountain men, French and Scots who came down from Canada and into Louisiana and who stretched themselves out across to the Northwest to get themselves more room. We were skinning and selling the whole time. We lived off the wild."

"Dead deer," I said. What I didn't like even more were the three rifles on each wall rack. Lots of rifles. I could count them if I wanted. More than the heads, more than the plaques and licenses. I didn't know about guns that much. I didn't know about rifles except what anyone would know. I couldn't imagine what anyone had so many for. So many I couldn't look at them because they looked back too. I could see the dead dead heads below them. I felt like one of them, staring away and watching at the same time.

"You got a lot to learn, boy. That there's elk. A buck elk."

I didn't care so much that he killed them. It was how killing them meant how much better he thought he was than me. How it meant he was a man, and I couldn't be one if I didn't blow away a dumb deer with a shotgun. That's what it seemed like to me. Like killing these animals was where the chores I was expected to do would lead, once I learned responsibilities.

And to not kill them meant I wasn't ever going to be tough the right way.

I nodded like I was getting it.

"It's my father's side," he said. "I'm an Okie child of the dust bowl otherwise."

The dust part. It was the lint in the laundry room where Cindy was.

"You know what that means?"

"I'm not sure, man. No. Really no."

"Means my family came here because there was no place else." He took a sip from a glass. It was whiskey, water, and one ice cube. I'd seen him do these enough times already.

For a second I stopped, and probably it seemed like I was interested. I wanted to think of—well, things to say, like I was supposed to, but I was waiting for what he wanted me to do, or what I wasn't, like that. I really wanted to take off. "Was there something else? You know, that I'm supposed to do?"

"You been on it good," he said. "You're being a good man."

I could never look him in the eye. I shot a glance as always and nodded. That was all I could make myself do.

"Remember that you're taking out the cans too."

Finally. I didn't remember because I thought I was only supposed to bring them in before I walked to school in the morning. That first time my mom ran out with me and helped. The second time she watched.

"It's a big help to me," he said. "You're a good man."

I nodded like the first time he said it.

"If you get out to the toolshed, you'll find a dolly."

The toolshed was where he kept the mop and bucket and light bulbs and water hoses and a wide push broom, which I used to sweep leaves from a neighbor's tree behind the carport and the stairs and walkway on the second floor—slate, Cloyd said,

showed dirt a lot, so it had to be swept a lot—and then the cement walkways on the bottom level.

"You don't mind, right? It's a big help. One less distraction for me, and the business I got plenty of distraction with
already."

"It's all right," I said. I noticed he was repeating things. I
noticed he was getting the whiskey look.

"Good man," he said. "Good man."

I can't say for sure, but I'd say this was the last time he tried
to talk to me. You know, really thought he was, really believed
it himself.

"Excellent," he said, swiveling away from me, dialing a
phone number off the Rolodex.

That work was something to keep me outside, not in there in
#1, and that made it easier to not do the other cositas, like talk
at that maple table with them. Doing the work made my mom
happy too, because it meant there was no junk between him
and me, and so she even started to slip me a few dollars to eat
out. I even liked working at this apartment building, don't ask
me why.

There were eight garbage cans. One was empty. After I
dumped what was in a couple into a couple others, it left me
with five to dolly out to the street curb. On my third trip a
man was standing near them, waiting. His name was Pinkston,
and he lived in #6, a one-bedroom. He wore a shirt that looked
like it had sunlight in it, unbuttoned one lower than the top, a
collar on it that to me seemed almost like wings that might lift
him up in a wind. He was strange in so many ways it was hard
to describe. His wiry hair was mostly white and had orange and
red in it, his face showed freckles you wanted to count, and there
was a river of a scar that cut from the side of his eyebrow, where

it trickled down, winding down to his jaw, where it got widest and disappeared under his neck. Its pink color was so much darker than his skin and hair that, even healed, it looked like it still hurt. His skin was so white he didn't look like a white person, but all I ever thought about was the scar.

"How ya doing?" he said.

"Hi," I said.

"Longpre made you trashman?"

I pulled the dolly from the can. He had moved one of the cans to the other side of the driveway entrance.

"Young man, these trash cans are not good for me today," he told me.

He pushed the other can away from the curb and closer to the sidewalk while he was talking.

"Here's my situation," he said. "You see, this Bird here is one I'm about to sell. She looks good enough to sex with, don't you say?"

It was old, and it had some small scratches anyone could see, and the back bumper wasn't perfect, and it seemed like there were a couple of tears on the bucket seats inside, but it was washed clean and waxed glossy and it was a T-Bird, and, yeah, it was a very bad-looking ride. I agreed with him.

"I wouldn't park here if there was another space, but you see how it is."

There was parking on only one side of this street, and parked cars stretched as far as you could see to the left and to the right, down the rest of the block to where it ran into the boulevard.

"But I think this is where I'm supposed to leave these," I said. "It's where they were the last times."

"And this is exactly correct, you are exactly correct," he said, dragging the trash can I just brought to the other side of the apartment building's driveway. "But when my good friend comes over to buy my Bird here, I can't have no garbage stinking up and disturbing. You see what I'm saying?"

"Sure."

"You all right, little brother, you all right." He watched a car slowing down the street until it passed. "I gotta get very little distraction, all signs gotta be pointing right and good and profitable. You see what I'm saying?"

"Yeah, sure."

I went away and rolled back with another can. He'd moved the other over there too, and I put this one where those were now.

"Getting dark. Cannot have these garbage cans in the dark next to my Bird. Bad sales psychology. See what I'm saying?"

"Yeah."

He pitched a smile that wasn't about only one thought, nodding, nodding. "I've been seeing you sweeping the upstairs."

Another car creeped and came to a stop. Pinkston went to it and bent down to the window, talked to the black man driving it. He pointed to the boulevard, leaned against the hood of his T-Bird when he got back.

"This is the one," he told me, quiet. "I'm feeling it itch."

When I wheeled out the fifth can, he was still standing in front of the T-Bird, and his customer was just rounding the corner—he had to park back on the boulevard.

"You her son?"

I nodded.

He nodded too. "Well, when it comes down to it, I'm on hers and your side, you understand me?"

Not even, but I didn't have to say, because he wasn't waiting for me to. He was making sure the doors of the T-Bird were open.

"I sell my sweetheart now, you make a five-dollar commission." He turned his head back to me with a smile that made me want to buy a car from him. "Whadaya say?"

"You don't have to."

"Now you stop that and take what I'm offering. You my good luck, see?"

"Okay then, sure."

He stepped toward the man with an outstretched hand, and I took the dolly back to the toolshed.

Cloyd was over by the front window, swirling what was left in his whiskey glass, no ice cube.

"He was talking to you?"

I made a yes look and walked to the big window.

"What'd he say?"

"That he's selling that car," I said.

"Selling a car."

"That's what he said."

"That one? To that black man?"

I didn't answer. I stared out the window too. There they were out there, talking next to the T-Bird, the passenger's door open, Pink bent over the top of it, almost laughing, talking it up, the man sitting inside with his legs on the curb.

"He's working some angle." He drank the rest. I already knew Cloyd didn't like black people. He didn't say so, but it wasn't like you needed to ask.

Cloyd turned away from me and started walking toward his office, when he spun back around. I noticed that the laces on his work boots were untied. I thought, that's what he does when he's getting drunk.

"Let me tell you something." He was way louder than he needed to be. It didn't even seem like he was talking to me.

I made a turn to his face, which seemed mad, but I saw the empty whiskey glass. He had it low and was gripping it more like he was about to throw it, rolling it in his hand. I'd turned my head away from the window but didn't move my feet. I waited for him to go on, but he didn't.

It was like he was chewing, his mouth full, and he had to swallow before he could talk. Then the office phone rang and he rushed to get it.

"What happened?" my mom asked, almost in a whisper. She probably couldn't help but hear him talking to me. He was in his office being too loud with someone on the phone. She said it more nervous than she had to. She was holding a hairbrush. It seemed like she came out of their bedroom, and I couldn't tell if she was coming or going. She was all sprayed and decked out, maybe a new dress and new heels, like she'd be when she was going out on a date or even shopping.

"Nothing," I said.

He was in his office now. You could hear him too easy on the phone.

"Why is he so . . . you know?" she asked.

"Why would I know?"

"Were you guys talking?"

"A long time ago already," I said.

"De qué?"

"Nothing."

"Sonny, I hear him."

"I think it was about French," I said.

"What?"

"Nothing," I said.

She went over to the front window too and started squinting out there. "Did you take his trash out?"

All she had to do was look.

She started seeing what was going on outside. "It was about aquel hombre, wasn't it?"

They were still out there, and the hood of the T-Bird was up, though they weren't even near to looking inside. "I dunno, Mom, okay?" I took the long way around her for the bedroom.

I was mad at her. I don't think I'd ever been so mad at her before. No, I didn't really like this husband of hers—the Cloyd, the Hernández twins were calling him, a lumpy wad that held it together—but that wasn't it, because I didn't care about him no more, bad or good. And even though I knew it was his decision about Goof, I blamed her and her only. I wasn't gonna say nothing about it unless one of them brought it up. What for? I wanted to show God how I was a man, not him and not her. But yeah I was so mad at her for letting him get away with it. I mean, I could understand why a dog shouldn't live inside an apartment with no yard, but couldn't she at least fight this dude a little about it? If she didn't care how I felt, didn't she care any about Goof? Didn't she even miss Goofy a little? Didn't she think I would?

For a while my room was being neat. That could be because I didn't have so much to mess up. My mom never picked up after me at home, before we moved here, except maybe once every few months, if somebody was gonna be coming over. For a minute she did almost every day. She even made my bed. I didn't think it was for good reasons. More some game. I don't think she was too happy. I was sure she would want to bust anytime. It's how she was. I put my blanket—that's what I slept with, a blanket, no sheet, and it was the same blanket I used at home, which she'd folded and left at the foot of the bed—under my head instead of the pillow, and I watched the ceiling instead of the television. And I listened. When I didn't hear my mom or them, I just listened harder. The curtains were closed, but the window wasn't. I heard the yelling from upstairs. Once I got used to it, I didn't have to listen harder, it just got louder. I wasn't sure if I couldn't make it out because it was in Spanish, or I wouldn't have been able to hear it anyways, even if it were in English. I used to feel better about talking Spanish. My mom used to speak it a lot more, and I used to hang out with my grandma, who didn't speak English, and I could talk with my primos who lived there with my tíos, but that all stopped once Grandma died. I never saw my cousins no more after that either. And then my mom only talked Spanish when she had to, which mostly she didn't have to, or maybe to say something to me in my ear when people were around. So I never spoke it either, never really tried. But I still could understand it, mostly, so I was listening.

The Spanish came from where that girl lived, in #4, which was a two-bedroom. I'd seen her like twice, and one time was while I was sweeping and I saw them around the TV. I saw her through the screen and window so good it was like she leaked through the mesh. She looked back at me too. Since I never saw her where I went to school, I thought she might go to St. Xavier's. I was sure she was my age, or close. She had a baby brother or sister who cried. Her family practically never went out, and she didn't either, not even when they went grocery shopping. Her parents both worked at night, swing shift, and they always went together.

The loud male voice up there, almost always yelling, didn't really stop, just went from closer to farther away, but a radio came on, and it was steady, and though it wasn't on very loud, it covered up the man's voice, her dad. She was listening to the same station I liked, the hits station, so I like listened to it with her and imagined her listening next to me. I liked her. She would like me, she had to. She was really pretty. Uu-ee pretty, made my stomach do circles. Like I said, I saw her twice, and that one time I knew she saw me back.

"You just check her shit out," one of the twins said. We were walking the tracks, going home slow, avoiding the worst grease puddles, kicking dented cans and throwing dirty rocks at them, seeing who could keep themselves balanced on top of the rail longest. "Look her up, look her down. Nod your head like a brother, like bad, you know?" He nodded his head slow, bobbing his head to the right, squinting his eyes, even though he had his glasses on.

The other twin was polishing his glasses with the bottom of his white shirt. They both wore the same short-sleeve white shirts, no tails, ironed too, almost every day. It was almost like they had a Catholic uniform, but the color of the slacks changed, and the pants didn't always match each other in style but the shoes were shined, both pairs black wingtips.

"I think I'd be getting more worked up for la güera, bro," he said.

"Who you talking about?" his brother asked.

"La blondie," he said, "who lives right upstairs from este Sonny. Remember he told us?"

"Oh yeah, that's right!" his brother said, like it was all as easy as that, and then he turned to me. "You see her again yet?"

They made me laugh all the time because they talked so smart but they were so fucking stupid. They knew as much about sex as they did these girls in the apartment building. I couldn't believe I told them anything.

Like, for instance, about the nudie magazine I ripped off from the mailbox. It's because it came in a brown wrapper and I thought I would, you know, take it. It was sitting there, and nobody was around. The label was addressed to the man in #2, a one-bedroom. He was Ben and he lived with Gina and they pretended to be married and Cloyd told my mom he knew they were only shacking up. Cloyd didn't care because they paid the rent on time and had professional jobs—he wore a suit and tie and left early. They were like "with it" people and, curtains always closed, they were either at work or closed up in there watching or listening to a complicated music system and a big television connected to it—I saw the TV one time because I passed by when their front door was open. If they were home, you could hear one or the other. So yeah, really I already knew who the magazine belonged to when I was bagging it. It was that I was supposed to take out the pile of throwaway ads no one ever wanted that the mailman put there for everyone. And the magazine in the wrapper could look like trash, because of that brown wrapper. That's what I would've said if someone saw me take it. That I threw it away. Both the twins were so impressed with my story they could barely shake their heads. Like doing shit like this was so dangerous. They both thought what I did was way fucking wild.

I was taking off the screens and cleaning them with a stiff brush and putting them back. It was the latest job Cloyd said I should do. So far it was easy, even on the second floor, because they were at eye level, but I hadn't been to the backside of the building yet. I would have to get those screens high up from a ladder. It was the thing I was asked to do this week. Cloyd was even saying—though not exactly, I admit it—that maybe I'd be paid something when I got it all done. I wanted him to, but the thing was it wasn't about money for me. Or only. He didn't have to know I didn't mind doing it anyways.

"Hey, cutie boy! You trying to sneak in on me while I'm in the shower?"

"Oh, sorry," I said.

Cindy was standing there with a towel wrapped around her, her hair and shoulders dripping wet. I was brushing the screen of #3 from her window. She'd pulled back her curtains to talk to me; then she drew them wider with the cord. The glass pane was already slid all the way open. She was smiling a lot.

The towel wrapped around her was short and her thighs, which I could see a lot of, were still drippy wet too, but I was too uncomfortable to look too long. I took the screen, which had been leaning against the stucco wall, into my free hand, and pulled it up next to me.

"I'm probably supposed to tell you before I take the screen off. It's that I'm cleaning them." I showed her the brush in my other hand.

"I see that now. I was hoping you were just going to come in and say hi to me."

I laughed kind of a nervous ha-ha-ha.

"Do you want a coke?"

"Sure."

"Then you have to come in," she said, turning away from the window and opening the door.

She walked toward her kitchen. I watched her moving away, shower water dribbling down her legs, and then go into the refrigerator and bend down some and get me a soda. I was still standing outside, the screen in one hand and the brush in the other.

"You can come inside and you can even sit down," she said. Then she smiled sexy at me again. She popped the can for me and put it on the built-in breakfast counter. "I'm gonna go dry off and put something on."

I went over to where she left the coke. She didn't shut the bedroom door all the way, and from where I was I could see where she was. I didn't think I should let myself find out more, and I didn't either.

"Go sit down and make yourself at home," she said from the bedroom.

The couch was this old one, both too saggy and too hard at the same time. I might not have noticed that if I hadn't been living in Cloyd's. His furniture felt brand new, even when it wasn't. Maybe old enough but never sat on. The cushions were hard in some better way. Our old furniture at home was about halfway between his and hers. Which meant her stuff was really gacho, really raggy and stained. I sat on the front edge of the couch and sipped.

She came out barefoot, in shorts with a drawstring and a white blouse. She was still not completely dried off, and she was taking the towel and rubbing her hair in it with both hands. I liked her hands and the way the light shined against the nail polish on the tips of her fingers.

She sat down on a stuffed chair that maybe went with the couch. The material on the set was worn, but at least there were no tears, though it seemed like it could rip any second, and I didn't want to be the one who did it. The TV set was the only thing brand new.

"It's nice to have someone here," she said. "I never get any company." She put the towel down. "Nobody except my sister. She comes over, sometimes a lot, sometimes less. Lately it's less because she's mad at me. I don't have any friends, not one!"

I wasn't sure what to say. I almost thought of telling her that the only friends I had since we moved were the twins.

"It all depends on whether or not she has a job," she said, "or, if she does, what shift it is."

"You're married though, right? That's not alone."

"Yes."

"Well, like, he's around then."

"*When* he's around," she said with a little nastiness.

"He's not here a lot?" I asked. I don't think I had seen him, but I did hear him. Since they were directly upstairs, you knew when he was there. We probably didn't hear her so much because, like now, she went around barefoot.

"He's here when he's not out."

"At work?"

"Well, yeah. But lots when he's out with his friends and drinking and who knows. He's here when he wants something, like sex, or to sleep, or to eat, or to drink, or to have more sex with me once in a while."

"What's he do?" There was something about the look in the apartment, the smell, something.

"For work?" She smiled right at me.

"Well . . . yeah."

"He sorts the packages for the brown trucks."

"Yeah?" It seemed like memorized.

"Oh yeah, right," she said sarcastically. She got up and got herself a soda and opened it. She plopped back down on the chair. The towel was hanging over the back and she rested against it like it wasn't there. "He started as a driver. But he said he had to run so much. Which at first he liked. But then it started making him too tired for when he got off, and then he hurt his foot. So they transferred him to the other department." She drank. She drank a couple swallows more. "I hate him."

That made me laugh. It just caught me that way, because she didn't mean it to be funny. She liked it that I laughed, though, you could tell.

"I do! I hate him!"

That's when I noticed she still hadn't dried herself completely under her white blouse. She was so wet in this one spot, and I could see how it curved down and up, where her nipple pushed out.

"You don't hate him," I said.

She glared. "How old are you?"

I told her I was sixteen, even though I wasn't.

"I'm not even nineteen yet," she said, "not for another month, and I feel like an old married lady."

I almost said how I thought she seemed older than that. "I guess that *is* pretty young to be all married."

"You seem older and more mature than that to me too," she said. "Or you're just so cute." She was smiling when she said that, flirty.

I felt good about my lie.

"I had to get married," she went on.

I was still wondering why she was teasing me about being big and strong. Like maybe instead of meaning it, she didn't. I wondered what her husband was like.

"Aren't you going to ask what happened to the baby? Everyone else does."

Even if I had thought of it, I couldn't because I wasn't going as fast as she was.

"I had a late miscarriage."

"Sorry." It's all I could say.

"He got me pregnant again eight months ago," she said, and she paused there and sat up in the chair, "but this time I went and had an abortion."

It seemed like she was talking to herself more than to me. I didn't know what I was supposed to say, if I needed to say anything.

"You're not against abortion, are you?"

How would I know? What did I know? I knew what it was, heard all about it, but, you know, what could I say?

"I'm glad I did it," she went on. She put her coke down beside the chair.

I sat there, fidgety now, mostly done with the soda, nothing to say.

"Maybe," I started, trying to think of something, "maybe your husband was glad too." Did that even sound right? I didn't know what I was saying. I was just saying anything.

"My husband?" she said. Her eyes were seeing some wall I couldn't. "My husband." She pronounced her words like she was practicing English.

"I thought you said you were married," I explained. I looked away, thinking I'd go back outside to what I was supposed to.

"No, you didn't say anything wrong. Just when you say it, *you,* it sounds different to me." She was looking at me. She looked at me like a girl would a guy. Before she wasn't really looking at me, and now she was. "His name's Tino."

"Oh, all right. That's who I meant. That's who I was talking about."

"He is my husband," she said.

"Okay."

"It sounded funny to me. Like I was listening to someone talk about my mom, not me."

I nodded like I understood.

"My mom had a few husbands."

"Okay, yeah," I said. "I know what you mean, I do see how you'd think that."

"Your mom and Mr. Longpre. . . ."

"Yeah," I said. I stood up. I didn't want to be talking about that shit with her. I had the empty can in my hand. "Should I throw this away?"

"Why don't you have another one?"

"I'm full," I said.

"What a butt you are," she said. She stood up too. "I thought you'd like my company." She took the empty to the kitchen and tossed it.

"I do," I said. I was getting a little confused.

"But you don't like me."

I was maybe gonna stay longer, but right then her telephone rang, and when she picked it up she said hi to I guessed Tino. I listened for a few until it felt fucked up to, and then I went back outside to the screen and brush. It wasn't much of a job to clean them, just a puff of brown dust jumping off. Didn't take very long to do both of hers, and when I slid them back into the brackets that held them, she was still on the phone, cuddling against it like it was a soft kitty, her knees up, touching her toes. I liked her toes.

The television cartoons were so loud in #4 that you'd think the curtains should be flapping in the sound waves. I knew she was there, but I didn't imagine how close to me on the other side of the dirty screen she'd be until she was inches from my face.

"I'm supposed to take this off because I'm gonna clean it," I said in English. I showed her the brush.

Her little brother, diaper and no T-shirt, wobbled over and stood behind her.

"Go watch the *teetee*," she told him in Spanish. He didn't. "Go go, Angelito, go on!" she told him again. This time he turned back and flopped down about a foot from it, as though if he didn't get so close he wouldn't hear it, blasting loud as it was.

"So it's okay I take this screen off?" I asked her. I said *screen* in English because I didn't know what the word was in Spanish. I didn't even know if she answered because I was completely distracted. I was seeing her but I was also seeing someone somewhere else. It was like when I shut my eyes and it was that dreamlight and colors that flew off that darkness, and so this was not doing what I was doing even as I was doing it. Strands of her long hair—black as in the best night, the same best black in her eyes—stuck to the edges of those eyes that weren't only hers either.

I did take off that screen, and she went on standing on the inside, watching me brush the dirt off. I couldn't say if she said anything. She might have, and I would've wanted to answer things back. I must have because I realized we were talking.

"Nica," she said.

That was her telling me her name, and it made me kind of remember where I was and what I was doing.

"Nica?" I asked.

"Yes," she said. "Nica."

"I'm Sonny."

"Sonny," she said, thinking. She'd said it a little different. Like it was two names combined, *son* and *nee*. "It's a good name."

It made me happy she thought my name was good, and I probably would've smiled right at her, but I wasn't able to look up, so I smiled at her dress. It looked soft like cotton, the color of beach shells, and it was wrinkled like the crinkly paper they draped from ceilings at a school party. It had a blue drawstring tied around her waist. Nobody wore a dress like that. It made her seem like a movie Indian.

"So what school do you go to?" I asked. I struggled with my Spanish. I was scared of how I sounded, how pocho she might know I was.

"I don't go right now," she said.

"Not to any school?"

"No," she said.

"I thought maybe you were going to St. Xavier."

"No," she told me. "Not right now."

"Then," I said, "you don't have to go to school." It was supposed to be a question.

She didn't want to talk about it, you could tell.

I put that first screen back. She followed but she came out the front door. "I'm right outside here!" she told her brother. "I'm not going anywhere!" and she turned away and waved good-bye.

Both curtains and windows were closed in #5, a one-bedroom, and I slipped out the first screen. Inside an old man whose name was Josep—a strange name to me—lived with a woman whose name wasn't normal either. The first time I saw him he was on the walk in a scratched-up wooden chair, doing nothing but sitting there. Sitting, only sitting, no newspaper, no book, no radio, nothing but his hands on his lap, fingers laced, in these old-man baggy slacks and an old-man button-up sweater and slip-on shoes that were so worn they looked like moccasins. He was looking out and away at the sky—full of telephone poles and wires and pigeons on them but like he was seeing something in or on them because he watched. He had a lot of silvery gray hair, thicker and more healthy than most viejitos, and long for an old man, and it was combed back nice, like he planned to go out soon or could if something came up. That first time I was sweeping he wouldn't even pick up his chair and move so I could sweep right there. I just went around, like I didn't even notice.

"How come you do this?" he asked. It was like he was talking more at the push broom. He had an accent from somewhere not close to where anybody I knew was from.

"The slate deck here, it gets dirty," I told him, "and it's supposed to be swept."

"No, no." He shook his head and a finger like I was way stupid, like I wasn't paying attention. "How come *you* do this?"

"Cloyd Longpre. I live downstairs, in Number One. It's that he married my mom."

He grabbed me by his eyes and squeezed. "He make you, or he pay you?"

I sort of twisted my head away to say nothing, or to make it an I'm not sure.

He shook his head slowly, backing off. When I'd finished sweeping, he went back to what he was doing before, which was sitting there, his hands back in his lap, fingers laced, gazing at the beyond in front of him.

In the bedroom that wasn't mine I listened for Nica's voice in all those voices up there—mostly her dad's came through. I was also having to hear my mom and the Cloyd arguing just a little too loud on the other side of the door. I probably was relieved that they were. It meant I could count the money I had hidden. Bueno, okay, look: The truth is that when I snuck into those houses, sometimes I took money away. At first it was only the change, especially if I saw dimes and quarters. Then I smarted up and checked only for bills. A dollar, a five, a ten, any of them could be sitting around, folded, piled, like forgotten or nothing to them, or in a drawer or a box under the bed. The worst time was that girl's house. Yeah, I did what I said before, I did that. But in her parents' bedroom, in a small drawer, I found an envelope with twenties, coming out to $200. You know? Most of the time I thought nobody'd notice, because—I dunno, but that was so much it's what got me scared. I also started taking from my mom or my sister if I saw it around, or when I decided to look inside their purse. Only a few dollars. I stopped that too, I didn't like doing it. At first, yeah, I spent it. That's what I thought I took it for. Even then I wouldn't spend very much. I'd go out and buy like a half-gallon square of chocolate ice cream. But then I made a decision to save this money, to use it right. Also because stealing made me feel shitty, and I didn't like that part much. So it seemed better that if I wasn't wasting it, if it wasn't exactly gone, just put away for necessary things, it wasn't as bad. When I'd collected small bills, I'd go over to a store and exchange the little ones into a twenty, and then I'd put it in this envelope with the others. Anyways, once in a while I liked to see it and count it, and this seemed like a good time for that. It was, I thought, hidden in a good place—I'd pulled up the bedroom carpet in the corner, next to where the bookcase was, and put it there and it didn't bulge out. I don't know why I liked to get it out and count it sometimes, but I did. It was a thick stack, and it now was up to $249. Probably there's some explanation I couldn't think of for wanting to do the counting. Probably I looked right then because I'd just taken $6 from Cloyd, and I'd put it away fast a couple of days ago. It was sitting there in his truck, on the bench seat, almost lost in a pile of receipts and fast food trash. Like he didn't care about it. To me. That was just the other day.

I hadn't thought about it much since, but while they were being loud at each other, I guess it got me to remembering what I did.

I could tell by the tone of the footsteps outside my door that they were headed at me. I stabbed the money under the pillow fast when my mom walked in.

"I want to sit with you for a minute," she said.

"Why?" I said.

"I just want to. Dame un minuto, one, please."

"Why, though?"

"Because I need to."

"Are you okay?"

"No. Yeah. No." She laughed.

"I don't know what to do," I said.

"Nothing you can do, nothing. Only I can."

"What is it?"

"Do you know that he cares about toilet paper?"

"What?"

"He cares about toilet paper. How much is used."

"You mean. . . . ?"

"Yes, when you make a coo-coo."

I started to laugh really hard. She did too. "En serio, he means this. I don't think I ever knew anything like this." I'm laughing, happy about my mom. "Like four squares. Algo así." She was laughing really hard too. "Shh! If he hears us!"

Bud and Mary were the couple who lived in #7. He did construction. You knew because he wore a T-shirt with the name of a sheetrocking company on it. He was muscles and shoulders under that cotton shirt, his skin darkened from sun, his forearms bulging out like they were biceps, his biceps swollen like calves. Mary was a substitute teacher. I knew that because she took over one of my classes one time. She didn't recognize or remember or even know me, and she didn't ask about where or if I went to school when I said hi then. Her face sagged as miserable as the rest of her when I saw her walking by my locker. At the table, she was eating chips from the bowl my mom put there, wearing her nice substitute teacher dress that, sitting down here, seemed like it was getting pushed at in more places about to burst. Bud made one of those glad-to-meet-mes, shaking my hand like it was a sport he always had to win and always did. My mom was cooking food. Really. She was even making something Mexican, even if she didn't know how to cook it any better than anything else. One time I heard the Cloyd on the phone. He said, *I love to eat them tacos,* and *now I even got myself married to a pretty little Mexican gal.* He said that. Really. The dude who my mom married. She had some rice on the stove, and something was going wrong there, because her face was way close to the burner, watching it boil through the glass cover. I knew something was more messed up when Cloyd complimented her on the *chili salsa.* He might as well have complimented her on the tortilla chips, because she bought them at a store too. She didn't correct him though. She had on a brand new apron. It was cute, she'd call it, probably from an expensive department store. She had a new dress on under it too, and she was fixed up like behind the stove door wasn't enchiladas but one of those too-dark restaurants she expected to be taken to before she married him.

My mom was already done with a tall drink of some kind and was asking Cloyd to fix her another. A whole lineup of colored and clear liquor bottles were out on the sink, and next to them was the silver ice cube bucket with tongs I couldn't believe anybody used but my mom said you were supposed to have. Mary was drinking a can of soda. Bud and the Cloyd were drinking beer and were the only ones talking.

"We can't let them take away the work from us," Bud was saying.

"But don't you hire them sometimes yourself?" Cloyd asked.

"Cheap as they are, shit yeah!"

They both laughed and laughed.

Mary was squirming like she wanted to move her underwear with her butt. She picked out the widest chips that were in the bowl in front of her. She ate one while she picked another, not stopping.

"It's just that I don't know where they think they are," said Bud. "This is my home, if you know what I'm saying."

"Please stop talking about this," said Mary. "I hate this kind of discussion."

Bud didn't like her comment. "Save some of the chips for the rest of us," he told her, shaking his head. "Does this topic get you perturbed, Silvia?" Bud asked my mom.

"God, I hate when you're drinking," Mary said after she'd swallowed again.

"So now you see how come we have such a good sex life," he told Cloyd. "We gotta make up every night."

The two men laughed.

Bud said, "Maybe we have to limit our conversation to the black race."

The two men laughed.

Mary said, "God, Bud."

Bud said, "Okay okay already."

Cloyd said, "He knows how to raise your hackles, Mary."

Bud said, "See, he knows I'm shittin' around."

Mary shook her head.

"So, what about these Southern Democrats? Isn't it only a matter of time they're in our neighborhood?"

"God, Bud," said Mary. She said that a little muffled because she was eating the tortilla chips and had a mouthful again.

"That's not gonna happen," Cloyd said.

"It's happening already," Bud said. "Lotta moving noises coming from just a few blocks from here."

"Bud, have you seen *one* yet living on our street? Have you seen *one* black living on any ten blocks around here?"

"I dunno. It's not like it's impossible if I haven't."

"You have not," said Cloyd. "It's not likely to happen neither."

"What's to stop 'em?"

"I own this apartment building," Cloyd said. "You think I can't let who I want to live here? That I can't figure out how to *not* let who I *don't* want to live here? We take care of each other by taking care of our own interests."

"Food's almost ready," my mom said from the cooking area. "Sorry it's been taking me so long. And I just know this rice could be better. I'm embarrassed."

Cloyd went for his favorite bottle. He got a glass and an ice cube and poured his whiskey in it and swirled a cube.

"The truth is," he said, "I don't want their problems." It was like he was going to take a swallow but he didn't. "Now you take the Mexicans. The Mexicans aren't making no problems. They're good, hard-working folks who take care of their family and pay their bills. It's not that I don't work with black people who ain't like that too sometimes—"

"I don't think we should be talking about this," my mom interrupted. "Can we please not? For me and Mary?"

The two men looked at each other, discouraged like the women told them they had to turn off a football game.

"Okay, so here's another one for you," said Bud. "What's the deal with my new neighbor? What's that freakball do? You know who I'm talking about."

"In Six?"

"Of course! He don't look like he's ever seen any daylight."

"He is sort of strange, isn't he?" Cloyd said. "Pinkston. You call him Pink."

"Pink? You kidding?"

Cloyd shook his head.

"How can his name be the color of his skin? I cannot believe a man who looks pink like that could be *named* Pink."

They were kind of laughing without laughing.

"He sells used cars," Cloyd told him.

"Used cars?"

"Parks 'em right outside on the street here. It took me awhile to figure it out. I'm betting he sells them like they're his private and personal property. I'm betting he tells them it's his old mother's or grandmother's dear car, practically never driven, something like that. How he hates to sell it because it's been in his family so long."

"Is that legal?"

"Probably not exactly. He's being a dealer without paying for a dealer's license, appears."

"Damn well knew he must be some kind of hustler."

"He pays me cash too," said Cloyd.

"For his rent?"

Cloyd nodded, but making sideways, thinking eyes. "Even when he moved in. All of it in cash."

"Ain't that something suspicious," said Bud. "It don't set off the alarms?"

Either Cloyd had thought of it a lot or never, I couldn't tell by his expression which.

"But then you gotta be impressed," said Bud. "Yeah, I couldn't get much of a read on that freak. He's something, he is some work."

My mom was carrying the food to the table.

"Don't you love Mexican food?!" said Cloyd.

"Here I thought you only married her for her looks," said Bud.

"I am a lucky man." Cloyd smiled at her. He was drunk, that stupid grin.

★ ★ ★

Los Flores apartment building was right off the boulevard. The boulevard was cars parked or moving. At night they cruised in slo-mo, checking not just what was ahead but the headlights beamed every screwy way from the banged-up cars, up and down and left and right, while the dim yellow from the streetlamps, because of the wino stink, turned the broken glass in the alleys and against the curbs and doorways of out-of-business stores into glowing, petrified chunks of piss, made the dried-up oil stains seem to come from beneath the asphalt, puddling up from the center of the earth. I'd made it a few blocks away to the corner diner with the bowling alley, Alley Cats, where I was going to eat most of the time. I ordered a large fries and a burger—Mrs. Zúniga put a pile of jalapeños in it, which I loved, and instead of mayonnaise, she put in her homemade chile—and a chocolate shake. The thick shake was really two because it was made in one of those silver containers and came out all iced on the outside. Mrs. Zúniga, who I think liked me to eat there, always gave me so much more of everything. I think Mr. Zúniga and her probably owned the place. To me it was going into a home except there was a bar and bowling alley and a cash register. Mrs. Zúniga did all the floors and dusting and dishwashing and cooking, and Mr. Zúniga had the tools, the register, the trash, the beer openers, and changed the channel on the TV up in the corner. They both were always smiling at me, winking and like that. Mostly her, I guess, not him. Not him at all. He was too business, watching everything going on or else distracted by what was going on inside his head.

There were only six lanes, and I was the only one bowling. There wasn't a time I went when I wasn't the only one bowling, and the customers on the stools at the counter got to watch me instead of the TV when I got there. The first time that made me do a lot worse, but not after a while. Mostly they were a bunch of viejitos with bad eyesight or lonely drunks and probably had nowhere else to go either, drinking beer after bottle of beer, and if they didn't say something nice when I left, which they didn't, it was only because their nose was sniffing the glass. I already put my favorite ball in a corner of the rack at the most distant corner, and I never had to worry about it getting moved. The holes in it were drilled maybe twice or something like that, and they were chipped all around, but I liked the way my fingers and thumb went in anyways. The ball made a little curve about two-thirds down the lane. I was trying to break my high of 207. I'd hit that the third time I ever bowled and I was so hyped about it I daydreamed about bowling a lot. The last times I rolled I wasn't even getting close. I was missing some easy spares, and then I wasn't getting any strings of strikes like I did that high game. It seemed like I was right there, in that spot next to the one pin, but they wouldn't all explode in that crash when it was a strike and I was leaving one or three or some split. It was no different tonight, and after the fifth game—which at one point I was sucking so bad it seemed like I might not break a hundred—I quit.

I was following a street that ran beside the railroad tracks. I don't know how long this sickie white dude had been following me. At first he was like trailing a car length behind, but when I noticed him, when he saw I did, he pulled alongside. His ratty car had electric windows with a strip of chrome at the top and the passenger's window slid straight down, and he had to lower his head to do his pervie look over at me from the driver's side. He had short hair that was long in some wrong way and wore glasses. I'm not sure if what he had was what you'd call a smile. He followed like that until finally I decided to cross over the tracks and walk the other direction and go back to Los Flores. Not a few minutes later, there he was next to me again. Inside

I was screaming at him to fuck off, calling him queer joto homo and shit. I don't know why, but I just didn't bother to go after him. Maybe because it was easy enough to cross the tracks again, where his car couldn't follow. This next time when he pulled around, he parked way up above me because I was walking against the one-way. He was sitting there, waiting. Did he think I would just walk right over to him? Fucking fucked-up freak maricón loser. I decided to make a break. I crossed the tracks once more, but this time I was running and I got onto a street that took me into a neighborhood with lots of trees and bushy shrubs and I kept on running until I found an alley and cut through it. It was a good run. Pretty soon I was on a bigger street. It was dark enough that if I had to I could hide. I ducked in a corner once when I saw some headlights coming from behind me, but it wasn't sickie dude.

I could see them through the window by the dining area, dishes and bowls still on the maple table. I didn't go in. Then they were in the living room area. I thought about going around to the other side, where my window was, and crawling through, but while I was walking that way, I saw that Nica's door was open upstairs. I could hear my heart beating, and it wasn't red but blue. It beat with circles that made circles. You know how when you drop a pebble in a pool of water? I decided to go see her anyways.

She was sitting on a golden couch, that crushed soft material, watching the TV but without listening to the sound. I saw this through her window, the curtains pulled open. It was like when she saw me, she couldn't look too hard or smile too much. Then she came outside quickly, talking soft.

"It's that Angel just went to sleep, and I don't want nothing to wake him up."

"So you take care of him every night?"

"My parents are at work, so I have to."

I was thinking of the layout of the two-bedroom apartment. "So he sleeps in the room with you?" There was a dented pillow and a ball of blanket next to where she was sitting. "Or you sleep on the couch?"

"Maybe it's better if you come in, so that nobody sees us out here," she said.

"How come—" I started.

"Shh," she said, holding that finger to her lips.

She was *so* chula! She was wearing a dress exactly like the other one I saw, only this one was orange-colored.

I tried to whisper. "You could turn some dials so that you can't see the TV either, so it doesn't make any light against the walls." The TV was almost that way anyway, too purple, the color gone. The program was a Mexican soap opera. We sat at different ends of the couch.

She didn't laugh but she smiled at me.

"What do your parents do?"

"My mom cleans at a medical center. Margarito, he cleans at an industrial complex."

"Then, they work at night and you watch the baby."

She nodded. "What are you doing out?"

"I walk around," I told her. "It's what I do."

"Your father and mother don't care," she said, more as a comment.

"He's not my father," I said.

"Margarito's not my father either," she said.

"But the baby?"

"He's my brother from my mother's side. My mom is married to him."

"Yeah," I said.

"Do you go out all the time? Whenever you want?"

"They don't really notice. I think my mom doesn't care, but if she did maybe, she don't notice anyway. Probably I've always been kind of on my own."

"So you go out every night?"

"Not really. Sometimes, not all the time. More these days."

"I wish I could."

"Come and go to bowling with me."

"Bowling?"

She had trouble saying that word, and I didn't know the Spanish for it. I stood up and made motions and dumb noises.

"Shh!" she said.

"You wanna go with me? There's this place right around the corner."

"I have never been to this bowling. But no, I can't go to this bowling."

I think she liked the word *bowling*.

"Sure you can. It's . . . fun."

"*Fun?*" She almost laughed when she said that word in English too. Like saying it in English was the most fun she'd had all night.

"Fun fun fun!"

"Shh!"

"You will love bowling. Especially when you get good like I am. Even if you always lose against me."

She shook her head, happy. "Are you good at it?"

"Hell yeah!" I said in English.

"You must get to go a lot."

"Not a lot. Only when I don't got nothing else to do."

"You have *fun*." She almost laughed.

"I eat there too. I like the hamburgers. You like hamburgers?"

She nodded, a big smile. I thought maybe she smiled because she liked me, not hamburgers. I was feeling happy.

"So come with me. We could go tomorrow, right after school even." I was talking about myself when I said that, but I heard the school word the same way she did.

"I can't," she said.

"What about the weekend? They're open on Saturday."

She took a little longer to shake her head, not because she had to think about it but because she didn't.

"Well, sometime," I told her. "Okay?"

She nodded.

We both stared at the TV. A beautiful woman was arguing with two men and a hot-tempered little grandma.

"My parents would get so mad if you were here," she said.

I wasn't sure what to say. "What time do they get home?"

"Not for a long time yet. Until the morning. You don't have to worry yourself."

"It's that I don't want you to get in no trouble."

"Do you want some water?"

"Sure!"

I walked with her to the kitchen. She got two scratched-up plastic glasses out of the cupboard and filled them from the tap.

"Want me to go buy us some cokes?"

"I'm sorry I only have water," she said. "Sometimes we have Kool-Aid, but not right now."

"I love water, it's the best drink. But I can go buy us cokes. For, like, fun. I know you can't leave. I can go and then I can come back."

"Maybe you better not. If someone saw you go and then come back. . . ."

"Next time I come over," I told her, "I'm bringing cokes."

That made her shake her head and smile—both soft like doing that too hard would wake up the baby.

"And some potato chips or something. You like little things like that, right?"

"Shh!" she said.

"I'm sorry," I whispered again.

We sat back down with our glasses, that novela show still fuming.

"I love this show too," I told her.

She did an *ay ay* and shook her head. "You like the *fun*."

"Serious, I watch it almost every night, and I hate when I miss it. Did you see it last night? Hijo de su, it got crazy!"

She put her finger to her lips again and made a face at me.

"Sorry!" I whispered.

I wished I could kiss her. I didn't know how I could. I was afraid she'd never want to see me again if I tried and it went wrong. So I only imagined kissing her—there was kissing on the TV screen in front of us and neither of us said anything. My mind kissed her lips and cheeks and around her nose and around her eyes, kissing and kissing her—her lips turned into a bright white against the blackness, tunneled into colors, purple and yellow and green and orange. She was her lips and their moisture was air and space but you could feel it. She leaned against me—and we were in a city of tall buildings and near a lake and a river and an ocean and sky and light, squares and rectangles like in buildings but diamonds and ovals and perfect circles too, and the air wet, floating us, and we were not here. I was so close to her, I was so close to her, her warmth was a kiss too and so we might spin so fast at first and then just spin until it got easy, even if it was like breathing underwater; might be as easy as falling asleep when you are so sleepy.

"Have you ever made out with a chick?" one of the twins, I think Joe, asked me. I was beginning to think I saw a difference between them.

"You're stupid," I said.

"My brother hasn't," the other twin, I'm saying Mike, said.

They were laughing like out of junior high.

"It's 'cause I skip past the kissing part," his brother said. "I go straight for the hootchy-kootchy." He bit the bottom of his lip and made his hands feel the top and grab a bottom, his hips pumping.

They were killing themselves.

We were in the middle of the tracks, and really they were making me feel okay too. When we saw a lowrider over there, colored glitter in the midnight-blue paint job, popping off like metal to metal sparks, rims so polished they were like raw sunlight, we went straight over to it. The twins mashed their faces into the tinted windows to see the insides.

"Hey you fucking putos!" a dude in a baggy white T-shirt and silver chains and black shades yelled. He was on the other side of the screen door and on the porch of the house right there. I don't think he was gonna do shit else, but those twins ran off like we were guilty of fucking the car up. I stood by it a few extra seconds to make up for them, embarrassed and mad.

"You dudes are such fucking pussies," I told the twins. "You didn't have to run, we weren't doing nothing."

Tugging their matching white shirts and looking at their matching black shoes, it took them a little while to think of what to say to me.

"I just didn't want to hurt the vato," said Mike, I think, after the long silence.

"Yeah, if I got mad, hijo de la chingada, after I messed that culo mamón punk up, I'd have had to kick the shit out of his ride también! It wouldn't be fair to that beautiful carrito to be all dented up por mis patadas."

"And then, you know what?" said his brother, getting into it. "I'd be so fucking pissed off still I'd go burn down his pinche casita feaissima! I'd have to fuck over his whole life and familia, dude!"

★ ★ ★

Her on the phone when I came in: *I can't be louder.*

Cloyd was wanting me to chop down weeds on the back side of the building. Everything else was okay, I just didn't want this job. I knew something like this was coming, though, because I already overheard him telling my mom one afternoon how I had to learn responsibility, how I had to earn my right to stay here. That he was teaching me to be a man. I wondered what my mom was saying to back me up—she wasn't loud enough for me to hear. Though I was also afraid to hear her. I hoped she was fighting for me, but I wasn't liking her so much, because she was the one who was married to this man and his gray uniform.

The weeds were really tall, some of them up to my waist. The weeds were why I couldn't clean the screens on this side of the building, which was what got him to assigning me the job. I did not like weeding. I was swinging this weed cutter left and right, right and left, just not very hard, and I scratched like ants were all over me. I couldn't decide if doing it would make it go away easier, which would keep anything like it from happening again. Already it seemed like I'd been at it forever.

"Chief," Pink said to me, shaking his head, "this is one job no God-loving young man is wanting."

"Hey," I said.

"I been watching you," he said. "My advice, little brother, is that you need a beer."

"Yeah," I said.

"You want a beer?"

He wasn't joking around. I grinned.

"Come on, young man. Let me buy you something cold that you well deserve."

I hesitated. And then I decided I definitely wasn't going to finish this weeding which I did not want to do, and maybe it was better to not be around to explain.

We walked away from the weeds and across the front grass of the building to the street. He opened the passenger door to a Pontiac. It was a yellow four-door with black leather interior, an automatic, an AM–FM radio.

"You like this?" he asked once he got in.

Sure I liked it.

It started up after a couple of halting groans.

"We need to get a new starter and solenoid for it," he said.

We pulled out of the parking space, and in a minute we were on the boulevard. The windows were down, the wind took over the insides, and, yes, I liked this a lot more than what I was doing before.

"You don't mind we take a little drive?"

He was going there already, but no ways I minded. Pretty quick there were only black people everywhere. Just when I started thinking about this, we both heard somebody hollering from the sidewalk. "Hey mister Pink man! Hey there brotherman Pink!" From a distance he seemed like an old dude wearing overalls and a cap. Once we pulled over to the curb and he leaned into the window on my side to talk, his right hand holding a tall can in a brown bag, I could see he wasn't old. He was hanging in front of a bar with several guys who stayed back uninterested, dark T-shirts, one of them with a rag on his head.

"What you say, Pinkston?" he asked.

"I got the word and nothing but," said Pink.

The man laughed maybe five times bigger than his size. "Straight from the Lord, straight from the Lord!"

Pink pulled out some dollar bills. "Since you standing here, can you see to getting us a couple of those?"

The man called over one of his friends and gave him the

green bills, then turned back to Pink. "How's business? You doing good?"

"I seen lots worse."

"That's good, that's good," the man said.

There was a wide space here. I thought maybe it was because of me sitting there, right between them. Neither of them had even glanced at me.

"I thought it was you," the man said. "Hadn't seen you around.

"Gotta work, gotta do God's business, if you know what I'm saying, and carry in some coin too," Pink said.

"Yeah, I hear that."

"We both know it," said Pink.

Two beers in two wrapped-up lunch bags were delivered to him, and he handed one to each of us. He still didn't look me in the eye even when he gave me the bag for me.

"We gotta go see about getting a starter for this," Pink told him.

"Oh yeah?" the man asked.

"She looks nice, wouldn't you say?"

"Oh yeah, oh yeah," he said, backing his head out the window, stepping back one, examining. "Oh yeah," he said again from there.

"We're rolling," Pink told him. "You be good."

"That's what *she* tells me!" the man said, laughing loud. "That's what she be telling me!"

We turned off the big street where the projects were, all those steel doors painted orange, and all those wooden houses with porches sinking like the roofs.

"You wanna drive this?" Pink asked.

I drank beer before, got drunk on it, but not malt liquor—I liked the drinking and being in the car with the windows down. I got even more comfortable because it seemed like he was in his own neighborhood. But I'd only driven a car for a minute one time, and that was in a shopping center parking lot on a Sunday when I told my mom I wanted her to take me over for a learner's permit which I wasn't old enough to get yet.

"I shouldn't be driving," I told him.

I made him really laugh.

It was either Victory or Victors Auto Wrecker, couldn't tell which because that last letter was missing. The weeds that grew in those cracks of the asphalt or in those dirt patches were dying of no circulation and whatever else could happen to them when nobody touched or cared about them—or of oil maybe soaking their roots and nuts and bolts and beer caps being pounded and crushed into them by tires driving over. No living weeds. Good beer or whatever it really was. I loved being here because I was not being back there.

Everything in every direction inside was smeared and then smeared over again by grease, especially the man leaning on the counter between old parts and a cash register. He was fat, but in the way that looks more strong and hard and muscular, and scary as shit, like if he hit you you'd be really more than bruised, more broken like bones in a chicken dinner, and if he squeezed you you'd be really so freaking squished. Black-skinned as he was, you could see the grease was a coat of wax on him too, except I didn't think he cared even if he noticed. What weren't streaked were his teeth, clean and white as nurses' uniforms. He showed a lot of them.

"I know now why they call you the big man," he said to Pink.

"You keep on listening to them women."

"You a nasty fuck!"

"You hear about last week?"

"Damn fuck sure did heard about her! Damn!"

They laughed, and they laughed, and they laughed.

"Proof only you don't care nothing about ugly!" that man screamed.

"Ugly? You crazy? She was too young to be ugly yet! Nothing but a brick house, built too good."

They laughed more, and the man gave himself and Pink a beer. Pink told him to get me one too. He brought me a coke—which was fine with me—shaking his head, saying,"You don't want to be getting too used to no drinking at your young age. You don't let this crazy cat lead you into wrong."

Pink shook his head at me. "That is a good man in the making, one who ain't gonna be led by nobody. Ain't that right, Sonny?"

The coke can stunk of grease too, but inside it was ice cold. I was nodding my head even before I knew what he said. After, when my brain heard, I wanted to say yes again. I might not have thought of it, but if I had, I would've. I wanted it to be true.

I still didn't want to have anything to do with that jungle forest of weeds along the side of Los Flores. I wasn't even close to getting it done. When I went there now, all I did was stand there and dream about when I got a car. Like Pink's Pontiac, sitting right there on the street. I imagined me and Nica cruising boulevards in it. We'd cruise east, then we'd cruise down to the beach. We'd even cruise Hollywood. She'd never been to Hollywood like me, a couple of times for me. Just telling her I went there and take her, I'd be in with her.

I don't know why I was so shy about going up to her. I wasn't shy! I must have wanted her to see me outside, doing whatever, and invite me up. Or I was afraid of something. There was her dad, and it seemed like she had to watch out with him, and the door was never open anymore—not like that one time anyways. She didn't go to school, you know? That was something from the

dinosaur times. She was like some Indian slave, like the twins
were saying. And I was hearing more yelling late at night than
usual. I didn't like to hear it—I hated that I did. He was always
telling her to do something else and then saying it wasn't right,
like that. Like how come she couldn't do it right without him
showing her again? Shit like that. Sometimes it woke the baby
and he cried too much and that was her fault too. I hadn't swept
the slate deck up there for a while, but how could I as long as
there was this pinche weeding to do? I wasn't ever going to finish this, I just knew it. I didn't try and wasn't going to either. I
ain't no slave, that was what I'd tell myself to say. I wasn't explaining to either the Cloyd or my mom about it.

So I was going to my room right after school, and then I
ran out to the bowling alley to eat a burger Mrs. Zúniga made
for me. It was all better going there, and they liked me so much
they stopped making me pay for my games. That kind of made
me hold back. I didn't want to take advantage. But I did stay
longer. I always got free coke refills. So I bowled frames, and if
I stayed out late enough, he was usually asleep on his chair or
even already in the bedroom and maybe my mom would be on
the couch watching TV. She never watched TV before. It was
crazy to see my mom in front of it. She'd even be asleep there,
the phone stretched out, and I'd go quiet as I could to that bedroom. Neither of them were asking me anything when they saw
me, but I figured out to say how I went to school or to some
friend's, like over to the twins for instance, even though I didn't
know where they lived.

It was hard to see in the night—no lights nowhere—and if it
were a hole to step in that went to the bottom of the earth,
you wouldn't know it was in front of you until you fell into it.
But it was also a little harder to be seen. I was going to see if
Nica had her TV on.

"What're you sneaking around to do?" I heard Cindy's voice behind me say.

I jumped, caught and guilty. I hadn't seen her or thought one thing about her for a while.

"You trying to steal more magazines from somebody?"

That doubled my surprise. I had no idea where that was coming from. She got up real close to me, where I could almost taste her breath and touch the hot coming off her bare neck and shoulders.

"I heard about it," she whispered. "Gina told me."

She was wearing a bikini top and some torn cut-off jeans, but once she said that, I didn't look.

"What're you talking about?" I asked.

"You know!"

We were near the window of Mr. Josep's apartment, and he pulled his curtain back to see us. Cindy grabbed my hand and led me, like I might get lost. It was like she wasn't even thinking I was up there for any other reason but to talk to her.

"You know," she said again once we were inside her apartment.

It was a lot warmer in here. Too warm. I think she had the heater on. Except she also had the apartment door and the windows on either side of it open.

"I don't either. I don't know what you're talking about."

"Oh, you don't know, do you?" she said, teasing. She put her hands to her chichis, pushed them together, and made a sexy face. "What can you think of now?"

That made it less clear to me. I did see how she was pretty good there. I let myself look at them when she did that.

Cindy was shaking her head at me. "You have to meet my sister," she said. "Do you know she posed for *Playboy* magazine? People talk about my sister's incredible body. She just isn't very pretty. They say I have the pretty face."

"*She* has the body?" I didn't mean to say that out loud. I was more thinking that Cindy was here in the living room, her hot living room, and she was in a bikini top.

"I know I don't look bad," she said, "but I'm supposed to be the pretty one. Wait till you see my sister, and then you'll know what I'm talking about." She went over to the kitchen counter. "I'm glad you finally noticed me, though. I'm not so bad, am I?" She was refilling a glass she'd been drinking from. "Hey, you want some of this?"

She held up a bottle of wine. She was mixing red wine and ginger ale.

"I don't know," I said.

She made it for herself without another thought. "We're all waiting for my sister's centerfold. They may only use her body. They can do that, you know. They do whatever they do and put in a prettier face on a better bod. Brush, I think they call it."

I'd sat down in the exact place I did the other time. "I think it's called airbrush." It was way hot in her apartment. "Do you have the heater up or what?"

"Yeah, I do," she said. "I like fresh air but I didn't want to be cold."

I looked around. There were windows open too.

She sat next to me on the couch, a little too close. Before I wasn't sure what to do in general. Now I wasn't sure of nothing.

"I didn't think!" she said. "Do you want ginger ale with ice?"

"It's okay," I said. "I'm full."

I was too hot and I wanted to look away, so I looked down. My mind was still seeing her pushing her chichis together and wondering where her husband was. That Tino. I wondered what he was like. If he was a big dude. He was the only one I hadn't seen yet, though I did hear him one time. I saw two dollar bills near a plate on the floor, sticking out from under the couch.

"How come you're so shy with me?" Cindy said. She scooted closer to me. "When you don't mind looking at naked girls in a magazine?"

"Whadaya mean by that? How come you keep talking about some magazine?"

"Sonny, Gina told me already. She knows."

"Wha'd she say?"

"Gina?"

"Yeah, this Gina."

"They know you're the one taking them, Sonny."

"I'm not," I told her. "How can she say it's me?"

"It's okay to look at them," she said. "You're a boy. You should want to look—"

"I don't take no pinche magazines."

"—maybe just don't keep them."

"I didn't take nothing," I said. "Why are they saying it's me anyways?" I was like upset, pissed off even. "Why would that Gina lady say that? Do you know her very well?"

She got up and was looking around. I pocketed the two dollars, probably because I was mad. When she came back she had an ashtray and she picked out a half-burned cigarette. I knew it was mota, it wasn't like I didn't know. I'd taken a couple hits of it before. Mostly I didn't want it to seem like I was afraid to get high with her, so I did what she did. We passed it back and forth really silent, not talking. When it was gone, she went back to drinking her drink, which was frosty on the outside because she'd made it so freaking hot in the apartment. She turned to me, like closer still, looking closer, and she seemed closer than ever.

"Have you ever been with a girl?"

I was feeling like I hadn't done nothing ever.

She leaned into me. "Kiss me," she said. Then she kissed me and her tongue was in my mouth, like she was the boy and we were making out. I wasn't thinking of that Tino. "Touch me," she whispered into my ear. She pulled my hand to her chest. "Go on, touch me." I reached my hand under the bikini top until it moved up and I was feeling her. She felt really good, big, soft. It was good. It was really good. She liked it too, but she was the one to make us stop.

"I bet you haven't been with a girl," she said, suddenly pulling away, acting like it was me who'd made all the moves.

The television in the living room was on and it seemed like my mom was asleep on the couch, the hazy glow of the TV a blanket over her. It was a weekday, and it was night, Cloyd was in bed already.

"Where were you?" she asked.

"I was out," I told her, surprised that she talked. I was feeling too much mota, and way strange. I wanted to go to that room where I slept.

"I wish I were too," she said.

That sounded like her, the mom I knew from before. The one who never sat around and watched TV. Or drank beer—there was a beer bottle next to her. That was crazy. My mom didn't drink beer, I think especially because it was fattening.

"I'm bored," she said.

The phone was next to the beer bottle, the cord across the rug of the living room. She'd had one put in so she could have her own phone and number and then she got the long cord so she could move around with it. I knew about this because, unlike a few, this was one of their arguments that was easy to follow. They were having these other kinds of raising-the-voice-a-little-bit discussions that weren't, if you asked me, much about what they were talking about.

"What do you watch?" she asked, meaning the TV. "I'm trying to like TV." She was serious even. "Can you put it on something you like and come sit with me?" She'd had her head on the arm of the couch, laying down, but now she sat up.

I walked closer and turned so I could see the television, but I didn't want to sit. "I don't watch anything regular. I don't really watch that much." At this moment, all mota high, it was impossible for me: TV was crazy! The noises! The light! The *normal* people in it were like nobody in a real world, the one I walked around in.

"You don't like the TV in your room?"

"Sure, it's okay," I said.

"You never had one before."

I nodded.

"You don't like it though?"

"I guess it's pretty good to have in there," I said. "I guess I don't always want to watch." I was wanting to leave. I wasn't going to try to explain to her how I listen to the radio and watch the lights and look for colors and get squares and circles and stars and my own planets and moons and suns, and all that, right into my head, especially since I was messed up good and this was really hard because the TV was fucking crazy light and sound.

"You want me to make him get you a better one?"

"TV?"

"Sí, m'ijo, a better TV."

I was so messed up it almost seemed like what she was saying was because I'd been smoking out. "No, I don't need a new TV set. Thanks though."

There was a fat, tall gray space here. I was trying to think of the right way to go away without making her ask me what was up or wrong or whatever, when what came up was that it was her too, that she went some places by herself too.

Then she just talked, broke into what I was thinking to myself and into what was playing on the TV. "I'm sorry," she said.

It sounded like it had an echo, like she was talking from a television. I didn't know what to say, what I should say, what she meant, nothing.

The silence became a fog.

"There's nothing ever good on," she said finally.

Her voice this time was like sunlight, and right then I thought of her that way: as a sun. She was the sun, and so much was winter, cloudy, dark, all moonless.

"At first I didn't mind," she said. "All I had to do was change the channel."

"Maybe you can call somebody instead," I suggested, looking at the phone. "You like to talk."

She looked at me. I think she realized I'd heard her talk on the phone. I didn't mean it that way, and I didn't want her to know.

"I was thinking of Ceci," I said. "Don't you wonder how she is?" I wondered about her, if my mom ever talked to her. She never talked about her, I never asked. I don't know why I was bringing this up, and now. It just came out of me.

The TV made all the noise for a little longer time, and even if our eyes were on it we weren't watching or listening to it, but wishing I hadn't said what I did. I was standing there.

"I've called everybody." So much time had passed, I'd already forgotten we were talking about the phone.

"I better go to sleep now," I told her.

"Buenas, m'ijo," she said. I swear there was disappointment in her voice. I'd never heard that in her before.

The stucco of the apartment building was painted a pale yellow, and bolted to its street side was a black wrought-iron sign, in a longhand-style lettering, two flood lamps in an ivy bed below aimed up at it: Los Flores. Beneath those words were three flowers branching out of one thick stem. I didn't know that much about flowers, but my mom told me they were margaritas, which I think are called daisies. Why I was so much in my head about words and flowers was because Cloyd was having me paint the sign. Which I didn't mind, because it wasn't the weeds along the side. He said he wanted me to be very careful about splattering black paint on the green wall, and because he worried about it, he told me to go easy, to take my time. That's why I was taking as long as I was. I went slow. I was taking my time and trying to do a good job.

Los Flores: It's that I really wasn't sure one way or the other, because I wasn't any expert on the Spanish language. I thought probably I was just wrong. Could be *flower* was a masculine word in Spanish, not a feminine. How would I know? There are words that seem like they should take a *la* and don't. A TV show, for example, is *el* programa. Or for *map, el* mapa. Or like the word for a fashion model is modelo, even if the model is not a dude. I mean, probably I was just making myself feel confused, so I had mostly accepted it standing up there on a ladder, painting the wrought iron. One day I remembered to ask the twins.

"Watch, it's this way," Joe said. "If it's the name of a family, then it's right. Me and Mike, say we wanted to open a bakery. We could call it Panadería Los Hermanos Hernández. So then *Los Hernández* means "the Hernández family." *Los Hernández* means "the family of." So *Los* Flores means the Flores family. Pero, *Las* Flores means "The Flowers." What your daddy the Cloyd has up there just means the vato's a dumbass."

"Un hija de puto," Mike said.

"You'd think he'd might have at least looked it up in a dictionary," said Joe. "Or somebody who's a relative, who has like a maid or a gardener he could ask."

"Yeah, or like he coulda checked it out in una libra de *quotetoes* por jotos," Mike said.

"This is probably why real Mexicans—you know, mexicanos —think we're such pochos up here," Joe said. "We grow up seeing words like that around, and then we get all used to them, and then we say them like that's how they are and we don't know how we got to be such pinches tontos."

"Hey, you know in the Lone Ranger?" Mike jumped in. "Como the Indian Tonto's name is pronounced *tanto*, right? Like his name's *too much*. That's pretty dumb, right? But his name ain't that, right? It's spelled T-O-N-T-O, *tonto*."

I added those letters up fast. "Ay, his name is *stupid*," I figured out. "Man, I'm so fucking stupid I didn't realize he was Mister Stupid!"

"Is too mush, Tanto," Mike said. "Es muy estupid, stupid."

I tried to tell my mom but she didn't hear me. She wasn't dressed for listening or like she had been in the kitchen for very long or like she was planning to stay there either. It seemed to me she was wearing another new dress, and she was smelling washed and bath-oiled and lotioned and misted, and the high heels were glossier and redder than her lipstick. She was opening American cans of Mexican salsa.

"He doesn't even know I buy este chile at the grocery store," she told me. "He thinks I make it. He even tells everybody I do."

"You do make it," I said. "Or you could."

She crinkled her face at me like I'd suggested she go out like jogging or something.

"You think I should cook for him day and night like he wants?"

I tried to think of what she did all day, now that she didn't have to work.

"What's it for?" I asked.

"It's for some client. Something to snack on while they're drinking beer and talking about their business. He says it's for a big contract. I think a whole housing development."

"That sounds big," I said.

She made one of those as-if-she-cared-about-that-part. "Like it would make him act like he has one extra dime to spare."

This was new complaining. She'd made some new move. At first I got thinking like, *Oh, no!* and then I got thinking like *All right!*

"Do you know what he told me this morning?" she said.

Oh yeah, of course I do.

"Do you know what he told me?" she asked again like I hadn't heard any of it the first time.

I answered no, even though I didn't feel like it.

"He told me again that I was using too much toilet paper."

I wondered what any of this was really about, where it was really going. . . . Nah, that's not right. I didn't wonder. I only wished I didn't have to hear any of it.

"Not in so many words," she said. "Just, 'I think you need to buy some toilet paper when you go to the store.' Or maybe he was talking about me not going to the grocery store enough. I don't know."

She struggled with the can opener. That was because she didn't want to use it. The other night I heard her telling Cloyd she was going to buy an electric one, and he was saying how they didn't last and took up too much counter space. She goes, I can buy a better one when it breaks.

I was trying to think of something else the hell to talk about. "So is that what you're mad about?"

"Why do you ask that? Who says I'm mad?"

"It sounds like you're mad."

"M'ijo, I'm not mad. I don't have to get mad."

"It sounds like you're mad."

"I'm not mad."

"Okay, you're not mad."

"Don't tell him I didn't make this," she said, as she poured another can into a big ceramic bowl.

"Tell him what?"

"That I don't make this salsita!"

"You should just tell him if you're worried about it."

"I'm *not* worried about it. I'm asking you to not tell him. Can you do that for me?"

"What are you gonna say when he finds out?"

"How will he find out unless you tell him?" She put a dinner plate over the bowl. "Will you take this outside to the trash for me?" She handed me a bag with the cans in it.

"You're afraid he'll see the open cans." Now I was smiling.

"Go throw them away, will you? Will you please?"

I went to the cabinet under the sink where the kitchen trash went.

"No, not there, Sonny. You're very funny."

"Why not?"

"Please? Can you please do what I ask for me without making me want to scream?"

I knew I couldn't tease her too much right then. Sometimes I could, but I could tell that this time she might not like me going too far. She hadn't hit me or threatened to since we moved in here. She was going out, and something was going on.

I was stuffing the empty cans under some other garbage—trying to do a good hiding job for my mom—when that Gina came from behind me with her paper sacks of trash.

"Caught you," she said. She wore plasticky blue pants and shoes which came to a point, sharp as a rosebush thorn. I don't know why it's what I kept noticing. Besides her short black hair, chopped to the bottom of her ears, I couldn't see her above her waist because my eyes were stuck on what was below. "What're you digging for?"

"I wasn't. . . ." I felt caught, not as much for hiding the cans only for doing something like it. I couldn't make eye contact with her.

"I'm your neighbor," she said. "Gina."

"I figured that," I said. "I know you're in, well, Number Two."

"The apartment next to you guys," she said. She was bones, way skinny, really small, all buggy eyes that watched.

"Right," I agreed.

"You're doing such a good job around here," she said.

"Yeah?" I wanted to move on. "Thanks, whatever you mean."

"Of keeping things swept up and clean! You're doing such a good job. The building's never looked better."

"Oh yeah, that. Cloyd has me doing it." I was dying, afraid she was gonna try to accuse me any second of lifting their magazines. I was glad when we were finally away from the trash cans and walking toward the apartment doors. "I don't mind. I kind of like working around here even."

"It looks *so much* better around here too. Really! It's always been kept up, but you're making it almost spotless." She stopped at the #2 door, hers. "It's great to meet you finally."

I started crunching on tortilla chips in the bowl sort of like I was out of breath and needed air and the oxygen was inside them.

"Don't eat those!" my mom yelled. She was practically skidding around the corner, she was banking her turn so fast. She was in a hurry. "Those are for him and his client."

"Isn't there a bunch more in that bag over there?" A bag was on the corner of the tile counter. I wanted these and I wanted them too.

"Please don't eat them. Please. Okay?"

I still had one in my hand, and I took a few more.

"And I want you to do something else for me." She reached into her purse and handed me a five. "Maybe just go get yourself dinner tonight. He'll be going out."

What was strange is that she said this like I wasn't buying my own dinner practically every night. I guess she was so distracted it hadn't occurred to her to wonder how I did that—how I'd been doing it. At first she would give me some money like this. But that stopped. I was using from my own hidden money pile.

"It'll probably take more than this to shut me up," I said.

"What did you say?"

"I'm joking around, Mom. You remember how people do that?"

"M'ijito, I don't have time," she said.

"I'm pretty busy too," I told her, "but I still remember how to joke."

She didn't hear a word I said.

"Speaking of that," she suddenly said, "are you going to finish that painting outside?"

"Speaking of that? What're you talking about?"

"I thought of it right now," she said. "It's that, well, I don't want it to turn out like the weeds."

"What's that mean, the weeds?"

"He talks about it. How you couldn't finish."

"Couldn't?" I was pissed off. "Wouldn't," I told her. "Didn't want to."

"Well, I don't think you should not finish this other too."

"I'm almost done already. He knows it too. I'm sure he knows. I'm almost done right now. Did he say something?"

"No. I just don't want him to."

"He better give me money for it," I announced. "He said he would."

She had actually stopped moving and was standing still, facing me even, looking at me, that's how serious the situation was.

"He said he was gonna pay me for that work," I said right back at her. "I wanna be paid."

"Don't make any trouble," she said. This was another kind of tone, with another meaning. It wasn't, I could tell, about me but about her and him, her and her trouble. "You hear me? I'll give you money if you need it. You know that."

I knew that? How did I know that? When did I know that? "I want it, and he said he'll pay me, right? He said he would. I believed him." I was feeling like I was on my toes a little.

"If he doesn't, I will. If you really need it, I'll get it for you."

If I really need it? I couldn't believe she said that. "He will." And no, she wouldn't. She wouldn't remember, and if she did, or I reminded her to remember, she'd either deny she offered or say she would later.

She stopped and, distracted, sponged the kitchen counter as if she'd already forgotten we'd had this conversation and then turned back to me, eye to eye. "Please tell him that I left the salsita in the refrigerator."

She had a note for him under the bowl of tortilla chips. "Doesn't it say that right there?" I asked.

"M'ijo, please tell him?" She drooped her head and closed her eyes for like two seconds, like a prayer. I was still thinking of him not paying me. "Will you please tell him? For me? Please?"

"Where're you going?"

"I've got an appointment at the beauty parlor," she said. "A late one. Then I'm going to a fashion show." She stopped and stared too much at me, then away like she was still staring, waiting for what I would say—I decided; I figured out— because she was lying. "Remember Nely?"

Nely was one of her better friends, one she liked to go out drinking with, talk about dresses and bras and makeup and men with. I did like Nely, how wouldn't I? She was the one who used to touch me the most when I was small, her soft hands all over my face and neck, and when she'd grip my shoulders and squeeze the muscles in my arms, she'd do it hard, like I was so strong, and like it made her feel muscles inside herself too. She'd tell me how I was a guapito, say it loud for everyone, soft in my ear. Of course I liked her. What I really didn't forget is my cheek against her soft chichis when I would be in her lap. I would pretend I didn't really know where my face was. In a way I wasn't pretending to not know where I was. Except I wasn't maybe supposed to like it, and she maybe wasn't supposed to let me.

"Didn't she marry some really rich guy?" I asked.

My mom made a face. Obviously she didn't want to talk about that, and she snapped at me. "That's who I'm going with is all," she said. "I haven't seen her since I moved here."

It wasn't nighttime yet, though it wasn't the bright afternoon anymore. I could paint the Los Flores sign. I was planning on that, planning on finishing this very day. Now I didn't want to very much. Outside the front door, on the grass I'd mowed and edged the other day, I thought of some other things I could do to get away from the two of them. I could go bowl. Or I could go sweep the walks, though I had been doing that too much, like that Gina said, and nothing needed it that much. Mostly I did it to get an excuse to go past Nica's door. Right then I decided to walk around from the front of the apartment building to look up there again. I was always watching the curtains, trying to figure out when she for sure was there alone, her parents at work. I don't know why I was afraid to just knock.

Mr. Josep was sitting on his chair, staring out. I didn't think he ever noticed me or anything else.

"Come." He waved.

"Excuse me?" I wasn't sure what he said or if he was talking to me even.

"Come," he said again, waving upward. "Go up the stair and come to here."

I took the stairs up and stood close to him.

"You want the chair?"

"I don't think . . . ." I started, considering. "I probably don't need one."

I was standing there, waiting for him, for what he wanted.

"You go to the school?"

"Yeah," I said. "High school."

"You like the high school?"

"No," I said.

"Good," he said.

He must not have heard what I answered.

It was like he didn't really want to talk to me but was working up the words, or his mouth was too full and he had to swallow. I stared out at what he might be seeing when he sat there. What I saw were dark electrical wires looping from one pole to another in the gray droop. And so many crinkly wood greased-up poles. I heard the traffic on the boulevard that I usually didn't hear, unless I was on that bed in the dark, now everywhere in the air like insects in a jungle. I heard a motorcycle revving, then popping. I heard an airplane but couldn't see it in the sky. I heard a dog barking, and then another dog barking. I saw the sky not like air but like gas, like clean fizz on a blank TV screen. For a second I started to imagine what he must see out there. Then he interrupted me.

"She doesn't go to the school," he finally told me, nodding at Nica's door. "She doesn't know any English."

"Yeah," I said. I didn't for one second think this was what he was going to talk about.

"That is not good," he said.

"Yeah," I said. I didn't understand why she didn't either. "Probably not, huh?"

"I practice my English," he said.

I was wondering what language he spoke. It didn't seem to me like his accent had anything to do with Spanish.

"I went to the school. My father wanted me to finish the school because it was good, he told me. He told me I would get good job and have good life because I finish."

"Yeah," I agreed.

"I have good job too," he said. "All my life, I have good job."

I was going to ask what that was and ask him about himself, like where he came from. It was supposed to be Spain, or Portugal, and though I never met anyone who was from Spain, or Portugal either, he sure didn't seem to be from there, so I was planning to ask one of those since-you're-talking questions when Cindy stepped out her apartment door.

"Hey you handsome boy, you! How come you don't want to visit with *me?*"

Even Mr. Josep's old chair creaked in surprise. First it was out of the surprise to hear any voice—made me realize how quiet it seemed before—and then at what she was wearing, which was a white bikini, which for a second or two didn't look like a bikini but panties and a bra. Either way, she had it to show. Even Mr. Josep not only shifted his body to see her but bobbed his head, almost shaking his eyes into focus.

"Why is that?" she said. She was standing fully outside the door, both bare feet on the deck, daring both of us to see whatever we felt like.

Mr. Josep turned his head downward very slowly, and then his hand waved above, in her direction, like he was brushing away a feather floating down toward his lap. "She want you to go there," he told me. "You go there."

"What is it about me you don't like?" Cindy asked me.

She was wearing a bikini that was supposed to make you
think of Hawaii. I was liking Hawaii.

"Were you at the beach?" I asked her, "or are you going
right now?"

"You want to? Yeah, let's go!"

She'd been smoking mota again, the smell strong in her
place. She had her wine drink in a glass going just as strong. It
was too hot in the apartment again, the heat up too high.
Clothes were spilled and draped around the living room, and a
few plates were off the walking path, and there were empty
glasses and beer cans and cigarette butts in ashtrays on a big glass-
covered coffee table. It seemed like more people had been here
than just her and the Tino I'd never saw. I started looking for
money.

It was going to be dark soon, way too late to drive to the
beach. "It's a lot of fun to go to the beach. I practically never get
to go."

"I promise you I'll take you if you say you want to," she said.

"Sure."

"Say it."

"Say what?"

"That you do. You have to say it."

"Do what? Say what?"

"That you want to. That you want to go with me."

"To the beach?"

I was confused, smelling her marijuana so much it almost
felt like I was already smoking it with her. I also kind of hated
being around drunk people—her now too—and also, maybe, because she was getting real close to me, fast. Close enough that I
could smell her winey breath. Close enough that I could feel the
cups of her little Hawaii bikini top brushing my chest and then
her hands on my wrists.

"Tell me," she said so close to me I couldn't remember what we were supposed to be talking about. "Tell me we will, Sonny."

I was embarrassed about being excited down there just for her being against me some when then, like that, she pushed her lips against mine and opened her mouth and sucked my tongue into it. For a few seconds or minutes we were making out and then we dropped onto that hard couch and she reached back and undid her top and guided my face to a nipple. Her skin everywhere was soft, and curved, and moist. I didn't know what I touched that wouldn't make me want to explode. She was pushing at me, hot as a sweat when you're working, and then she undid me and was playing with me down there and breath sounds came out of her and probably me too. When my eyes closed, it was the desert, black space and sparkly stars, so up there it made me feel both old enough for this and way young—thought of and seen so much, it had all been too far away or hidden from what I knew about—a sky too high and faraway that I could have never seen it from this city if I were to look up, straight at it, as someone kept pointing it out like constellations I didn't see. I think she would let me touch her anywhere, but I didn't because I wasn't sure, even as she pulled down my pants and my chones and had her hand on me there. I couldn't take it and I was telling her she would have to stop, I couldn't hold back if she didn't stop, but she didn't want to and I couldn't stop myself. I started falling away, into a black so black I couldn't see nothing but the fireball streak of light swirling through it—I couldn't tell if it was going away from everything or was going to suddenly crash.

She got up, putting her little pieces of bikini back together as she went into the kitchen. I was still pretty much in shock. A good shock. It felt really good and I couldn't talk.

"I wanted to take you into bed with me so bad," she said in the kitchen. She was drinking water. "You came too fast."

As bad as I felt, meaning good, what she said made me feel the other bad. I wanted to yell at her for saying it, and I wanted to do it again now, but now that a minute or two more went by, well, I didn't say so. I wanted to steal something of hers and as my eyes went around I couldn't believe the front door was wide open. I was scared too about what we did. What if someone saw? What if that Tino dude walked in?

"You haven't been with many girls, have you?"

Maybe she was meaing it nice, but I didn't like it that she made me out to be a punk. Except, how could I defend myself? "I've been with a few." Almost dressed, I was standing up, near the front door.

"A few?" Her tone made it clear she didn't believe me for a second.

"Yeah," I said. "Shut up," I said.

"Have you even been with one?" She wasn't laughing at me but she was like, what, an older sister catching you making up bullshit. "You can tell me."

"I done it before." Okay, mostly I was lying. Okay, I was lying flat out. Though in a way I wasn't. I had a girlfriend last year, and I did everything I could with her, she just wouldn't go all the way. And she'd never considered touching me down there, at least she never did except accidentally.

"It's all right," she told me. "It's sweet."

That got me really mad for a few seconds, until I decided maybe it was better to not say nothing else. I didn't want to lie to her and—well, she'd know and I'd really feel fucking dumb. "You didn't even know the door was open, did you?"

"Oh no," she said. She really didn't. "That is bad!"

I closed it hard and locked a deadbolt.

It could have been that that got her going different, because she changed moods and started cleaning up the kitchen, piling pans and dishes into the sink. I saw her put her jug of wine in a lower cabinet. She'd gotten nervous and excited. It was the same kind of energy she had when she saw me, but now it was more like not drunk or sexy.

"What time does he get home from work?" I asked.

"See those plates? Could you bring them to me?" She barely looked at me when she said it.

I stacked them and took them to her, even another two she didn't ask for, and a couple of glasses sitting around. She was running the water hard into the sink, loud, making dish soap bubbles mound high.

"I'm gonna go on and take off," I said.

"I'm sorry," she said. "I think I'm feeling guilty." She wasn't looking at me. "I should have cleaned up the apartment earlier."

"Oh," I said. "Yeah."

Her wet, soapy hand grabbed mine as I turned to leave. "I like you, Sonny," she said. She kissed me on the lips. It was a lot different kind of kiss. "I like you a lot."

Cloyd swiveled toward me as I was trying to pass his office as fast as I could. There was a man with him in a slobby suit. Cloyd was already red-eyed, and he was wearing that hick smile I hated the most and swirling that ice cube. He had on his gray work uniform, still starched from a laundry, like he hadn't sweated in it today. His bottle of whiskey was on his office desk like it was the latest trophy, shiny below all those dead deer with blank marble eyeballs.

"Hey you," he told me. "Come and shake hands."

I was already past, the corner I'd be turning in front of me. I did not want to talk, I did not want to turn back, but I did.

"This is my son," Cloyd told the man.

That pretty much took me by surprise. Mad. I probably frowned. I felt my whole body want to go all diarrhea sick.

"Milt Womack," the man said, extending his big hand. He was so fat his belly was squirting out between the buttons on the white shirt he was wearing. Even if I wasn't very knowledgeable about ties, I could tell the one he was wearing was like from a hardware store and probably bought used. He stunk like gym socks.

"You shake his hand like a man," Cloyd told me. "Give it a good grip!"

So I even had to do that again.

"There you go!" Cloyd said.

"It's good to meet you, young man," said Mr. Womack. He was very impressed by the advice I was given.

I wasn't going to say anything, but I could tell Cloyd was about to give me more suggestions. "Nice to meet you too," I mumbled.

I stood there. I couldn't figure out how to plain leave yet. I'd say it was something like standing at a urinal with old men on either side of you, or a coach who's telling you how much tougher everything was for him, or a vice principal who's not saying nothing because he's so much better than you. It was like I was getting old and wrinkled before their eyes.

"He's a handsome one, like that mother of his," Mr. Womack said.

Cloyd approved of that comment. "Yeah, she is one pretty Mexican gal," he said. "I am one lucky man, all right."

I was one disgusted dude.

"You play sports?" Mr. Womack asked me.

"This one, strong as he is, says he don't like playing sports," Cloyd answered.

"No?" Mr. Womack said. "You look like you'd be an athlete."

"He don't like playing sports," Cloyd said again.

I couldn't look at either of them. "I guess I'm gonna go."
I was squeezed up.

"You feel like coming out, having some dinner with us,
you're welcome," Mr. Womack said.

Cloyd drank, hick-smiling at me to tell me not to say yes.

"You do like steaks?" Mr. Womack said. "I'm buying us
big steaks."

"Well, there it is, he's buying!" Cloyd said, pouring himself
some more whiskey first, then tipping some more into Mr. Womack's glass. "That's the best part!" The two of them hoo-ha'd.

"You gotta get good grub while you can," said Mr. Womack,
"because I know this cheap bastard Longpre ain't feeding you
steaks, is he?"

"Listen now, you don't gotta go let him in on that! I don't
think he'd even noticed yet!"

I knew hahahaha in English. I knew jajajaja in Spanish. I
wanted to learn how it was in French.

"You know," Mr. Womack said, turning to Cloyd, "I barely
get to see my boy now. About the same age as you, Sonny."

"My own got all grown," Cloyd said. "Can't believe how
fast they grow up."

They both turned their gazes up at me and kept them there,
like they were both suddenly all religious about life.

"Thanks," I said, "but I think I'll go finish the painting
outside."

"That is one very fine attitude," Cloyd said. "Even if really
he don't want to go out with us old farts."

If there was a way to bust the dude about him not wanting
me to go with him, I would. I almost wished I could say I wanted
to go, to see how he'd deal with it. "I'll be finished today," I
said. "I'm almost finished right now."

"That's good news," he said.

"My mom was saying you were worried about it," I said.

"Worried about it?"

"That I'd finish the painting. That I wouldn't. I'm just about finished right now, though."

"No, no, not worried," said Cloyd, talking more for Mr. Womack. "I saw the work." He swallowed all that was in his glass. "He's painting outside," he told Mr. Womack. "Doing a fine job too."

"That's good," Mr. Womack said. "Learning how to work is good."

"He's been doing lots around here for me," said Cloyd. "I gotta be truthful."

I went to get the ladder I left along the side of the building, in the tall weeds I never cut, but it wasn't there. That scared me, because if it got ripped off, I'd hear how I should have put it away. The paint and the coffee can with the brush soaked in turpentine weren't there either. I walked around to the back, where the shed was and saw that aquel Tino had gotten home, his car—front-ended, rear-ended, and side-smashed—was in its slot. My stomach got twisted sick. The ladder and paint and brush had been put back in the shed, but not by me. I balanced them all so I'd only have to make the one trip out to the front.

"Hey there, young man."

Pink waved, leaning against a long, polished, heavy bumpered four-door Buick, obviously waiting for a customer. I liked seeing him and I probably would've gone over and talked to him, when Cloyd came around from the front door and over to me.

"Womack's taking a leak," he told me, "and then we're on our way for some supper." He was out of the gray uniform and in a clean shirt and a clean pair of pants, and his hair was comb-marked a little bit. "How you been, Pinkston?"

Pink waved to him too, but he was already on his way in the other direction toward a black man and woman, both Sunday dressed, who'd parked the car they drove to look over one of Pink's.

Cloyd stared at the three of them for too long. "Don't know when I'm getting back," he said finally.

I thought he would be talking to me about the ladder. I was setting it up under the Los Flores sign, about to step up.

"Tell your mom," he said. "You hear me? That I don't know when I'm getting back."

I nodded. It was too weird for me. Everything.

"All right?" he asked.

"Like, tell her you'll be back late or what?"

"That's right."

"Okay," I said. "If I see her."

"She probably won't be getting back earlier than me," he said. "Don't ya think?"

"I have no idea." And I really had no idea. And now I didn't want any. This was getting to be a bad subject. I made like I wanted to finish painting fast. It would be getting dark really soon, looking like his voice was sounding. I did want to finish. I was up on the ladder, almost about to paint, and I could feel him down there, not saying anything.

Just as suddenly, happy came back to his mood as Mr. Womack came out the front door. "'Bout time!" Cloyd said to him. "I'm starving!" He took off, more hungry to get away from me, and the two of them went to Mr. Womack's shiny new car and settled in. "We're off for them steaks."

"You sure you wouldn't want to come eat with us?" Mr. Womack asked.

"Thank you," I said, shaking my head.

"That's a good boy you got there," Mr. Womack told Cloyd, but he wasn't listening.

Finally it was streetlights and the building floodlights, on by an automatic timer, glaring at the fresh paint. I wasn't sure I didn't splatter the black, especially at first, after I got going a little too fast. Right then I didn't care. I just wanted to finish no matter what. I forced myself to get it done, and I was relieved when it was. It took me longer than I thought it would, even working fast. I was starving. I decided I'd go inside and eat those chips first thing.

As I put the ladder and paint back in the shed, I saw that Nica's door was open. I hadn't seen her parents leave, but then I never did. They seemed to come and go without footsteps. Only one time I saw them on their way out, from the back. Her dad was short and husky and was one of those dudes who walk like he's as big as anyone, even though I was already taller than he was. Her mom had a braid that reached to her skirt. It's what you saw first, not that she was so tiny. Which was not like Nica. It wasn't that I thought about Nica so much that it seemed like she took up so much more space. It really was that she was bigger than both her parents.

"Are you alone?" I was standing way away from her door. It was quiet, the TV was off, not even the radio was on.

"Angel's asleep in the bedroom," she said.

"I meant, you know, your mom and dad."

She nodded. "Angel went to sleep right after they went to work." She was smiling, but at the same time the smile didn't seem to be about being happy.

"It's like three in the morning in there," I said. "Not a sound."

Then she looked at me, like she was scared. "I can't go out there," she said. "I have to stay close to him."

"Of course," I said. I stayed close to the railing.

"You don't want to come in?"

"I can?"

"I can't go out there," she said.

"I'll talk really soft," I said too loud when I was inside. She made a face at me.

"I'm sorry!" I said.

She gave me a real smile, happy. Happy to see me, happy that somebody was over, happy I visited her, that it was *me*.

"Don't worry," she said, a little hushed. "I think very soon he won't be able to wake up."

I was thinking how she was in this apartment all the time.

"Do you know the neighbors, the ones over there?" She was pointing the opposite way from Cindy's.

"Mr. Josep?"

"No."

"Pink?"

"No, the couple."

"Oh, yeah. Them. Number Seven. Yeah." I sat down on the couch. There was a crowd of pictures of the baby, Angel, on the walls. There were a couple older ones too, ones that weren't in color but were more yellow than black-and-white. A big mirror with a gold frame so wide across the room, a black and red fan, gold trimmed. There was a picture of Jesus, that profile of him my mom one time said was a shampoo ad. It wasn't that she didn't like the church anymore, she'd tell people, even if she didn't go. Other times she'd scream at me, saying how I should be learning some religion, how I wasn't confirmed. In Nica's apartment there were crucifixes, and there was a black statue of a Guadalupe.

"Bud and Mary, in Number Seven," I said.

"They asked me if I could babysit."

"Really? Babysit?"

"She did."

"Really?"

"What do you think?"

"I think they don't have children."

"They do," she said. "Why else would they need a babysitter?"

"Maybe you're right," I said. "I didn't hear they had one though."

"My father told me he thought it'd be all right if I did it," she said, her voice saying it fast.

"Yeah, I guess you'd make some extra money." I didn't think she made any, so it wouldn't exactly be extra. "Right?"

"My father said so, that he thought it'd be all right."

"I guess if you don't mind doing it." I didn't know what to say. I still didn't think they had a baby. "You would want to, right? 'Cause, I dunno, maybe you get tired of babysitting."

She took a few seconds, but she wasn't going to admit to that, if it were true. "You could go over with me. I was thinking that."

First my heart stopped, then it took off. I was already sitting so I stood up. I even forgot I was hungry. "Yeah," I said. "Sure!"

"You would go over there with me?" she asked.

She really wasn't sure if I would! "Are you kidding? Of course!"

"That would make it better."

Now I was so happy. "We could buy pizza," I said. Maybe I could still think of food.

She looked like she was gonna say yes because she was smiling.

"Hey, I'm hungry right now," I said. "What if I buy us a pizza right now? Are you hungry? Because I'm hungry."

It was like she was trying to say something in English. But then, finally, her face made a not-sure, like I was saying we should run out of the apartment and walk on the streets and, before we got back, we should take one of Pink's wheels for a joyride and then start making out in the back and then we'd get back later than her parents do from work, and all this while her little brother was screaming and crying, Where's my sister?!

I was too worked up, and I had to convince her it was only about food, about pizza. "It's that both my mom and Cloyd went out to dinner. I got my own money and I wanted to buy one for myself anyways. It's not nothing. I mean, it's pizza, and we can clean up the mess. Is that what you're worried about? Or maybe you're afraid because I'm here and I'm not supposed to be? Is it bad that I'm here?"

Walking fast over to the hallway to listen to something I didn't hear, she put her finger to her lips to shush me.

"I'm sorry!" I whispered. I was probably as loud as I was excited.

She went on listening to the bedroom where Angel slept, her finger still crossing her lips.

"Look, I'll go downstairs and order the pizza," I told her as quietly as I could. "So that I don't have to talk loud on your phone."

I think she was so confused she couldn't say no. And me, I was happy, and I also wanted pizza for both of us.

I about hopped the railing to get downstairs. I pulled up my money corner and added some to the $5 I found in my mom's purse—I don't know why I did that. I wasn't sure how much I'd been using lately, but I'd been into it a lot. I spent it at the bowling alley on Mrs. Zúniga's food at Alley Cats so I didn't have to eat deer meat or whatever, but now that I might need more, I needed to start getting it somehow, somewhere. What if Cloyd didn't give me the money for painting? That would suck. That would really piss me off. I'd have to get it out of him. I'd make sure I got it some other way. And how come he didn't bring it up when we were talking about it? When I stepped outside again, I felt around in the sky like it'd be out there, like if I squinted hard enough I'd make out the answer.

I went back up the stairs so fast to Nica's and my brain was beginning to scheme when I remembered, just as I got to where square light was beaming out the windows on either side of her door, that I forgot to call for the pizza, forgot what I went down there for, forgot I was hungry. I tapped on her door and it was like she was waiting right there. When she opened it, she put a finger to her lips.

"I'll go down and wait until it comes," I told her. "I already ordered, so I hope you like what I picked."

She nodded with her finger at her lips. I think in her expression she really liked the idea a lot.

I sat in Cloyd's swivel chair. I went into his office since he wouldn't be back for a while and I'd seen the telephone book on top of the desk. Those guns, those rifles up there, they made me pissed off. I wouldn't look at them, I didn't want to. His phone was one of those heavy black ones whose dial made noise when it spun the number. Every object weighed heavy in his office, like everything was or was almost made of melted hard stone— the desk, the cabinets around it, this swivel chair, even the tile floors were gray. The thick green padding on his chair was probably vinyl, but it looked like sheet metal too. I flipped through the bulky Yellow Pages and made the pizza call and wanted to go right back up but decided not to until the delivery man came. I thought how, to be smarter, I better be quieter when I went up to Nica's and not seen—not by Gina, Mr. Josep, or Cindy. I put the phone book back exactly where it had been. I didn't want Cloyd to know I'd sat at his desk, that I'd been there. I was as careful as I would be if I'd snuck in. I opened his desk drawers. A drawer with boxes of bullets and shotgun cartridges. Another with letterhead sheets of paper and spiral receipt books with plastic covers and lots of pens with companies' names on them, black and red markers, tubes of white glue and airplane glue, nail clippers, erasers so old they were miniature bricks, tangled paper clips, new and rusted tacks and hooks and a couple of empty bullet and shotgun shells, a hunting knife and a pocketknife, screws, long and short nails, lead pennies, and some buffalo-head nickels that got my attention as much as the silver dollars. The biggest drawer was on the left, the one with the most papers stuffed in it, business contracts, so many there wasn't any spare room to slide so much as your finger in if you had to. Don't ask me why I pulled the drawer out all the way, and I can't say how come I was pushing those files around in the first place, looking between them, or why I happened to look in the very back. Except I did. I did. And I saw a brown envelope and I got it out and I counted the pile of hundreds in it. There were ten of them. I counted three times. One thousand dollars. It made me crazy scared but also not. I felt the marble deer-head eyes over me. I looked right back up at them, and then it got to maybe they'd be cool with it.

I was like that longer than I should because the bell for the front door went off without me waiting and waiting for it. I only panicked for a few seconds because Cloyd's money was still out. I got up and paid the dude for the pizza. It smelled really good. Yeah, I was still hungry, even if sometimes I kept forgetting I was. When I went back into the office, I put Cloyd's secret stash in the far left corner where I found it. I was very careful. I was even conscious that I hadn't taken a bill out of the sequence they were in.

"It's sausage, mushrooms, and green peppers," I told her, keeping my voice way down. I had to say sausage, mushrooms, and green peppers in English because I couldn't think of the pizza words in Spanish. "I hope I picked okay, I wasn't sure what you'd like."

She was smiling! She was more excited than me, I swear!

"We do have to be quiet," she said, "but he's asleep for the night."

The TV was on. It was another one of those really dumb novelas in Spanish, but I didn't say nothing. She'd gotten us plates—all scratched-up plastic—and made lemonade. It was real lemonade too, from lemons and sugar. A lot of sugar. It was sweet, too sweet for me. She'd made us each a glass while I was gone. I kind of wondered if she'd ever eaten a pizza before because she sort of seemed like she hadn't. She was cutting it with a knife and fork at first. I told her how that took too long and I think she got embarrassed but since I didn't make a big do out of it, pretended I was watching the show on TV, she picked her next slice up from the box with her hand like I did. She ate it like it was burning hot, like the littlest bites were how it had to be eaten, and she held the slice with both hands. Me, I was too hungry, but I controlled myself. I wanted to seem, you know, like, polite. I didn't eat as fast as I wanted to. I even pretended I didn't want to eat the last three pieces. I kept telling her to have them, they were hers, but she wouldn't, so I went ahead and overate one more bite out of one and dropped it in the box.

She picked up the plates and glasses. She washed our dishes and I dried them and she put them away. I told her it was fun to be doing this. She laughed. She laughed really good. She didn't say and I didn't have to ask that she didn't want her parents to know I visited, let alone that we ate pizza in the apartment. When I walked the box to the trash cans in the back, I admit it, I ate one more slice before I threw it in.

The TV was off when I got back. I wasn't sure if I was supposed to leave.

"No, you can stay a little more," she told me.

She was so pretty, she was so fucking chula!

"Can I tell you something?" she said.

"Sure." We were sitting on either end of their gold-colored couch, facing the dead green screen of the TV set. If you stared into it deep enough, you could see each of us sitting there on the curved couch, way away from each other. It made me think of how I could get closer to her.

"You know what I wish?" She had a faraway face. "I wish my name were Cathy."

"Cathy?"

"I hate my name," she said.

"I like Nica better," I said.

"I hate my name."

"Well, okay, so then I guess what you gotta do is dye your hair blond."

It wasn't that she didn't think I was joking. More that she didn't seem to get it.

"I don't like my mom's or dad's or my brother's names, not any of them."

"What's wrong with theirs?"

"You know, everybody who is Mexican is named María, like my mom."

I didn't think that was exactly true but I didn't think I could say anything. I know I hadn't thought about this as much as she seemed to have.

"I hate being Mexican sometimes," she said.

"Not much you can do about it now," I said. Yeah, it surprised me what she was saying, made me laugh, though she was so serious. "You know, if you think about it, I don't know. Who else can make tacos? Who else you gonna get nachos from? Nobody else loves jalapeños or green chile like we do."

"What's green chile?" she asked.

"You see what I mean? You're not even that Mexican." I guess I thought everybody ate green chile.

She still didn't seem to be getting me. "So what's your dad's name?" I asked.

"Margarito," she said, after a few seconds. She was watching the television like it was on, answering somebody on the screen, until she looked over at me. "Do you understand what I say? His is such a *Mexican* Mexican name."

"Uh, a little. But the thing is, he *is* Mexican, so there's a good reason for it. You know, my mom tells about how gringos name their dogs, like Concha or Paco or Chuy. We had a neighbor whose shepherd was named Pedro. Understand what I'm saying? My dog was named Goofy. What if I named her Judy?" I was smiling right at her, hoping to make her laugh some, hoping my Spanish was good enough that it wasn't too confusing. I might've laughed alone and to myself, but I cut myself off. "It's probably your dad's parents were Mexican, if you think about it, and they didn't think about it. Didn't maybe have many names to pick from that weren't." You could tell she didn't seem to get any of my joking around too well.

"Where's your dog?" she asked. "You said you have a dog, but I never see him."

I wanted to ask her how she could if she never went out of her apartment but I thought I better not bring that subject up right then. "Yeah, I don't know. They said that she's. . . . nothing. They didn't bring her to the apartment when we moved here."

"What's your name?" she asked. There wasn't that long a time between that last question and when she asked this.

"My dog's name?"

"Yours."

"Ay, you don't even know? And here I bought pizza."

"Of course I know . . . ."

"You eat pizza with me but you don't know my name? I didn't think you were that kind of girl."

"Already you know what I mean. Your real name, your real first name in English."

"Sonny? That's Spanish?"

"Already you know what I am saying."

"Hey, you ever seen that movie where this actor Marlon Brando was Emiliano Zapata."

"Marlon Brando?" She got the syllables kind of right, but if she moved one or two this way or that, it wouldn't have made any difference. Probably it was that her English wasn't that good and she had to consider what I said. She was probably laughing but didn't show it or something. "Your real name," she repeated. "I wonder what your whole name is."

"So you never seen that movie?"

"What movie?"

"*Viva Zapata!*"

She looked at me like I was still teasing.

"Marlon Brando is American. I used to think it was crazy that Marlon Brando played Zapata."

She looked at me like she didn't understand anything I was saying.

"It's a movie, he's a man."

"Your name, tonto."

I started laughing. "You saying I'm an indio?" I said that in English.

I think she thought I wasn't talking in any language.

"Everybody's named after somebody," I said in English.

She was staring at me, not sure.

"You still want to know my name," I said in Spanish.

She didn't have to say yes.

"My name Sonny." I said the words like I just learned to say them in English. "You say Sonny, I'm here. Except you call me other names, I promise to come too, especially on babysitting night, and I carry pizza."

"I like American names a lot," she finally said, giving up on trying to follow me.

"I like yours. Nica's a cool name."

"It's from Veronica," she said.

"I like that too. That's a cool name. But I don't see how you can pull a Cathy out of it."

"I like American names, and Cathy is so American. It's happy. You see? Like your name too. It's a good, happy, American name."

"So should I call you Cathy from now on?"

"I like the name Veronica," she said. "It's good too, don't you think? And I like when you call me Nica."

"Yeah," I said, "I think it's very cool. I've never known a Nica before you."

We heard noises which I thought were outside the front door, but she went to the bedroom to see how her brother was sleeping. When she got back, she kept looking around, being distracted. "They shouldn't come home for hours yet," she said.

"But you're worried about it. That's okay. I'll leave right now if you want."

She nodded. "I'm sorry," she said.

"I don't want you to get into trouble."

"I never have any company. I like it."

"Yeah," I said. "Me too." She was always here alone—with her parents and brother. I really didn't think she went out of the apartment ever. "They'd be mad if they found out I was here?"

"Probably my father."

She was so chula. Her eyes, the white of them, the black of them. Her eyelashes. Her eyebrows. Her nose. Her cheeks. Her lips. Her chin. Her neck. Each strand of her hair in place as alive as the ones that floated in the breeze while I stood at the open door, wishing I knew how to make her kiss.

"Can we get pizza when we babysit?" she asked. "I don't get to have pizza, and it was *fun*. Thank you."

"If you remember my name."

"Stop."

"You could call me Marlon Brando, because it's more American. Or Pancho Villa, who you have to like, right? That'd be an all-right Mexican name, right?"

She wasn't listening to my words again.

"They might not like it if they found out. And my father for sure wouldn't let me go there if he knew."

"Your mom and dad will be at work then, right?"

She nodded.

"Then nobody'll ever know except us."

There was no moon outside so I didn't think anybody'd see me, all quiet except for the car fizz behind and in front and the electric buzz of a power box on the telephone pole above, and the TV over there, and even over there too, and in the building next door, and I could even hear a throbbing bass line not so far off, not the pumped-up car that passed by, its windows letting in and putting out, speakers aching. Up the stairs I wanted to listen in Cindy's window for, like, a few seconds, but I was afraid Mr. Josep might come out and see me. Cindy's husband was in there, that Tino, talking fast, and it could've been mad talk. I only wanted to hear a few sentences of his voice and maybe I could have stood there, but I went back down the stairs. Yeah, I got myself scared of the dude, scared of what would happen to me if he found out. I wished I could see what he looked like exactly because I was already inventing him. I combed his black hair back, with Tres Flores brilliantine. First I put a scar on his face, but that was Pink's, I realized, so I took that away and saw acne digging up his cheeks. I had him wearing hard black shoes, too sharp at the toes, too polished. I had him in cheap shiny nightclub shirts with collars too floppy, the cuffs unbuttoned, the long sleeves sometimes rolled up. I tattooed him because he probably was in the navy. I didn't like the way he looked or dressed and I didn't like the fucker. I'd say it wasn't possible for anyone to like him. I started seeing how I'd fight him if he came at me. I didn't make him out to be much bigger than me if he was—he had to be small—but he was more experienced, because he was older and tough, mean, unafraid, especially of a kid like me. I'd just hit him any-where I had to, cut loose, go crazy, hurt him! I'd bust the dude's fucking nose and crack his ugly yellow teeth. He was a culo and I wasn't going to back down. He was only a cheap drug dealer.

It took me a few to slow myself back off. My eyes closed, my mind was swarmed by white gnats of light that kept me from sleeping. I was counting ten bright-green hundreds. I was feeling Cindy's chichis. I was kissing Nica's lips at her front door, and I was in love. I was defending myself from Tino, popping his face, busting him up, a knee in his mouth, kicking his jaw, uppercuts, loaded rights to his nose. I must not have heard Cloyd come in. He might have already been home and I didn't know it. It was when my mom walked in that I heard the mutter of conversation and the speech getting faster. I didn't want to know, didn't want to hear it. On my back in the bed, I started to listen to Nica's radio, on above me. I imagined her balled up asleep, a small American-made transistor radio near her pretty face. I was hearing my mom and him out there for too long. They were arguing, and I could make out words if I let myself, but I didn't want to. I shut my eyes and went. Sound went into color and shape and I traveled up or down or wherever it was and I listened with other ears and saw with other eyes and the bright lights didn't make me turn away but stare. I was traveling toward it and I felt good, like black air was water above me and around.

"I don't know," Joe said. "If I were black, I wouldn't want to be called a nigger. I'd jump all over anybody who'd call me that."

"But if they act mayate," said Mike, "they're gonna be treated like mayates."

This was because of these black dudes who were parked when we passed by them, waiting for someone. Their lowrider Impala was painted a purply blue, with silver glitter in it, a bright white interior, oversized dice dangling from the rearview, mohair around the steering wheel, chrome rims that hadn't been washed in so long they looked like tin hubcaps. They were laughing and carrying on, giving us some shit about being Mexicans—about hair grease and farting beans. Two of them had rags on their head, like they themselves weren't the cartoon characters.

"Still, probably people shouldn't be calling them niggers," said Joe.

"They're acting like it," Mike said, "and they were calling us names first. Like it's us."

"Maybe it's just us, me and you," said Joe, "because we're twins."

Because the black dudes started it by laughing about the way they dressed.

"No," said Mike.

"We get teased all the time," Joe told me.

"They were calling us Mexicans, dude!" said Mike.

Joe smiled at his brother. "We are Mexicans."

"Yeah, but we aren't *Mexicans*. I hate it when they're throwing it like it's a bad word, like it's a pendejada."

"He's right about that," said Joe.

"Our grandparents were born here too," said Mike. "We're living in their house still."

"That's true," said Joe. "We should tell them to go back to Mississippi and get off our land and leave us alone."

"The gringos too," said Mike, pissed off now about everything. "They're the ones who are the inmigrantes, not us. They crossed our northern border. We were here already, just not picking cotton."

"Sometimes our old man talks like that," Joe explained. "That they couldn't be happy enough with all they get—we give them a chair at our table, offer some tacos, but they start shooting too much tequila and want the whole house."

"He's right too," said Mike. "It's true. Isn't it true? Our family has been living here before people heard of the English language."

"Our grandfather was a carpenter," said Joe. "He built a lot of our house."

"But he had to work as a laborer," Mike said.

"He worked for the union," Joe said, "and he always had a job, and he was always working."

"Yeah dude!" said Mike. "He built all the freeways."

"We got brothers who do construction too," said Joe. "We're going to be the first ones to go to college."

"That's what our family says," said Mike.

"They've been telling us that forever," Joe explained to me. "Our family thinks we're smarties—"

"Smart-asses," Mike interrupted.

"—just 'cause we get good grades."

I checked out the Los Flores sign in the light of the day. I'd splattered a little in like two places, but it was no big deal, couldn't be. My mom was standing in the living room with a couple of department store bags, on the phone. But she was weird too. It was in the air. Sometimes I'd be able to pick up on it, and I could tell something was up. That Bud from #7 was standing at the Cloyd's office door, facing forward, but he turned when he saw it was me.

"I didn't know they had a baby," I said to my mom, once I was past them. She looked at me like I was nuts but didn't explain.

She went into their bedroom. I wasn't going to follow her at first.

"What's wrong?" she asked.

"Nothing," I said.

"Entonces?" She acted like it was me. Maybe that I was at the door of *their* bedroom. She'd bought clothes. She'd bought a blouse and a skirt and she was trying each one against different others in the closet.

"So did he like that I finished the painting?"

She didn't act like she knew what I was talking about.

"The flowers sign outside, remember? I painted it."

"You did?"

"Remember? You said he thought I wouldn't. We were just talking about it, remember?"

"Good," she said, distracted. "Good."

"I guess he must not have said anything to you then."

"Must not have," she said. She was studying a particular combination in a long mirror, holding them against her.

"I was wondering if he said anything. Wondering if he was gonna pay me."

"Don't bring it up with him."

"Why?"

"Because I'm asking you not to."

"But why?"

"Because I'm asking, okay, m'ijo?"

I didn't want to talk about food money to her—she'd stopped giving it to me. I never ate with them, so what'd she think? But I'd never talked to her about money before. I felt like taking some from her right then, though. That's how I could get it. And now I knew where that envelope of hundreds was.

I turned around and headed toward that bedroom I slept in. Bud was by the refrigerator getting out a beer as I passed. "Wanna a cold one?" he asked.

Cloyd heard him from his office. "Yeah, get him a beer too!"

"Nah, it's all right," I told Bud. Bud was even bigger than you'd think at first. Solid, as wide as a wall, muscles squeezing out in it and all over his arms. He was wearing a T-shirt, and he'd been sweating in it.

"Hey, come in here for a second," Cloyd yelled.

I didn't want to. He was drunk. You could see liquor squirting around in the veins of his eyes.

"Did Pink sell a car to those colored yesterday?"

What'd he say, *colored*? Qué cabrón, como anda. "I dunno what you're talking," I said. Bud came from behind me and handed him a bottle of beer.

"You could have one, you know," Cloyd told me.

"Yeah," I said, "but no. Thanks anyways."

"You don't want one?" Bud asked.

"No," I said. "I'm all right."

"I'd never turn down a beer if I got asked at your age," Bud said.

"It'll grow you some pubic hair," Cloyd said.

Bud laughed.

Cloyd sucked at the tip of a cigarette with a metal lighter. "You lit any of these up before?"

I didn't answer. I let him know I didn't answer.

"Have you ever smoked?" Cloyd asked.

He thought I didn't understand the question the first time?

"Probably not." Bud answered for me.

They chuckled in some tough, we're-big-men way, like they were so wise and so experienced. I knew right then they'd been talking about me. I wanted to do something, anything.

"Did you want something?" I asked Cloyd.

"Whadaya mean?" he said.

"You called me in here."

"You did," Bud agreed, but smiling at me.

"Damn," said Cloyd.

They laughed.

"You were asking him about them blacks," Bud told him.

"Oh yeah," Cloyd said. "You were outside there when he was showing one of his cars."

"I was painting," I said.

"Yeah?" said Cloyd, taking a long drag on his cigarette.

"I finished it too," I said.

"The painting?"

"Yeah, the painting."

"You put the ladder and brush back in the shed this time?"

"Yeah."

"You clean the brush?"

"Yeah."

"Last time I had to do it for you."

"It's that I went to get something and forgot."

"And so I had to clean things up and put them away."

"Whatever. Sorry."

"What's with that clown selling to them blacks anyway?" Bud said to me. He turned to Cloyd. "Guy looks like a circus freak."

I wished I could tell him how he was the one with the clown face. He could kick my ass so easy, and I didn't want it to happen easy.

"I don't like it," said Bud. "I don't like them being around my home."

"He's making money on them," Cloyd said.

"Who cares? I don't like to see them standing around where I live."

"Gonna have to get used to it," Cloyd said.

"You wouldn't let them move in here, would you?"

"I didn't say I would," Cloyd said. "Fact I wouldn't. But that don't mean they aren't coming. They're all around us, multiplying like Mexicans." He heard himself say that and he looked up at me, embarrassed for a couple of seconds, and then lifted his beer bottle. "At least for Mexicans it's because they're of the Catholic faith."

"Why can't they live where they live," said Bud, "and we can live where we live? They got their shithole neighborhoods, why don't they keep themselves over there? All they gotta do is clean up after themselves."

Home was where we used to live. Where my old friends still lived. I guess home was when I had a bed and a bedroom and called them mine. But I didn't want to live there no more. I didn't want to go back there. I was like my mom—new. And I was a boy then and now I wasn't. It's that I was seeing big money. I was seeing Cindy, and I was in love with Nica, and, yeah, confusing. I lived here and I was sitting on the cement walk—with apartment windows and doors with numbers on them, stairs and walkways and rails and carports. The Cloyd went on talking hillbilly with that Bud. I could hear them. Talked about my mom. When they started talking about me, said my name once, I went farther away. I was wishing I could say *fuck you* in French. *Foquez-vous*. Saying that in French made me smile and feel stronger and even laugh about shit. The dude owed me. Maybe I would have cared more if I hadn't found that drawer with the money. Yeah, now I was scheming. I was like making reasons why it'd be okay to lift it, you know? Like, didn't I need some coin too? I was working around here, doing a good job of it, a *fine* job of it, and I'd been spending mine and that wasn't right either. He should pay me like he promised and then I probably wouldn't be thinking nothing. He shouldn't be laughing at me with that muscle-head from #7.

No, the building didn't need sweeping but it was all I could figure to do. I got the push broom out of the shed and went to sweep around the carports, where I'd never been. I was avoiding the grease puddles when Bud's wife pulled in. She didn't have a baby with her either. I was still trying to figure out when they had this baby around, if they had a baby. Getting out of her squeaking car, she had that already-an-old-lady face she wore most of the time, her body about as wild as that plain dress she wore.

"And how are you?" she asked.

I almost couldn't hear her.

She had bags of groceries. I knew I was supposed to ask if she needed help. I went on sweeping instead. I don't think I even heard her get so close to me.

"Is Bud with your dad?"

"Cloyd Longpre's not my dad," I said. She smelled like old lady powder, dusty and stale. Definitely not like a baby just diapered.

"Okay, that's right." You could tell she really was sorry because she got almost scared that she'd said something I didn't like. "I should have said your stepdad."

I was trying to seem polite.

"I hope Bud isn't getting drunk tonight," she said. "Is your mom with them?"

I nodded.

She got tight, kind of pissed.

Then I said, "Not with them. She's doing something else, she's out."

"That's good," she said.

It was happening everywhere, everything was about taking sides.

"Cloyd drinks," she told me, cutting off some of what she was going to say. "Bud comes back drunk."

What'd I care? I had stopped sweeping to be polite. I felt really stupid standing there, both of us stiff and stuck like we were waiting in line. I was like *uh, uh,* trying to move on, but then nothing was coming out of my mouth.

Finally she started grabbing at her grocery bags like she'd never lugged any up before. I had no choice. "I guess I can help," I said, "if you want."

She did want that. There were four and I got three of them and followed her up the stairs. Mr. Josep was sitting out on his chair. He waved at me with the back of his hand, either because he wanted to talk to me or he was saying hello, I couldn't tell. Mary didn't seem to see him, she was so focused on the keys going up and opening the door. "Right here, please, right here," she said. "Thank you so much, thank you so much."

I put the grocery bags on their dining table. There was a cat, and the apartment stunk like a really dirty catbox. The cat was making noise and following her, jumping up, then down. My eyes were checking around this place they lived. Kind of like when I was alone and did it, but I wasn't.

"I know you missed me," she told the cat. "I know my baby missed me."

Baby.

"Let me give you a coke," she said.

I told her no.

"No?" She was surprised and scattered and worried. She wanted me to have one. "It's the least I can do."

I didn't really feel like it. "It's that I'm sweeping down there."

"You can have one. I know you can. It'll be okay."

She had uncapped a bottle and was holding it. I couldn't not drink it.

"It's okay," she said. "You can have one."

I didn't know if she thought I wasn't allowed or I was very bashful.

"So," she said.

She was wanting me to say more than I possibly could or would. And that's what I meant. I didn't feel like this. I didn't want to have to listen or say anything back and be all polite.

"Your mother's very attractive," she said. "She's beautiful."

What was I supposed to say? Was I supposed to if I thought something? I wanted out.

"Everybody thinks so," she said.

I figured if I nodded, it'd be enough. So I did.

"Beautiful clothes." She was unpacking the grocery bags. The cat was on the table, craning and stretching to be petted.

"She buys them in stores." Maybe that came out more sarcastic than I intended, or maybe more honest than polite.

"Of course," she said.

I drank the coke like I was thirsty, like my brain didn't need much else. I'd tipped the bottle and chugged, and when I was done I clunked it on the table and made out that I was born to be gone.

"Well, I couldn't have gotten these up here without you."

"No problem."

"My husband was too busy," she said from behind me.

I was already turned away and moving toward the door.

I was sweeping near Tino's dented GTO—I just missed him, still didn't know what he looked like for real, because the car wasn't there before—fading black, with black bucket seats coming apart along the seams, and on the driver's side the foam rubber was leaking out. There were empty beer bottles and fast food trash on the back floorboard. A plastic hula Virgin Mary swung from the rearview mirror. For whatever reason, I'd started sweeping faster and sloppier until I put the push broom back in the shed and rushed by and ignored Mr. Josep when he began to wave at me to come up and also, when I passed #2, that Gina, who pushed open her curtain to look at me and probably say something "nice" though maybe not, who knows. I pretended I was too much in a hurry to hear her or stop.

Cloyd and Bud were loud drunk, sitting in the office, and my mom was in the living room. On the maple supper table was a bucket of fried chicken, and I was hungry, and there was plenty and there were a couple of jalapeños that maybe my mom got because of me. It made me feel almost happy, believing she got some food I might like so I could eat there. I took a plate to where she was and she shook her head *no no* at me, like we'd already been talking, like there was a secret. Like them, she had a drink going too. The TV was on but too low to hear unless those guys drinking in the office were quiet, which they were not. She made a secret between us, eyes toward the other room where they were. I ate near her without saying anything. It was almost never that I was around my mom like this. Even before, at home, she was always either out or moving around getting ready to go out. And we never ate anything like fried chicken, though it wasn't like she was eating any. She didn't like fried chicken.

"Hey, Sil!"

She made one of her faces at me, nodding like, Here it is finally, then shook her same head without moving from the chair.

"Hey, my luv-ly wife!" he yelled from the office.

She still didn't flinch. It wasn't like she was really watching the TV show she had on, only pretending. She was far away. She was taking side streets, making turns that kept her going. She was scheming too. It's where I learned it.

I was eating fried chicken. It was good too. My mom was touching my hair and we didn't have to say anything to each other. I turned the volume up some. There was no way we could hear it if it wasn't turned up.

"Sil?" He scared us both when he came around from the hall side and found her. He was blasted. He had the dumbest look on his face ever, smiling like—well, I'd heard him do that a couple of times. He'd cut one, then say, *Speak again, sweet lips, I'll find you!* He thought that was the funniest shit ever.

"You feelin' better, Sil?" he said like I wasn't even sitting there. I couldn't see what kind of face she made. I ate the fried chicken, and then I got up to see if there was any orange juice in the fridge. I really did like orange juice, and if it was around I didn't think anybody'd notice if I drank some.

★   ★   ★

The neighbors on the other side of the fence had their television
close to a window. They talked with accents I didn't think anyone anywhere could understand. They sounded old. I wasn't even
sure they were speaking English, though they at least did when
what sounded like the grandma would yell at a child who was
there too. *You stop! You be good! No!* Unless that was to a cat. It
couldn't be no dog. Sometimes I thought I heard a little kid voice
in the muffle. They might laugh about something they would
see on TV—the TV never went off. There was mumbling between the old woman and the old man, and first only their sound
would stick to me. And then it was sounds a little closer or farther, and every day I listened one and the other got louder than
before, and the night world of this room I slept in closed and
expanded into another into what wrapped me like a blanket I'd
mummy myself in. Those noises swirling up into air and off the
boulevard blew onto me like wind, like static or exhaust fumes
or cooling puffs from a bird's wings, or the hot breath of a loose
dog panting. I could even hear a spider—I am telling you I could
hear it—I could even see the sound the same as I could see the
wind that came in blue-white through tree branches, and silver
leaves shook, floating down yellow, crumbling into brown under
a gray cat's creep through blue overgrown grass. The walls of
the bedroom and ceiling creaked with a *fump fump fump* from
above, not just water swooshing up or down or in or out but
moving white through the space between the wall on my side
and the wall on the other and through the air I heard it somewhere, not where it really was. I could hear the kind of air that
didn't move, if I listened for it. There was music in it, and the
sounds spun lines, squares and triangles and circles, colliding and
crossing and twisting into new shapes, and then I'd be dreaming. I could feel it like a boat or a train or in a car, wandering on
sand or floating on a rubbery raft or staring down from the edge

of a steep mountain, hanging there like air floated me, until I'd ride a bicycle I found as fast as I could, bouncing on some path cut out, parting in front of me, or stepping on some rocks hot on my feet and I'd see so many people there until there was only one left who would pass me as I went on and then I'd feel alone, be alone, sometimes scared that I had dreams, except they were good like I'd eaten an orange or a tangerine.

"I never remember any dreams," said Mike.

"I do," Joe said.

"Oh yeah," said Mike. "Those wet ones."

"That's not what I meant, pero, you know, now that you mention it."

"You should see his magazine collection," said Mike.

Joe slugged Mike.

"Sonny won't think it's bad," said Mike. "Do you, Sonny?"

"Nah." I told them how I'd taken those magazines from the mail slot. I don't know why. It just came out. They wailed big *ay*s and *quela*s because they thought it was dangerous.

"It's not shit," I said. "It's not."

"I couldn't fucking do it!" said Mike.

"If you bring yours sometime, we'll show you ours," said Joe.

Mike gave him a look.

"Sonny won't think it's bad," Joe said. "Huh, Sonny?"

Mike gave him a look again.

Joe shook him off. "We got this collection."

I didn't say nothing. I was listening.

"There's this one," said Joe, "where this ruca with the biggest titties you've ever seen is like bent over, like ninety degrees, and they touch la fucking tierra!"

Mike wasn't happy about Joe talking about this. He was rolling his eyes while he was cleaning his glasses.

"These magazines are the really serious everything-goes kind, not like the ones you're ripping off," Joe said. "Like they show the chicks' pelitos down there, and they show their legs open a la madre, really wide too."

"Can we talk about something else?" said Mike. "My brother talks about anything. You know, some things you don't have to tell everybody."

"I'm not saying anything so much," said Joe. "My brother makes it seem like he don't like to look, and he looks, I know."

Mike shoved Joe. "Shut up, will you? Will you shut the fuck up?"

Pink was under the hood of a Bel Air outside The Flowers when I was walking by. It was a good-looking one, even jacked up in the back a little. He had tools out and grease on his white white arm with the sleeves of a dark satiny dress shirt rolled up. His hair, which was both bristly and long at the same time, had a streak of white in it, which made the yellow rest of it look even more fake.

"This one's yours, you want it, little brother," he told me.

"I wish."

"You gotta move yourself up, my man. You got to, you wanna get anything or get anywhere." He pulled himself out from under the hood. His smiling teeth were whiter than you could imagine, and they were big as show-off jewelry—which made you realize he was not really a small dude. Because his skin was so colorless—the pink scar was it—his size wasn't what you usually thought about.

"You have a buyer yet?" I asked.

"Maybe. It's why I do this. All it needs here is a tune job. But see I sell my automobiles to black folk, as you know, and this kind here is not their brand. That's why I'm thinking of you. You gotta own this automobile, you got to. You a good young man and I'm cutting you a deal. You tell your mama to get her new daddy to buy it for you. I say the fine lady could sugar him up to anything she wanted sugared, including buying you these wheels."

"I'm not really old enough. I don't even got a license."

"Shit, you told me, didn't you, and I didn't remember. But no matter, no matter, I wasn't no sixteen when I started to drive. Where I came up, it don't much matter."

"Where are you from?"

"Why you asking?"

He turned and answered so quick, the blow of it hit my face. "Nothing, just curious," I told him, "just wondering."

"You're not asking 'cause of Longpre, are you?" He was talking like I was pushing and he was about to hit a wall except I saw a lot of open street behind his back. "Is Longpre asking questions about me?" That got him a little too agitated, and he backed off and stepped forward. He even shut his eyes when he shook his head to disapprove of himself. "Listen to me. We're buddies, ain't that so?"

I nodded.

"And in my experience, and by numbers, you aren't cozy with your stepdaddy. Am I right?"

I wasn't sure how honest to be or why I should be. "It was my mom that married the dude," I said.

"There you go and there you have it, it's what I'm saying, that's how I understand it." He got his breath close to me and would've put his hand on my shoulder if it wasn't greasy. "Young brother, what we say to each other, it's between us. You see what I'm saying?"

I was looking at his scar, which could seem raw and wet.

"Right?" he said.

"Okay," I said.

"All right, all right, that's good, that's real good, real good."

★　★　★

I saw my mom, but I didn't think she either heard the door or saw me because I was shooting through fast. She was dressed to go out again, only it was a dress I'd seen before. It didn't even seem very new. She had too much perfume on, in my opinion, because once I was inside, I thought I remembered smelling it from outside. I wanted to tell her even as I was also wanting to pass by without saying nothing. It wasn't like her, at least I didn't remember her having so much smell ever before.

I was already in the bedroom I slept in on the bed I slept on. I'd heard her when she said she wanted to talk to me but I closed the door like I didn't. I did not want to talk.

She opened the door. "Don't you hear me?"

"I guess not."

"What's the matter?"

"Nothing."

"Are you mad at me?"

"Mad about what?"

"There's nothing," she said, "so let's drop it."

"I didn't bring anything up."

"I have to go out," she said, "but I won't be very long."

"Okay," I said. "See you."

"I'll be back before Cloyd comes in."

I didn't care.

"If he comes in though. . . ."

"I won't say nothing."

"I was going to say. . . ."

"What I'll just say is you weren't here when I got in."

"Okay, that's good, thank you."

She was still standing there. "So?" I asked.

"Oh," she said. "Este es algo que no te vas a gustar, que you won't like."

"What? What is?"

"What I have to talk about."

Nothing was being said. "I thought you were in a hurry," I said.

"Okay, es que . . . it's that Gina, the woman who lives next door, who lives with Ben—"

"The ones who live in Number Two. I know their names."

"Yes. Well, she came over. She said you've been stealing some magazines that belong to them."

"Whadaya mean that she said that? Did she say she saw me take magazines?"

"I don't know if she said she saw you. I think she says she thinks it's you."

"I didn't do it," I said.

"That's what I told her. I told her you wouldn't do that."

"Good. Thanks."

"She says it couldn't be anyone else."

"I don't know why it could only be me."

"Well, what she says is that before we moved in, they never didn't get the magazines. And now—"

"Well, I didn't do it."

"Bueno. I just wanted you to know what she said."

It made me mad. I didn't like to be accused of shit. I decided to go out, get out of this bedroom I slept in.

"Where you going?" she asked me on my way.

"Out there," I said.

"I won't be long tonight, okay m'ijo?"

She wasn't saying what she really wanted to say, which was about what to tell him.

Though there wasn't much blue sky, Mr. Josep was sunning himself on the deck outside his apartment and waved me over. As I went, he pushed his door open and dragged out another wooden chair. I went ahead and sat there next to him, but he wasn't talking so it felt kind of awful, so much I swore I'd never be nice like this ever again. I was watching for my mom to move out and get in her car, but she didn't. It was smoggy, so all you could see were electric poles that were close, a few pigeons on them. I could hear the TV on in Nica's apartment, a Mexican talk show, but there was so much noise coming from everywhere, my ears hurt like all of it came from being near his chair.

"How is school?"

I wanted to fucking moan! "Fine." I should've gotten up right then and ran. I wanted to hit something. I wanted to steal something. I wanted to go to his office and get that money.

"School is best thing you do," he said.

I got up. "I better go do my work," I said.

"Wait. Sit one minute right here," he said.

I didn't, but I didn't walk away.

"You like her, don't you?"

I didn't really want to talk, I really didn't. I nodded.

He winked at me. It was stupid, an old man's dumb wink.

"Good when you are your age," he said.

I didn't know or care what he meant, and I wished I weren't there.

"She is the bad woman," he said, winking.

It took me some seconds to realize he was talking about Cindy and I was talking about Nica.

"I say bad," he said, "and I mean good. Good for you for being a man." He was smiling.

I remembered that he saw her that day. I slowed my brain, came back.

"Only you have to be careful," he said. "You know, because of husband." He wasn't even looking at me. "Two or three days ago, it is me," he said.

I thought I heard him say two or three days ago, but that didn't make sense.

"He is bad," he said. "I mean bad, bad for you. You understand?"

Cindy's TV was on, a game show that hurt the ears. The apartment was hating the noise too—drying pizza slices were curling up as they tried to escape the box, fast food bags were torn raw and cups flattened out, aluminum cans of beer and soda even wrinkled away and, the biggest losers, cigarettes were crushed in and on them. The apartment stank but not of a smell, not just of drugs and wine and beer but of something fucking up.

"Where have you been?" she asked. She turned away from the door and flopped onto her couch, swinging her bare feet onto the cushions. "I didn't know if you were ever going to visit me again."

"What?" I said, teasing.

"I didn't know. . . ."

"What?"

She turned the TV down.

"I haven't been seeing you around," I said, the only thing I could think of saying. There were clothes hanging on chairs and at the edges of the floor. "Like down in the laundry room."

"So did you forget where my door is," she said, "or how to knock on it?"

I didn't say anything back and the game show got quiet for a longer time than usual.

"What's been going on with you?" I asked her.

"I'm lonely here, and I'm bored."

I nodded.

She wanted me to say something else.

"What're you watching?" I asked.

"Whatever's on."

I was still standing, looking to not sit. Now I didn't feel like staying either. Whatever brought me up here. I'd forgotten this fast. I think I'd been mad and now I wasn't and I wanted to get out.

She lit up one of her mota cigarettes. She smoked some, then she passed it to me. At first I didn't think I would. Then we passed it back and forth a few times.

Suddenly she wasn't watching the show, she was watching me. "Come here."

Not thinking enough, I did.

"Do it to me this time," she whispered.

I wasn't sure what I heard because I'd never heard what I thought I just heard.

She put my hand under her T-shirt. Then she put her hand on me. She led me to the bedroom. She took off her top and her cut-off sweats—no underwear. She fell on her back but then just as quickly sat up. I hadn't done anything yet but stand there. She dropped my pants and put her mouth on me. She pulled me onto her. She rolled us and got on top of me. Time passed. Still light out, a faded white coming through the curtain, it blackened in my brain, then the colors and shapes were crossing the back side of my eyes while I watched her and her body with the front of them. She whispered what to do, how hard, how soft. She moved my hands, made them like her hands touching herself, had them touch her where I wouldn't have gone otherwise. When she said she wanted me, she made me want so much I ached like I lost something permanent in me down there, the pleasure hurting so much I couldn't imagine it working ever again. Then, we did it all again, its world so far from where we really were, the light so far away from wherever that was.

Until I remembered where I was. I remembered because the two eyes opened and there was a photo between the piles of envelopes and cream jars and shoe boxes and brushes and everything on and falling off a bedroom dresser. Of her and Tino, the drug dealer. I couldn't look straight at him, into his photographed eyes, so I made mine go to his white teeth smiling and then my brain saw a rack of guns like Cloyd's and then I imagined I heard one but I couldn't hear it go off. Which is how it is, I heard.

"I better get outta here," I said, getting up fast. "You're gonna get me killed." I was a lot more scared than when I, like, took something.

"He's at work." She didn't care what I said, or she wasn't worried, or she really didn't care.

"We don't even know what time it is."

"It's all right, he's at work."

"But what if he comes home?" I might have sounded mad. I was almost dressed.

"He's at work," she said again, but now she was getting up. "So you're gonna leave right now? You're gonna leave me here? Please don't leave me here."

"What're you saying I should do?"

"Stay. We can watch TV."

"Watch TV?"

"I don't wanna be alone," she said in a girly voice. "Please?"

Now I was dressed, and we were both standing in the bedroom. I noticed his clothes all around the floor too.

"Please?" she said. "I hate being alone. I'm alone all the time. Please keep me company, please stay. Please?"

"I dunno."

"You don't know how much I hate being by myself, I can't." She got close to me. She put her arms around me like it was Valentine's Day and we didn't do what we already did. She kissed me on the neck like she was my girlfriend. "I like you, Sonny. You know I like you, don't you?"

I felt the danger like I'd just felt the pleasure, only it hurt higher up, in the stomach. I felt the confusion like I wasn't on my own feet.

"He'll never know," she said. "I promise, Sonny. I promise not to tell him ever."

We walked into the living room together, but she turned toward the kitchen and opened the refrigerator door. Another game show was on. She was saying something but I wasn't listening. I sat on the edge of the couch and fought to tie my shoelaces. In one of his T-shirts, she came over smiling, thinking I'd changed my mind. Not for a second did I think of staying. "I gotta go," I said, and I was out the door.

Cloyd was in his office, and he spun and squeaked in his metal swivel chair as I tried to get by his office door.

"Where's your mother?"

I wanted so much to get to that room where I could just lie on that bed. "I dunno, man."

"Don't talk to me like that!"

It was like I got hit in the face but I didn't feel the pain there yet. It's that I was not expecting him to yell like that. I wasn't even sure what I'd said.

"You talk to me with respect, you understand?" He was standing up.

"I'm sorry," I said. "I didn't know I wasn't."

"Don't *ever* talk to me like that again!"

He was drunk, the red in the bulbs of his eyes at the bottom like it sank down there, or they were the roots growing off the blue above. I nodded at him but turned my sight away. I was too afraid to walk off and I wanted to so bad.

"Goddamnit," he said. He was still fuming. "Goddamnit!" he said again even louder, swirling his whiskey around the one ice cube so hard I thought it would come over the lip.

I hated that I was afraid to leave, to scratch an itch. I hated him.

"You don't know where your mother is?"

"No," I said.

"What?"

"No sir." It's that I couldn't think of what else to say.

"Where the hell is she?" he said.

When he finally turned to me I shook my head.

"So where the hell is she?"

"I dunno," I told him. "She wasn't here when I got home either."

"She wasn't?"

"No sir."

"Where the hell would she be?"

I shrugged my shoulders, I shook my head. I hated him, I hated this fucking asshole. Now I didn't even want to go to that bedroom I stayed in. Now I didn't know where I should go to get away. That's when we both heard her Mercury rolling down the driveway.

I couldn't go to that bedroom. I wasn't about to stay in this apartment.

Then my mom came through the back door anyways.

"I didn't say nothing," I told her as softly as I could as she came in. I think she heard me, too.

Nica was sitting there beside Mr. Josep. She was outside. What would she be doing outside? It was almost dark enough that I wasn't trusting it was her for a few seconds.

He waved for me to come up, like they'd been waiting for me there.

"I tell her about Russia," he said. "I tell her about when I am in Russia."

"You are?" I asked him.

A tiny red light was blinking into the glass of her apartment window, a reflection, a blip between and under the electrical poles. It seemed like I was the only one distracted by it because it reminded me of the Cloyd's bloodshot eyes. "Is everything okay?" I asked her. I said that in English. She was outside. I'd never seen her outside her apartment. It was like seeing her in a new way. It made me think everything could change for the better.

"It is not what you think about Russia. I was young and I came from Spain." He said that in Spanish, which I couldn't believe, which I couldn't understand for a second, because he still had an accent that was like having a full mouth.

"Spain?" I said.

"I want to live in Spain," Nica said in Spanish.

"Yes?"

"Yes," she said. "Don't you?"

I stayed in Spanish too. "I don't. I don't think so. But I don't think about it much. It's that I think about France." They both listened. They didn't laugh. "Paris, France. I want to go to Notre Dame, you know, the church, not where they play football."

They both stared at me but not like I was a nutcase, and neither of them laughed. It was more like they wondered if I said what I meant.

"I wish my name was Carmen," Nica said.

"Yes?"

"Don't you think it's a beautiful name?"

"It is a beautiful name," said Mr. Josep. "Very beautiful name and very beautiful music."

"I am going to name my daughter Carmen," she said.

"But you're not from Spain, are you?" I asked him.

"I want to tell you a story," Mr. Josep said.

"About Spain?" she asked.

Mr. Josep was all hyped up in his voice, but his body was as wooden as the chair he sat on.

"No, no, I am talking about Russia. Hear me. It is beautiful, it is beautiful story."

"He was going to tell us a love story," Nica said.

I couldn't believe she was standing outside.

"Yes," he said, "yes! Hear me! I was with her." He turned his head, like he was checking on something on the other side of the walls of his apartment. He did have a wife who was always inside. "Her name," he started, putting his finger to his lips and shaking his head so little that it wouldn't make noise or something, "is Alexandra, Sasha. I am in love with her. I am afraid she does not love me. I am afraid she does not like me. She is more beautiful than I deserve. The Russian people, the Russian women, they are beautiful, beautiful. I don't want to scare her and I don't know what she is feeling with me. She is a good girl in the heart and the spirit, and we are taking a walk. We have not kissed, and I am afraid even to hold her hand. I do though. Does she like me? I do not know, I do not know. We are walking and since I am not from there, she leads me to the river. It is named the Neva River, and it is stupendous. Rich like the most beautiful black hair, which is more black than black, and on its surface the whitest light hits it, like jewels floating on top of small little waves. It is evening but the sun never sets in the summer, it is always in the sky, always daylight and hot. We are sitting at the bank of the river, at the edge of granite rock. Our feet are hanging and the river is splashing us only a little. It cools us from the heat to sit there. It is very peaceful and, like a poem, very romantic. Sasha is sitting next to me. She is close but not yet close enough and I wish I can kiss her but I am afraid because I don't know and I do not want to spoil what I have. Because I am happy. Look how this is, you see? I am happy to be alive, to be with her thus. But then, wait, you see? I look and I see it. Up the river, an object is floating. I am not sure what it is until I see it and, yes, I am sure that it is a dog. It is a big dog. I don't want her to see it and I don't want to tell her. I don't want to leave but I am afraid if she sees this dog she will want to run, go and go, and this time of us together will be over. The dog is coming toward us in the river. I am sorry to see the dead dog but in truth I am not thinking of the dog, I am not. I am thinking that our time together can all be destroyed, and that it is our destiny to be destroyed, dead as the dog. Then, yes, finally, it cannot be stopped, she sees it. 'Oh, Josep, look!' she says. She is breathing with sadness, exactly as I believed she would, and she has put a hand over her mouth. 'Yes,' I say, 'it is a poor dog.' The dead dog is not twenty-five feet away, floating down the river. It is dead, dead. But it is not as you are thinking. Instead of wanting to leave, Sasha moves closer to me. Closer. She puts her arm around me, and she rests her hair on my shoulder, and I put my arm around her, which she wants. Now it is better! The dog is dead, yet I am lucky because I am in love and I feel as a man full of his strength."

We all heard Angel crying. It hadn't been for very long. He'd started to cry while we were listening to the story.

"Did you kiss her?" I asked him. "Did she kiss you?"

"I have to go inside," Nica said. She was sad. "I have to go back inside now."

Mr. Josep stood up too. "He is fine."

"I have to go in," she said as she shut the door, the sunset light against the glass of her apartment's window gone.

I saw it. Or it's what I didn't. The darkness was not light. The darkness was what might be a wall and might be a bottomless hole. It was not light. No sun and no moon. Death was not light. And the light, the light was what could be seen. Light was what shined and sparkled and was happiness, and death was like sleeping alone—it was not light. Light could be still and be watched or could pass under like a freeway was under you and you sat there. It was a spray and flow in the face when you couldn't not notice it and you didn't always unless it came at you so hard.

I was sleepy, maybe even asleep, and light was making shadow and felt good, like the shape of a nipple and pushing against me, and my hands are on her, and she is a bright ball except small, and smaller—if I could get closer, if I could see it but it was too far, or so little, because I can almost not see it easy. I'm fast, I'm more, I'm more. I'm seeing, I'm hearing, I'm touching, I'm tasting.

I needed to get up, or I needed to wake up. I was too alone. I was confused. I was all alone and it was dark behind and around me and I was alone and I was scared to be alone. I didn't want to be this kind of alone. Nobody but me. Nobody else but me. I didn't know what I should do and I didn't know what else to do. I imagined going to my mom, but she wouldn't. Not her either. No one.

And so I woke myself up—whatever you call it when you get up from this and it's still before the birds. First I went to the magazines I'd hidden. Nobody else touched them. I don't know why I got so worried about having them. Nobody knew and nobody'd know unless I told them. First I thought about hiding them better. Then how I should give them to the twins. I pulled the bookcase over and pulled up the corner where I hid my money. I wanted to make sure it was how I left it. I was spending too much and I needed more and I didn't think I was gonna get any money unless I took it. I stood up and I went into his office and I sat in his swivel chair. It squeaked so loud I about jumped out of it, feeling busted. I didn't move, though. I waited. I almost went back, but then I opened, slowly, that desk drawer. The envelope hadn't moved. I closed, slowly, the drawer. I kept my eyes low enough but I stared back at all the killed eyes in his office, eyes like Goofy's, and though she watched me sometimes, hers were never sad.

Me and the twins started walking the high beam of the street curb near the railroad tracks, balancing above the half- and full-out smashed paper cups in the gutter, near where dumpster trash blew up and out and off like moths unless they gummed up and tangled in the sticky weeds. There was a stink of a fire somewhere, which could not be called campfire smell and was something more likely horrible, like a house fire one day or two ago, and, yeah, also there was that nasty ammonia of wino piss new and old as everywhere as oil and grease and dried turds that, yeah, better be only dog doo, please. For me, it was not much like we were walking in wild nature even when we got behind one of those houses in an alley with bushy green growing all around it. First of all, mostly it wasn't green in the right way, because smog and grease and gas fume was stuck on it, and there were a lot of broken branches, sticks really, and then a car parked on the front yard was usually a dead one, and out in the backyard there'd be a couple trashed-out classics, but they were wheelless, dented, with broken windows and rotted tires and missing radiators—a bad place to make a life of getting in the back or seat behind a wheel. To me, death hummed through power lines and were not like cute clothes-lines swinging low in the air and didn't make it feel like a clean spring morning. So for me it wasn't no great outdoors when our fun was tossing rocks at shit, even when the best ones—and I got me one of those rocks I wouldn't throw, a round one—and bigger ones that were chunks of broken cement made a nothing thud into and against trash cans, or when you had to be hopping over drying-out piles of bird shit—sure, you gotta watch your step out in the wild, I know that much, but barely tied-up dogs with drooling chops, leaping and snarling, gagged by rope that held them, wanting to chew us like we were bloody butcher bones still wet in the marrow. Nah, this was no wildass exciting danger in the woods. Maybe it was for these twins, but for me we never for one moment weren't where I knew this wasn't any nature hiking. Even if there were a couple of lemon trees and pomegranates in that alley, or oranges in that backyard, and over there an avocado and an apple tree and yeah there were tall palm trees and banana plants, and little palm bushes, and all of it would seem like it was the jungle pushing itself over a backyard with a gang-tagged wall—maybe the twins saw things around them in a better way than me. They kept telling me it was my messed-up and no-fun head until these lowriders threw a can that landed close, either by accident or not, and sprayed all over. Those dudes laughed and screamed "Cuidense, putos!" and rolled up their tinted windows and spun off. That at least changed them for a couple of minutes.

Mike made the most flipped-out noises about them, cussing like he'd do something if they came back or we chased them down. Joe, who I finally knew was not Mike, was even saying, "Pinchas culeros gachos."

It wasn't asshole police he hated, even though now they were cruising by. They were still going on about those other dudes so much they were blind. I wouldn't have interrupted nothing either, until that fuzzy-haired sickie from that other time, I swear, backed off his perv ride, checking us out slow, and maybe he did think his drooling eyes might get us all so heated up that ay ay, que pasó pues, mister, like we'd be dumb-shit all over to him, all turned on and wanna jump in. I told the twins how I swore it was that same freak who'd followed me before, and Mike got to wondering which kind of culo was worse, one with tinted windows and a car club plaque or ones with power windows smeared with saliva and none of us wants to know what else.

"You'd think he could at least focus on girls," Joe said. He wasn't upset about the lowriders like Mike was. "Though I guess that'd be sick too, pues, even más sick."

"I hate living here sometimes," Mike said.

"Yeah, let's tell Mom que por fin we will agree to move to Beverly Hills," said Joe.

"Chúpame, güey." He wanted to get into a fight, even if it was only his brother, even if it was only with words.

Sure, the twins weren't like dudes who'd be able to fight for you or even with you—they'd fucking run so far, so away!— and they weren't putos, but they were kind of pussies. Still, by now they were guys I'd stand up for. I was past liking the twins. I hung with them during these school walks anyways, no matter. They were the only dudes I really knew since I'd moved here and I wasn't trying to meet anyone else at that school. They were the only friends I had. It was that I didn't think we would be living very long at Los Flores. I don't know why I got to telling little things about any of it to them. Maybe I liked the dumb way they got worked up whenever I told them shit. They made it seem like my life was a joy ride, like I was traveling, and their envy made me stronger. They heard me too much, and every little story I gave them seemed to pop in their sky like fireworks. It's that they never hung with nobody outside their own family, and they were always like they were, dressed like they dressed.

"You *made* it with her?" Joe couldn't walk and say this at the same time. "Straight up! Did you put it *in* her?"

The way his voice sounded—something almost like being at the top of his lungs but squeaking—made me laugh so hard I couldn't answer if I wanted to. I hadn't told them anything exact and didn't plan to, but it wasn't like I was saying I didn't neither.

"She's married, right?" said Mike. He really did forget, just like that, about the mood he was in. "That's crazy, dude! That's really fucking loco, loco!"

"You mean being in her apartment?" I asked. I really was wondering if they thought it was as much about being in her apartment, just that, whether that was like crossing the line.

"Fucking A, B, and C!" said Mike.

"And putting Z in her!" said Joe like he was a voice in a Nazi movie.

That really made me laugh too hard for a long time.

"Yeah, I think that'd be something that'd make her old man not like you there," said Mike.

We'd moved off the curb and were standing on the wooden ribs of the railroad tracks above the gravel river of rocks, leaping between their iron spines, going miles forward and miles backward—couldn't tell which way was coming, which was going. I was standing on train tracks, gray dirt air above and around, the twins in my ears, and my brain going into married Cindy's apartment doing the dirty magazine thing or I was wishing for Nica, seeing her and me looking at each other in the gold-framed mirrors of her parents' apartment, silver and gold and white, black and brown, and how could my mom be living with a hickabilly named Cloyd Longpre while I slept in some room with a checkered red camper bedspread, and then my mind's hand was pulling open an office drawer in the dark. There was this boy part of me that wanted to hop and laugh and twist around like the twins and call it crazy crazy, who wanted to ask all the dumb questions they asked, the ones I couldn't answer for sure. I liked it that I was going to be a man soon. The twins hadn't even kissed a girl. I hadn't been telling them about Nica very much, probably because that would've made them feel bad, you know? So I let everything be about Cindy to them.

"What's her husband like?" said Mike. "Is he big?"

"Con big pata or small pito," said Joe, "a pinche gun's all it'd take!"

"Yeah, dude, I'd fucking do you with a shotgun, dude, you putting el panchito to my woman!" said Mike.

"Simón vato, I'd fucking blow you and your huevos off!" screamed Joe.

"Her too!" added Mike. "How would it be if that was *your* old lady?"

"For being in her apartment?" I asked. I was still hung up on that.

They both moaned at the same time and it made me laugh again, made me feel happy I knew these dorks.

"Once you were in there, yeah, how could you not cork his wife?" said Joe.

We were all laughing like kids talking about caca and farts.

"En serio," Mike was saying, though Joe seemed like he might pee laughing. "Seriously."

Both their eyes were bigger than the chichis they saw in their nudie magazines.

I was nearing the front door of #1, walking and not watching what was around me, my brain climbing and hanging upside down from schoolyard monkey bars, so I nearly crashed into Pink. I don't know why I didn't see nothing of him or where he came from or how or why he was standing there. He had on a thin tank top and he'd combed his wavy, kinky, peroxided hair. Probably he was looking Elvis because he really was that way and I hadn't seen it and paid attention before, and maybe it was only because his skin was so white that his scar was so especially a cool pink, a baby girl's bedroom color, like it might light up a dark room.

"Hey there, chief," he said. "You got a second?"

I was still like waking up.

"You know, to talk to you," he said.

I nodded. He put his hand on my shoulder and walked me to that Bel Air.

"This is my proposal," he told me. "I wanna give this baby to you."

"You do?"

"That's right."

"Give it to me?"

"That's right."

"Like, whadaya mean?"

"I wanna give her to you."

"But I can't even drive it," I explained. "I'm not sixteen yet."

"Holy shit, that's right, that's right, I forget! Damn, you still a child, ain't you? You ain't no virgin though, are you? I don't think so, I don't think so. Look, nothing don't matter none, none, it don't. You want her, don't you? You want her?"

His talking was moving in a way I couldn't keep up. I must have nodded yes though. I wouldn't say no, that's for sure.

"We make a deal," he said. "Whadaya say, little brother?"

"A deal?"

"That's right. We make a deal. We make a deal that benefits the both of us. You see?"

"I guess. You know, not really."

"No? You saying no?"

"No. I don't mean I'm saying no."

"So we got a deal then?"

"It's that maybe I'm not exactly sure what the deal is." We were standing next to the car, and he'd opened the passenger door and was motioning for me to sit inside. "You haven't told me yet."

"It ain't much. It ain't nothing."

I wasn't looking at him but he was smiling, he was winking even if I didn't see his eyelids wink. I sat inside like I was told to. It felt good to sit there too, bad-ass thinking it would be mine.

"Yeah?" I asked.

"Come on, whadaya say?"

I was staring at the driver's seat and the steering wheel.

"I got the car for nothing, and I ain't gonna sell her no way, and she's meant for you."

"You're saying you're gonna give it to me? Come on, how much would I have to pay you?"

"Have I once been talking one dollar bill?" he said. Then his tone changed. "You got money? It wouldn't be much. Not much." He was looking at me without his face.

"I dunno," I said.

"We'll work out the dollars part," he said. "We can do that, we can."

"Not sure what my mom would say," I said.

"Listen, we can talk about that later, can't we? Let's talk about what I was talking about, you understand me?"

I was dizzy. I thought I wasn't hearing English. "No," I said. "I don't think I understand."

His eyes and his head and his shoulders and then his body were checking around like shit was about to hit. His eyes were checking the cars parked on the street, and he lifted his head up to see up the street if any cars were coming. He did that in a flash of seconds. Then he was back around on the other side of the parked cars and the streets, seeing if anyone was watching us, trying to hear, or any second, any second. He did that way long. Then finally he got inside my head and was looking in there, making sure. I felt him crawling in there and it felt like a long time too but it was probably only a few more seconds.

"We just be working this out," he said. "I just need you to be working with me, little brother. You see?"

All I could see was the steering wheel.

"What I'm saying, what I'm saying, is that I think me and you, we be like partners."

Then he tossed the car keys in the air and I caught them like I was ready for them all along.

"Start her up! Yeah, that's what you gotta do, you got to start her up!"

The truth was that it was a stick shift and, though I'd barely driven a car one time, I'd especially never shifted a four-speed.

"Go on! See how she sounds! I'm telling you, she is yours, she your girl! She wants you to take care of her, love her. Love how you want is how she wants."

I slid over as he made moves to take the passenger seat.

"Put your foot on the clutch real sweet," he said. Then he messed with the stick. "I put it in neutral, so go on, start her."

I'd slipped the key in the ignition and I turned. My foot pushed the gas pedal too hard and the engine shook the car.

"You gotta learn it good is all. It's got a lot inside, too much, but you'll get used to her. But see, you see how you like it."

It was fucking bad and we weren't even moving!

"So we gotta deal, right?"

"Maybe. I guess. I want to. What do I have to pay you?"

"Nothing right now, nothing. What I want is something else right now."

I clicked on the radio and punched the buttons. They all worked.

"Look, what I want," he said, "is for you to talk to me when I need you to. Understand?"

This time I turned my head to him. "Huh?"

"Little brother," he said, "all I need is you to listen for me is all. Be some wide-open ears. I'm speaking of your stepdad. You know how your stepdaddy is, don't you? What I want is that. I got a question, you got an answer. We be partnered up, see? You inside knowing what's going on is all. Understand?"

"Kind of," I said. "Not really."

"It ain't no big deal, ain't nothing, not really nothing, probably nothing. You'll see, you'll see."

I turned off the engine and offered up the keys.

"No no, uh-uh. You go on with them, they stay with you. You come start her and you take care of her because she yours now."

"I dunno, man."

"No no, it's okay, it's good, you do what I'm saying. I make a deal, I keep my word. I trust you, and you trust me."

"I'm not sure," I said, but I didn't give him the car keys. I put them in my pants pocket.

"What were you doing out there?" my mom asked when I came in.

"What're you talking about?" I didn't want to tell her about the Bel Air.

"With that man," she said. "I saw you in the car with him."

"Nothing. He was just showing me it. It's clean, really clean. A Bel Air."

"Cloyd doesn't trust him."

"So that means you don't either?"

"Listen," she said, just like that changing the subject, and tone. "I'm going out for a little while—"

I made a sound that made her stop talking. She was already dressed—low-cut front and back, draping like curtain—ready to go. She was perfume dusted. She was sitting on the edge of the couch, the maple coffee table against her knees, brushing on nail polish.

"What's the matter?" she asked.

"I dunno."

"Say it," she said.

"Where are you going?"

"Out with Nely."

I let the air move in the room. "You are not. Where really?"

"Stop it!" She stood up and it looked like she was about to

hit me or maybe throw her jar at me so I tensed up. "Why are you saying that?"

I didn't tell her.

She put the nail polish brush back in and screwed down the top and then sat, her fingers up to blow on them. It was like we were waiting for the commercial to talk again, neither of us able to move away.

"I'm not happy here," she told me.

I didn't expect her to say that. We used to talk a lot, and she used to tell me a lot, but I didn't expect this and wasn't sure I wanted to know much more.

"I'm a little bored," she said.

I nodded.

"I just need to get out some." She said that more like a question and left it there to see if I'd say something. I didn't. "It helps me to go shopping."

Now that she was lying again, putting it on like lotion, it almost made me feel easier too.

"So you want me to like tell the Cloyd something else or what?"

She didn't like me to call him the Cloyd. "He thinks I should just be here all day and dust."

That one did make me smile. It was crazy to imagine her dusting.

"Es que, he thinks I'm spending all his money. He's such a tightwad."

I didn't need to nod.

"You can just tell him I won't be back too late." Happy, as though she'd forgotten there was anything else before this, she handed me a few dollars. "Maybe you can convince him to buy a pizza for both of you."

"I don't want no pizza with him."

"Stop it, m'ijo, please."

"How come you don't tell him what you want yourself?"

"Because then we'll have an argument," she said like I was dumb for asking, "and then I might not be able to go or even want to."

"I don't want to," I said.

I hadn't seen her get that look at me since we'd moved here. I thought she might hit me like she used to hit Ceci.

"M'ijo," she said, "I'm asking."

"I don't want to eat dinner with him either."

"Please. Please stop right now."

Probably because I didn't say anything else about it, she changed too. She grabbed my hand and pulled me close and kissed me phony. "I better go quick," she said. She went digging in her purse. Small as it was, she couldn't seem to find whatever was supposed to be in there and she gave up—her keys were already in her hand—and then she was saying good-bye.

Bud pulled his truck in, stopping next to where I was still standing, and rolled down the window.

"Hey," he said. He had to be especially loud because his pickup was louder. He drove one of those huge ones, with tires out of a cartoon and the paint so waxed it looked like it could drip off.

"Hey," I said back. This was like a handshake thing again, and mine was not hardass enough, so I was sure that's why he made a face at me.

"Dad home?"

You knew he said it to irritate me. "Cloyd's not my dad. He's not home either."

"Your mom, she's not here, right?"

I nodded.

"Where'd she go?"

"Out, I guess." It made me pissed to have to talk.

"Out, huh?"

I took a long time. "Yes sir."

"Out." He stared at me.

How was it his business? "Yes sir," I told him.

"Dressed up?"

"So see ya later." I pretended I didn't hear his question and turned and stepped up the stairs. I heard his truck go on toward the back parking area.

"Where have you been?" Cindy said.

The apartment was lots worse than the last time.

"Get in here," she said. She shut the door behind me like she didn't want anyone to see. At first I didn't like it, but then I didn't want anyone to see me standing by her door either.

"So where have you been?" she asked again.

I scooted things to make room on that couch for my butt. She was standing, a T-shirt and gym shorts. The TV flickered, a rerun with a laugh that made you stop whatever you might need to be thinking, which fought with another TV show on another station going in their bedroom. It was mixing too much up, and it'd make anybody feel confused.

"I don't know what to do with myself," she said. "I'm going out of my mind! I'm so glad you're here. You want something to drink?" She was in the kitchen, pushing dirty dishes around. "I don't know what to do," she said.

"About what?"

"About anything, about myself." She was drinking a wine cooler, and she made me one and handed it to me and at the same time she was drinking hers. "I don't know what he's doing. What should I do?"

I sipped while she was almost chugging. "I'm not sure what the trouble is you got."

"This," she said. "Look at this mess."

"Maybe just pick up," I suggested. "It wouldn't take so long."

She looked at me like she couldn't believe I could say that, I could misunderstand so much. She plopped in the chair and stared at the TV.

"How's school?" she asked, turning to me.

I made a sound.

"You need to do good in school," she said.

"Okay, Mom."

She laughed. "I'm teasing. I'm not serious."

"Can you turn that down?"

She did. "So what about Gina? Did Gina talk to you?"

"Talk to me about what?"

"You know."

"No."

"You know."

"Are you talking about those magazines again?"

She grinned.

"Screw her, screw what she says!"

"She says it's you."

"Yeah, well she told my mom too. Except my mom knows I didn't steal them."

"Gina says she knows it's you."

"Knows what?" I gathered myself. "Let's talk about your life, man," I said, fucking mad. "What does this Gina know about you?"

"You mean about us, Sonny? Are you kidding? I wouldn't say anything."

I was so mad. I wasn't talking about *us*, but it did seem like a good one.

"And you can't either," she said. "You know that, right?" She had a different kind of look on her face now. She wasn't laughing now.

"No," I said.

"Sonny!"

"What?"

"You can't. If he found out. . . ."

I stood up and went straight for the door and out, and I didn't even slam it.

I pulled some money from my corner, and at the bowling alley I ordered a coke and some fries. Mrs. Zúniga stopped me.

"*¿Por qué siempre cenas aquí, muchachito?*" She always spoke to me in Spanish.

"I dunno," I said. I almost always answered in English at first. "Because I like the way you cook? It's the best. It's my favorite food ever."

"*Ay, que demonio eres,*" she said, shaking her head.

"No, really, it is, I do. Over there, where I am living, I don't like to eat. They got nasty food."

"*¿A dónde vives? No vives con tus padres?*"

"With my mom. At The Flowers apartments, that's what they're named."

"*Pues, bueno, ella tiene su trabajo alli, por eso.*"

"Not exactly."

Mrs. Zúniga put chopped up green chiles and grated cheese over the fries I ordered. God, that was really good! She also gave me two bean tacos, with cheese all melted in. They were really good too. Every time I came here, I wondered why I didn't bowl more, and why I didn't just eat here every single day. I guess maybe I was kind of embarrassed. To not have friends, to not want to be home. Like the way she was asking questions now. It's why I always got some lanes no matter if I really wanted to or not, even if alls I really wanted to do was come to eat.

Bowling, lately, I was having a little trouble with this extra last-second hook. No matter what I did, it seemed like the ball wanted to smash left of the one pin. I was even missing to the left on spares. It was only a matter of adjustment. At first I tried not turning my wrist. Then I tried using it. Not long ago I'd gotten all these high scores, so I had whatever it was right then. I was working on it, and I was having a sucky game, and I cussed loud this once when I missed a way-easy spare, and that's when Mr. Zúniga shouted at me that if I didn't watch my mouth, he wouldn't let me bowl here again. At first I didn't like that, but then I stopped myself. He wasn't like la Mrs. Mr. Zúniga never said nothing to me, except when I was leaving and I paid him at the register, and then it was only a thank-you-very-much. When he yelled at me right then, those drinkers who sat watching me blank-eyed were still blank watching me from their bar stools, like it was nothing. I was the only one here bowling ever. I was always the only one here. I took my time, I didn't bowl, I didn't leave. I didn't want to screw up. I didn't want to get mad because I wanted to come here. Mr. Zúniga didn't even charge me for as many games as I played—three was the most I ever paid for, and mostly not even that, only for the food.

I was thinking that if I was calm, didn't let myself get pissed off, if I concentrated, I'd roll strikes. If a pin didn't drop, I'd probably pick up the spare if I only took an extra second and focused before.

It was not my best day, but once I made a comeback, to 192, I quit, and I was back to feeling okay, like a kid skipping on the sidewalk even. I shouldn't have cussed. I liked bowling. I liked throwing the ball, aiming. I liked the smash of it.

"Thank you, Mrs. Zúniga," I said.

"*Que le vaya bien, muchachito,*" she said.

"I'm sorry," I told Mr. Zúniga at the cash register.

He didn't act like he'd said anything or I'd made him say something. Like most of the time, he practically didn't look at me. "Thank you very much," he said.

* ★ *

It was black outside, but the streetlights and headlights and bill-board signs on the boulevard were lots brighter than in daylight and I was hopping over the widest sidewalk cracks when I kind of lost my balance and accidentally bumped into some old white man with hair growing everywhere and a scary nose that was so smashed up it looked like it didn't come with his face but grew on it, like something that smelled and not what he smelled with. I made him drop whatever he was holding.

"Stupid punk," he said.

"Fuck off," I told him. I was sorry, but he didn't have to call me names, and really I was sorry I made him drop the paper bag he was carrying.

"What the hell?" he said. He looked in his sack, a glass bottle inside broken, wetting the cement. "Look what you did!"

I shoved at him because he was kind of trying to grab at me. "Hey, get off of me," I told him. "Get your shit off me!"

"Lemme tell you something!" He was all bent into me, and spit was popping out and spraying.

"No," I said.

"You speak English?" he asked.

"Whadaya think you're hearing?"

"Lemme tell you something," he goes again. He was too close—he could spray his spit into my face, and he kept trying to touch my arm. We were standing in the dark and shadow of two or three stores that were closed. There were cars parked, probably for the bar across the street, making a wall on the other side of us too.

"Lemme tell you something," he says.

This time he took hold of my arm and I reacted to it, fling-ing him off me, but because he kept his grip, he swung some, and, once he lost his balance, he banged into the glass window of one of the stores.

"Goddamn you!" he screamed. He took a second or two and then he came back and he took a real swing at me.

It was one that was easy to dodge, but when another caught me in the shoulder, I came back. I threw at that old man right in his stinky hocico, and then I hit on his face again. He didn't fall, and he was saying something to me, so I hit him again too—más harder, because, though he was a little dazed, he wasn't going to stop—a couple more times and then he did drop.

He was on the sidewalk and he was down and I should have walked off. But I didn't. It's that he was still saying something. "What?" I asked him. I was jacked up. He was saying something, but I didn't know what. I moved closer, standing over him. "What're you saying?" I asked louder. He didn't say. And then I did something I'd never done. It's because I could see his wallet bulging from the back pocket of his pants. I reached down and took it and I walked away.

I was carrying the Bel Air's keys on me—they were heavy in my pocket—so I jumped in behind the wheel and was about to start it up when I saw Nica's mom and dad leaving for work. The car wasn't parked right in front of the building, but it was close enough, so I made myself get lower. I didn't want them to see me. It was dark, so lights were on in #1. I was sure my mom wasn't home yet and wondered what the Cloyd would be doing in there while he was waiting for her. Then I went ahead and looked inside the wallet—was it just old, or was it soggy from so many years of sweat? It only had thirteen dollars, until I also found a twenty folded small in a little slot. The rest of the wallet was empty, not even a driver's license or a business card. I was feeling sick. It was sad that this old dude didn't have nothing. Why'd he have to go after me? It was his own fault, but I felt sorry and dirty.

★   ★   ★

I didn't even see Mr. Josep sitting there until I got too close and he saw me. He was in his chair, staring out, staring at me, I think smiling because he knew where I was going.

"The baby crying there," he told me.

I guess he would hear that.

"Sometimes *she* is crying."

I knocked on her door, careful and gentle, like the wood was part of her and she was sad and I didn't want to hurt her. Maybe she didn't answer because she didn't hear. "She's in there, isn't she?" I asked Mr. Josep, like I didn't already know. He nodded, not looking away from where he was staring, which was not at me. The TV was on loud, a movie in Spanish. I knocked again. I couldn't make myself do it any harder though, I don't know why. She didn't answer.

"Probably she not hearing," said Mr. Josep.

I put my ear against the door, like that would help me.

"Probably you wait a little bit," he said.

I passed his office and he wasn't sitting there, only the animal eyes and those fucking guns. I was at the bedroom door and his voice came up behind me.

"Where's your mother?"

I wasn't as deaf as I was pretending to be, though I didn't need hearing to feel and smell his breath when it was at my neck.

"Where's your mother?" He had his whiskey glass in his hand.

"I dunno, man."

"Don't call me *man!*" Then he punched the wall right next to the door and it left a hole. "You hear me?" He shook his head at it, like I was the one who did it.

"Sorry," I said. I was. I was trying to get myself ready. What if he came at me? If my body didn't step away from him to put distance between his fists and me, my mind was figuring out how to.

"You don't know where she is?"

"No," I said.

"No?" He was so loud it didn't sound like *no* exactly any-more, just like a sound of anger.

"No sir," I said as calm as I could.

He turned, leaving the door open. I hadn't clicked on a light. I wanted to close the door but I couldn't, it might cause some-thing, so I let myself down on top of the bed. I felt space all around me. Him gone was more like air that came in and I was being lifted up. I heard him from his office and he shouted out a word I didn't even recognize. I was trying to hear all the apartment, but the silences came through too loud, and though my eyes were open I was seeing as though they were closed too—shapes were bobbing into the darkness like dust in a block of sunlight coming through a window. I almost couldn't help but watch this mental show, as hard as I was trying not to. Then my mom got in and the strong lines jumped in brighter. He was yelling so furious there was no making out words, and his sounds were jagged, with sharp bleeding edges, and the whites were sparks from cutting metal.

It went like that until the big bedroom door shut. I took out my flashlight. I peeled up the corner and I counted out what was left of my bills, adding new ones to the count. I'd been spending too much money, but it didn't matter no more how much. I'd already made the decision, even though this was the first moment I'd admitted it to myself. I listened for Nica's breathing. I could hear it.

I handed the magazines over to the twins. They were awestruck and speechless—well, almost.

"It's that he don't need to look at pictures of them," said Joe.

"Yeah, 'cause the boy's seeing it cerquitas y for reals," said Mike.

"In color," said Joe. "Fíjate, in real güerita color too."

"Ay ay," cried Mike.

I'm cracking up, they're such stupids! I didn't even tell them she dyed her hair. "No, dude, come on, it's that I want your French book is all," I said. I traded them for a French language textbook—they were studying it for I have no idea why, but it was good for me. The deal was that they could report it lost. It didn't matter so much for them because there were two books assigned, one to each, and they studied together with only one. And they wouldn't even get in trouble for it, like most, because they were A students.

"I don't believe him," said Joe.

"Ni yo tampoco," said Mike.

"I have a personal question," Joe said to me.

"Yeah?"

"Is she a blondie down there?"

Mike howled long like a coyote. His reaction was as crazy funny as his brother's question, and I was almost crying.

"Pues, todo que tenemos son estas revistas," Joe explained.

"Cómo no que you never seen no blondie?" said Mike. "There's a few at school."

"But we never seen those pelitos de aquel chango, pendejo!" said Joe. "I'm always wondering if they're the same color," he said to me.

"You never seen any of those pelitos, never ever!" said Mike. "For all you know, they could all be turquoise!"

"How do you know I haven't seen any?" said Joe. "What about our prima Norma that time?"

"¡Ayyy, que sucio!" screamed Mike. "She's like the stack of manteca in the grocery aisle, pero without being in those square boxes!"

"Still," said Joe, "you said I never saw nothing, y ay está."

★ ★ ★

The French textbook was perfect for me. It was a lot easier than I expected too. Words and a few verbs and adjectives that I could teach myself, and the twins, laughing, gave me some of the pronunciation. I decided I'd learn a few sentences to mess with the Cloyd's brains. I probably wouldn't have to say much, if anything. Just leave the book around so he saw and maybe he'd ask. Then I'd say something. He was supposed to be French. He said his name was anyways. I was thinking of Nica. How I could say words to her. That'd be all romantic, right? Made me smile. I wanted to make her laugh. If I could make her laugh, she might want me to kiss her.

I was so gone inside the book, trying to read and pronounce in quiet whispers, I didn't notice when my mom came in.

"It is good that you're studying so hard, m'ijo," she said.

Her wrists were weighted with clangy silver, and liquidy stones dangled from her neck and ears. Her hair had some touch of new styling or color, something.

"*J'aime la pizza*," I said.

She laughed. "What?"

I liked that she laughed, because it proved French was funny and not only to me.

"*J'aime la pizza* and *j'aime l'orangeade*." It was because *limonada* wasn't in the textbook, but the second I said this drink word out loud—which was maybe what we call orange juice and not orangeade, because the book taught with pictures—I knew I'd just make the one I wanted up when I said it to Nica. I couldn't wait to learn more sentences. "It's French," I told her.

"That's wonderful, m'ijo. You are full of surprises."

"*Mais oui, ma mère.*"

She came and sat on the bed next to me.

"*J'aime le taco aussi.*" I'd been laying on my stomach, but I turned sideways and sat up to say that.

She rubbed my head like I was still her little boy.

"I made that up. I wonder what *taco* is in French."

She laughed. "Taco," she said. "What else could it be?"

I guess she never got it when I was making a joke. "It's what I think too. Like *enchilada* is enchilada, *burrito* is burrito."

She was shaking her head. "I didn't know you were studying that. I should know it though, shouldn't I? A good mother would know."

She had stopped making my bed and doing all the clean-up in the room lately. There was no more trying to keep up with whatever it was before. "I decided I should learn it for when I go to France."

"What?"

"You know, when I get to visit Notre Dame."

"Sonny, what are you talking about?"

"Cloyd said I'd go to Notre Dame, right?"

"Sonny, please, what are you talking about?" She copped a tone with that.

"Does he know where you're going?"

"I'll be back before he gets in."

I looked at her.

"Don't."

I looked down.

"He had to drive way up north and isn't getting in until late. Later than I will."

There were two big black dudes in Alley Cats, which was usually only Mexican people. They were drinking a couple and talking to each other. They seemed like men who had good jobs to me, because they both had those kind of shirts on. The regulars at the bar were acting the same as always, sitting there squeezing their beers and whatever was in the red glasses Mr. Zúniga used for drinks. He was the one scared about it, these dudes were scaring him. I could see it easy, like everybody else. He was moving in short confused steps, not doing whatever he wanted to do right. For instance, he was even talking to one of the most regular regulars, which he never did, named Rufino Cervantes, and we were hearing Rufino Cervantes say how he was born in San Antonio but raised in El Paso, then how it was for Mr. Zúniga when he was stationed at Fort Bliss army base, how it was, right at the border, and those wild bars where the GIs and Mexicans fought and even shot each other sometimes. I'd never heard Mr. Zúniga talk about anything to anyone else before that didn't have to do with the business.

"*¿Traes tu hambre, muchachito?*" Mrs. Zúniga asked me.

"Yeah, I can eat."

"*¿Y qué vas a comer hoy?*"

"*J'aime beaucoup les hamburgers,*" I said.

Mrs. Zúniga stared at me like I was talking a foreign language.

"I'll take a cheeseburger, with fries."

"I woulda believed this joint served Mexican food," the black guy closer to me said. It was that I was sitting near them, a bar stool between us.

"It does," I said.

"Oh yeah? So what you recommend?"

"Hamburgers or cheeseburgers."

They both laughed easy and loud. Neither of them seemed to notice, or care, that the place had become all about them, no matter who else was talking or whatever was going on the TV. "What the hell kinda Mexican food you used to?"

"It's Mexican now," I said. "It's that all you do is let her make it with jalapeños, and she puts her salsa de chile on it too, and then it's Mexican—as Mexican as it is American."

"Sounds hot," he said. They were both laughing.

"Sure, but you said you wanted Mexican, and it's good too."

"We want two of them then," said his friend.

Mrs. Zúniga nodded at them. "Something else too?" Usually, when someone only spoke English and was new, Mr. Zúniga took the orders and told her in Spanish.

"What else you got?"

"*Tenemos un caldo de pollo,*" she said nervously, not to them but to me. "*Viene con arroz y tortillas.*"

"A chicken stew, rice, and tortillas," I told them.

They looked at each other.

"They got beans too," I said. "They're really good, man."

"I ain't eatin' those Mexican beans," said the one farther from me. "I don't wanna be around you eatin' 'em either."

"I say we'll stay with the Mexican hamburgers," said the one closer to me.

"Cheeseburgers," said the other. "Double cheeseburgers."

They ordered another couple of beers from Mr. Zúniga. They finished everything—the beers in a couple of gulps, the burgers in what seemed like three or four bites—faster than I could make it through any of mine, and then stepped out as loud and with as little movement as they had sitting there, telling me I was right, that was good, and politely thanking Mrs. Zúniga. When I went to pay, Mr. Zúniga shook his head, like he was talking to himself. "Thank you very much," he said. He was washing dishes, not wanting to talk anymore to Rufino Cervantes or anyone else after those men left.

I sat on the driver's side of the Bel Air and I stepped on the clutch and practiced shifting. I was feeling the gears, where they were. I could see The Flowers from where I sat, but I didn't think anyone could see me because no one, except Pink, would be looking here. Close as the car was, it seemed as far away as a dream of driving it. I might have started it up, until I saw my mom driving out, her car bottoming a little too hard as she came out the driveway and onto the street in her distracted hurry. Her leaving was good news. I didn't feel like talking. I didn't feel like sweeping either. I could go in and be alone. I took off for the back door of #1. I almost didn't turn around when I saw Gina driving up behind me. But I didn't want it to seem like I was avoiding her.

"Hi, Sonny."

"Hi."

"You doing good?"

"Sure."

"That's good."

I nodded and shrugged and got really self-conscious.

"The place is still looking really great."

"Yeah. Thanks."

"Okay then," and she winked at me and went the rest of the way down the driveway.

I was walking fast, I thought, but not fast enough. Because it was Bud pulling in the driveway, right after I made the sharp turn toward the back door I wasn't through yet.

"Hey tough guy," he said from inside his truck. He'd leaned away from the steering wheel and rolled down the passenger's side window and his body was still on both sides. He'd been sweating or still was. He was looking dirty. "Your dad around?"

I knew he was saying that to grind his mean into me. "Not in years," I said. "Maybe he's with your mama."

"What'd you say to me?"

"Nothing."

"What I heard sounded like you said something to me."

"I didn't," I told him. "I said no."

"I swore it sounded like you were getting cute with me."

"I gotta go in."

He was nodding and nodding, and right at me. "So you don't know if Cloyd's there?"

"No. But I don't think so."

"You know when he's supposed to get back?"

"Probably not until late."

"That so?" he said.

What was I supposed to say?

"I saw your mom," he said. "Driving."

Now I wished my thoughts were my actions and would bust all into him, would do something to his fucking face.

"She was in a hurry."

"Why're you telling me?"

"No reason. Thought maybe you might know is all."

"Know what?" I hated myself for talking to him.

"You tell me."

"Sorry, but I don't know what you're talking about," I said. I wished I wasn't afraid of him. "Hey, if you don't mind, I need to go in now."

"Hey," he repeated.

If I moved it wasn't because I was trying to.

"You watch how you talk to me, all right? You understand?"

I couldn't understand why he was this way with me either, what I'd said or done. I didn't like this face though, I didn't from the start. Maybe he knew it. "I wasn't trying to talk to you bad." But maybe I shouldn't like him either. Maybe I didn't because I shouldn't. Maybe it was that he didn't like me from the start and that's what. "I gotta go in now."

"All right then."

"Okay."

It was the time of night for lights inside, but still not so dark that you couldn't see. For a couple of minutes I was mad at myself for being twitchy, then I let myself get mad but smart and that got me a little nervous. I was thinking, This is the time. I paced around the darkening apartment, thinking thinking thinking how it would play out *if*, though mostly how bad if I got caught and how really wrong—really really—it was. How scared would I feel once he found out it was gone, once he started looking? How I wanted to and how that feeling felt like it was talking back and not being afraid of Bud. Thinking, I do it cold, I stay fucking cool, ando suave. How if I didn't do it, if I didn't do it *now,* I could feel worse later. I stopped pacing. I went to the office and the drawer and pulled it out and there was the envelope. He hadn't touched it, it hadn't moved since I took it out and put it back. I wondered how often he looked. No, I could not touch it again. If I touched it, it could only be to take it. I shut the drawer and went out and walked back and forth and then I was doing laps from the kitchen through the dining room, by the maple table with lazy susan thing of salt, pepper, napkins, toothpicks, and like on it, spun into the living room past the elk, trout, owl, leather furniture—quick through the hall and not into the bedroom I slept in but turn and back into the kitchen and around again and around again. This was, definitely, the time if I was gonna do it. This might even be the only time. If I'm gonna do it. If if if. If if if. If I'm gonna do it, do it. Now. Do it. Now.

I went into the office again, all the dead eyes on me and not seeing, the Goofy noses smelling, and I sat in his squeaking chair and fuck the rifles. I sat, it swiveled, it squeaked. If he even saw me in the chair, ever, then I could never do it. I decided! I went into the kitchen and grabbed a dish towel and came back and I opened the drawer like an oven and I took the envelope. I shut the drawer. My heart was crazy beating in my legs and arms and fingers. I was panicky. I hurried the envelope over to my spot in the bedroom I slept in but it was too much to put there, a lump not too fat but so serious it seemed like it.

I was behind the parking stalls, where the trash cans were, looking for a better hiding place. I wished I didn't do it but I couldn't put the money back because I'd even crumpled the envelope holding it. It was like there was no way I could go back, I'd be guilty no matter. I couldn't think where to go, where to hide it.

"Sonny."

My body jumped like it was him, even though the voice obviously wasn't.

"You taking the trash out?" Gina asked.

I said something but I don't know what.

"Are you all right?" She seemed to mean it.

"Yeah," I said.

"You sure?" she said in a funny voice. She stood there holding a plastic garbage bag.

She didn't believe me, but I was positive she didn't see me drop the envelope.

"Yeah," I said. "It's not trash day."

"Oh," she said.

"It's that he likes me to put them in the fewest containers."

"O-kay." She said it like that was two words.

"Let me take it for you," I said. I looked in several containers. Then I put her bag in one and I picked up another bin and dumped what was in it on top of the one I put her trash in.

She watched. "Thank you then," she said.

"Sure," I said.

There was no turning it around, no explaining. I wished I didn't but it was done. I couldn't give this money, say, to the twins to hold. I couldn't tell nobody. I was in that bedroom again and sorry. I stuffed the money between the two boyscout books. *Voilà*. Saying something in French didn't even make me smile enough and that I knew I was real fucked. Not much of a secret place but who cared. Because if they were going to look in this room, they'd find it no matter where I hid it. Then again, nothing was going to happen so fast. It could be a week, or two even. Then again, it was a good place in another way. It wouldn't be a place to look first. I was not going to mess up. I knew how not to mess this up. I wasn't tired but I fell on my back and closed the eyes and I was safe deep inside a mountain and I could hear and not be seen. I could hear whatever I wanted. The wind calmed me, until it was pushed away by the other building's neighbors talking. I still couldn't tell what language they spoke, but their sound made me feel like I was going away. I went there. I was going to make a sharp turn, any second, like a turn too flat on a ground around it that was too flat too. I'd made it before. I could still feel this curve on me, when, going so fast, I went up what should have been a down. Then Nica's father's voice interrupted, and I could understand him as well as I heard him. He was asking where were his ironed pants, why didn't she iron better, how hard was it to iron? That cat outside started hissing and I saw a lizard staring back. I saw a spider at the top corner of the room's sliding glass window, still, hanging stick legs up from a thread. I got off my back, taller, shorter, ready, getting ready because I did it.

"Sonny. Up here."

That was Cindy, leaning over the balcony and looking down. She was in something low-cut, and she wasn't wearing a bra.

"What?" I said.

"Come up," she said. "Come over." She was kind of whispering, kind of shouting.

I didn't want to do anything messed up. "Not right now," I said.

"Sonny!" she said. "Come up here!"

"Not now," I said again. "It's too late."

"Sonny." She started coming down the stairs.

I met her halfway and she took my hand. I didn't want that. But I went into her apartment. The TV was murmuring, the place was all junk and dishes and glasses again.

"You haven't visited me."

"Cindy, I need to do some shit."

"Come on." She shook her body at me, then she put her hands on my pants. "I want to play."

"Are you crazy?"

That made her back off.

"Sonny," she said quietly.

"We're both gonna get shot."

"That's not going to happen."

"You're gonna get us both—"

"He's working late again tonight."

"I gotta book, man."

"Please don't."

My hand was on the doorknob.

"Sonny, I'm broke. I'm lonely. I'm bored."

She was sitting balled up, soft as a pile of pillows, as I opened the door.

"Will you come by tomorrow then?"

I only wanted to watch out safe behind the windshield, and what I was watching was Pink talking it up to a black dude, counting money the guy gave him, signing papers on the hood of a Lincoln I'd never even noticed before. They shook hands in some black way and the man got in and drove away. Pink talked to him with his hands, kind of nodding as the man went down the street to turn left.

He jumped in on the passenger's side, his white teeth even whiter than his skin. "Oh, yeah, it is a beautiful night, little brother. A beautiful, beautiful night."

I was sure he was right.

"Ain't it so, ain't it?"

It was hard not to feel better because of him. I nodded.

"And what're you doing out here, my little brother?"

"Sitting." I smiled. Made myself smile.

"You are sitting, aren't you?"

I nodded again.

"So you like your car here, don't you? I knew you would. You been driving it?"

"I can't drive it. Like I said before, I don't even got a license."

"Oh come on! You been driving it, ain't you?"

"No," I said.

"All right then," he said. "All right, that's all right."

"They'd both pop if I did," I said. "My mom and Cloyd."

"All right, yeah, I understand." He sounded calmer, made a shift with what seemed like his body. "We all partnered up still, you know, about your stepdaddy."

"To be honest," I said, "I'm still not really sure. It's that I don't know what I'm supposed to do."

"Ain't no nothing, no big nothing. Like I told you. You just keep me up on things, keep your eyes and your ears open. You keep me up on your stepdaddy."

"What, though? I mean, keep you up on what?"

"Nothing, nothing. You know. If you hear something, if you see something."

"Did he say anything?" she asked me. She stank of cigarettes and cocktails.

"About what?"

"He's still gone," she said, talking as her eyes roamed. "He didn't come back. I don't know what I'm thinking." Her body sighed all over. She plopped down onto that special favorite leather chair of his and she was taking off her high heels. They were bright blue, color coordinated with the baby-blue dress she wore. "I am so happy I got here first."

I sat on the sofa, not sure what next. "You like that owl?"

She looked at it. "No," she said. She looked at it longer, then she laughed. I listened to her laughter. "I guess I never thought about the owl. No, I don't like it, no. Tú no te gusta tampoco, you don't either, do you?"

I shook my head no, but not hard. I meant my question.

She was laughing. She laughed too much because she was drunk. She took off her earrings sloppy and tossed them on the coffee table in front of me. She rubbed her feet. "Why are you asking me that?"

"It's that it's kind of cool and I never seen an owl before this one, so I don't hate it. I hate the fish up there, and I don't like these duck lamps for real, even if what I think is how lots of people maybe would like it all. But that owl—well, I think I don't hate it but not how the Cloyd loves it, you know?"

"Ay, m'ijo!"

I shrugged. "I always call him that."

She laughed. "Ay, m'ijo, we moved away, didn't we?"

She wasn't wanting me to answer.

"He stares," she said. "He's like knowing what we do, isn't he?"

"Or she."

"What?" she said.

"It could be a she. Neither of us knows what's a male or female owl."

She laughed, too drunk again, and rubbed her feet. "Like an abuela! But abuelita no puede decir o hacer nada, can she?"

"Are you okay?" I asked her.

"Of course, yes. Are you, m'ijito?"

"I miss Goofy."

She put a finger to her lips.

I nodded. "*Bon soir.*"

"Angelito's asleep," she whispered, shaking her head in a good way, smiling, "but if we're calm, we can talk."

"*Toujours*," I said. "I'm always calm, *n'est-ce pas?*"

She looked at me like I was making it up.

"I said, 'I'm always calm, right?'" I said *right* too loud.

She shushed me again, but she was still smiling. Talk French, make a smile. She was happy to see me. And then she took my hand, and she sat us on the couch. Some really dumb Mexican variety show was on TV. A woman in a nurse uniform swatted at the bedridden old man's hand grabbing at her butt when his ugly red-haired wife wasn't looking, the laugh track volume up high.

"You're not watching this, are you?" I asked.

She didn't care what I said. "I have a job to babysit," she whispered.

"You already do that."

"No, you clown. Over there."

"Yeah? That's real cool. You're going to be rich."

"You can come over. With me." She was smiling like she was talking French.

"Of course. With pizza!"

She was a little girl in a white chiffon dress and black shoes and a pink ribbon. "But you do not tell!" She was a little girl.

"No, not possible."

"They can't know."

I wasn't sure which *they* she was talking about. I was feeling confused. I don't think I could get anything straight. Maybe something was wrong with me. Because I didn't understand. For example, why would I get to be there, in #7, just down the walkway, but not here, in #4, where I was anyways? And who would be watching Angel if nobody else could? I didn't ask questions, I couldn't. "But I don't think," I decided to say, "those people, Bud and Mary, have a child."

Really, I was sure they didn't. I was kind of sure she didn't know, but then it didn't matter if she didn't or her father didn't. She was always in this apartment. Even if she only got five minutes over there, it was better.

We were still sitting in front of the TV light and the noise, and it's what I wished for every day. Another program: a man holding a weeping woman. She was wailing so hard her hair shook. Nica shook her head and turned it down.

Instead, she talked, happy. Nica told me that in her pueblo above Xalapa, that big city below, their home was painted blue and yellow, and she loved the red flowers that grew against the walls. The fog rolled up to her and, since she lived on a mountain, sometimes she would stand in a cloud that lowered from the sky. She stayed with her cousins there. She missed going out and playing.

"Playing?" I asked.

Her eyes would never see into mine. As though to look straight at me was wrong. As her lips moved, I didn't see curve in them, only sharp-cut lines. Her nose too, they weren't for breathing, they were for someone to draw. She wasn't real. She couldn't be real.

Nica's mother was from Veracruz, from a big family. Her mother was the first girl in her family. She loved her mom. She still loved her mom. Her father? Her father she didn't know. This man, the man here, Margarito, he was not her natural father. He married her mother. He said he was from Mexico, the capital. Angel Fidencio was their child. She loved her baby brother Angel, she really did. She loved taking care of Angel. She said everything was fine. She said she liked living here in the apartment. Her mom had work, her stepdad Margarito worked, and it was good for everyone that she was here to watch Angel while they did. She hoped they didn't have another baby. She hoped that things would change eventually. It was not the first place she lived with them. It was different when they were alone, her mom and her, when they came across. Yes, she loved to listen to her radio. When Angel was asleep and he was next to her, she could listen to it. He liked it too when she was next to him and he was awake or asleep.

The commercials were full of action and she was watching the TV, but it seemed like she was more near me, she was moving closer. Her hands could almost touch me again. The TV had a broken purple color in it, and her hands weren't real in the strange light. I wanted to kiss the not-real hands. I wanted to go to the not-real place with colors I didn't know. Like the world away from this city, if there was no smog, like where she grew up. Or if we were kissing and we were there, that black-and-white I knew. I was shaky, and I was happy. I was so happy I was next to her but I was also afraid to stay and didn't know where to go. Where was I going to hide that money? I was sad. I was fear and sadness except where I saw a glow on her, like in a saint's painting. The glow didn't come out of her but gathered around her, collected around her, came off her—or it was a light behind her that she was blocking, and its too-bright light was on the other side of her face, and so the fuzz was a circle around her.

She was happy that I was sitting with her too. She liked it that I was there! Still, I jumped up. "I better go," I said suddenly. I needed to go. "It's pretty late." She sagged, her body deep into the couch. I couldn't see what it was in her eyes, not directly anyway, because they didn't look into mine. "I don't want you to get in trouble with your family."

She didn't move.

"I'm bringing the pizza, and we'll have it over there."

"I want you to be there when I am," she said softly.

"I do too. I don't want to go now either, not really. I don't. I just better."

"I wouldn't say nothing," said Joe. "So what if the baby's a kitty-cat."

"A él, le gusta màs la otra kitty-kitty," said Mike.

"Shut up," I said. "Don't say it, don't say shit or anything like it."

"Her dad probably didn't know she was talking about a cat," said Joe.

They kept a distance as we walked.

"I think you're in a bad mood," said Mike.

The pervert cruised past us slowly. It was like he never washed his car or changed his shirt. Both were kind of red but with so much dirt they could be called as brown as his stiff bristly hair.

Joe said, "It can't be the same dude, it can't."

Mike said, "It's the same dude."

We saw him turn around way up there.

I'd picked up a rock. It was a big one, baseball size and heavier. It was a good rock.

Joe said, "We should do something to him."

Mike said, "We should fuck him up."

"You could anyway," Joe said to me, "but we'd help you out."

"We couldn't help him out," said Mike. "We wouldn't know how."

"Yeah," said Joe, "we're fucking pussies." As he said this, he about tripped over his brother.

"That's not the same," Mike told him in a whisper. "He's not gonna get mad about that."

I smiled. I wasn't smiling because I wanted to laugh, just everything they did made me want to smile like a French word. And I wanted to smile. When the sickie came toward us, now from the other direction, I could see his insect eyes behind his glasses. I think he thought one or all of us was in the game. I got a little closer to the curb and he steered his four-door closer. When he got near enough, I stepped out on the street and threw the rock as hard as I could at his face. It cracked against the windshield—a break but not the explosion I was wanting—and the rock ricocheted off. He hit his brakes, and when he did the twins stopped walking and ran. The twins didn't see I had the rock until I threw it. I was in the street, looking for another rock, and when the sickie realized, he pounced on the gas— not to hit me—and made a big curve around me. The twins were running over the railroad tracks and were across the other street, holding their books like girls squeezing their arms against a tight sweater. They were not good runners either, and they didn't look too good running. They did not hear me yelling at them. The twins always made me smile, no matter what, like French. It made me smile to see that sickie dude driving away hard.

After school, I'd rolled a 229, the score I wanted against that windshield. It was my highest score for a while, and I was walking strong. I was feeling lots better about myself. I was proud of my power inside and my aim, my roll. My shot. I wished I didn't take that money. In another way I was like, well, not sorry. Then again, I couldn't be. Then again, it didn't matter, it was done.

On our way back, avoiding the hijo de su madre puddles and globs of slime or maybe grease or none-of-us-wanna-know, while it seemed to me our shoes were only digging into an island of ugly gravel rocks on either side of the railroad tracks that made the crunchy noises at our feet, the twins kept going how we weren't just walking in what was once upon a time the ocean, we were cracking the crust of ancient earth, crushing shells of cellular lobsters. Our feet were like maracas, a stepping jungle music, and we were doing a cumbia that had to be heard with a brain. That's what these guys told me, and they got straight As, so I couldn't say nothing much. My own theory was that maybe they were smoking the mota.

"Hey, so, what is it like?" Mike asked, almost shy. His brother got closer too.

"Like getting high, fucker. Whadaya think?"

"Ay, vato," said Mike. "Honest, come on. I mean, is it like beer, or whiskey, or es como tequila?"

"Those are nothing," said Joe.

"Cálmate," said Mike, shaking his head. "You always exaggerate, cabrón."

"No siempre," said Joe, soft. "A little, nada más sometimes."

"I guess it's like being inside her," I said after a few seconds, trying to be serious, "except all the time." It's what I could think of.

Both of them made groaning noises.

"It's that it's the only time I smoke is when I'm with her."

They both made more noises and stuck their tongues out like they were having a spaz attack.

"He's no Catholic," Joe told Mike finally.

"Not gonna be a priest anyway," said Mike.

"Dude, you're our pre-Conquest warrior hero," Joe said. "Un indio que toma el polvo de las uñas de águila, and the heavenly white moon is shining down on your beautiful maiden's big-ass chichis y nalgas."

"La blondie Azteca!" said Mike.

"When I'm on the bed at night," I said, "I do hear shit."

"Stop snorting eagle nail powder, dude," said Joe.

Mike started making sounds like we were in outer space.

"That's not the music, vato," Joe told him.

"I'm Catholic. What the fuck do I know about my pre-Spanish, pre-Columbian musical heritage?" said Mike.

"It's there, hermanito, in your cells," said Joe.

"It's in your skin color and on the bones of your nose," said Mike.

"Your nostrils don't look exactly Swedish," said Joe.

The route was our regular now because of me, and the twins were cool with that because they were into busting malt liquor bottles and pickle and peanut butter jars—this one of mole sauce didn't bust, and we cracked up about how tough Mexicans were—against the iron rails. We hadn't seen the sickie since that last time. He was there though, lurking. I was definitely planning to bomb the fucker with fat rocas, dent the shit out of his stink ride. I juggled my favorite monster rock between my hands, back and forth, ready: big as a softball, hard as a shotput. Every day I expected it to be his day to get to know the real deeper me better. I left this one rock where I could carry it in the morning, then I'd leave it at the other end to pick up on the way home. I wanted muscles flexing with each hand-to-hand toss, my blood to run so quick inside me it'd come squealing into my ears, the rushing wind in a conch shell. It made me feel like I was gliding and getting lighter, floating, a bubble coming up fast from below.

I skipped Alley Cats to get to The Flowers early because, the night before, Cindy looked her dirty way at me and was going how she was really lonely, so I was all Oh yeah, I'll come up, why not? I was getting in an y qué? and also an y por qué no? mood lately a lot, seemed like. I was going like, yeah, that's right, yeah, I *don'* care you like it or you *don'*. Fuck her candy-sales husband. Nobody was around in the afternoons, so it wasn't like I had to watch how I said what.

An ambulance was way up in the driveway already, the back loaded with Mr. Josep's wife, and there were even neighborhood strangers around, setting up sodas and chips, like it was a TV set. My mom was near—glossed and sparkling, ready to be gone, going wherever she'd go to—and Cindy was at the top of the stairs, and Mr. Josep was coming out of his apartment door. Bud, a construction site stuck all over his workboots and jeans and T-shirt and face and arms and hair, was below too, eating a white-bread sandwich that sometimes would hang on his lips, which made it seem like he was distracted about something else. Maybe he really was only around for his lunch break, late. My mom hustled up the stairs to steady Mr. Josep down, and he accepted her arm. They were talking in Spanish, and I swear that made Bud growl out loud. He held his position like he had a memorized speech ready. Mr. Josep was dressed as neatly as every day, slacks ironed, shoes polished, a vest buttoned, his silver hair combed like an old important politician. He bent down to get in the back with one of the emergency workers, but like he was weak and sick, and then the ambulance whined in reverse and turned onto the street, rushing forward with a siren running.

"How bad is Mrs. Josep?" I asked.

"Her last name's not Josep," my mom said, ticked I was so dumb. "They told me she didn't look good. They weren't hopeful."

"They weren't married?" I asked her.

"Sonny, Josep is not a last name. It's his first."

"Really?"

"Poor man, este pobre viejito. He is upset."

Cindy turned back into her apartment. It was as though I was the only one who ever saw her standing there, because nobody else looked at her, and she didn't look at or say anything to anybody either.

Bud stepped up into my mom's face, though more like he was holding out on what he really had to say. "So, you're saying you didn't see him?" It might have been the subject he wanted, but it wasn't what he wanted to talk about.

"No, Bud, please," my mom said. "Please don't raise your voice."

"I swear to God I saw him."

"I just don't know, Bud."

"He don't answer the door, even though I know he's in there."

"Well, I don't know what to tell you," my mom said. It wasn't clear whether she was telling me or him or herself. She checked herself over, her clothes and shoes and jewelry, up and down, making sure nothing was wrinkled or dirtied, wiped on or off, hanging wrong. She squinted at her purse. It was wet black vinyl, and sunlight bounced off it and onto the nearby walls like it was a mirror, making flashes that seemed more like from a camera snapping photos of her. "I'll be back," she said, like an announcement. Her high heels tapped the sidewalk toward her car.

Angry still, or maybe always, his mind not on what he was seeing with his eyes, Bud backed off but not away, watching her at a distance, and close, like she was a movie star. "Hey," he said.

"Yes?" my mom answered, tired of him.

"So you're going someplace?" This time it was it, what he meant.

"Excuse me?"

"Wondering where you're going."

"I don't think I'm married to you."

"That's your loss."

"Is it now?"

"Why are you all dressed into the tens?"

My mom fumed. "I'm leaving now." She dug around for her car keys and when she found them she opened her car's door, got in holding the hem of her dress, making sure to catch what might show to somebody looking to see, and slammed the door shut.

★   ★   ★

Cindy'd already been smoking mota and drinking wine and something was making me think there was more serious shit too, something else. It was like a burning smell, except I didn't know if it
was a real burning or in my head.

"God, it's about time," she said. She went up on me and
kissed me, her hands moving inside my pants and onto my butt.
"I miss you."

I liked it, but her talk I didn't like. I'm not sure how to
explain what it was, if there was a name for it. There was. Tino.

"I do like you, Sonny," she whispered, kissing my face and
neck.

"Don't say that shit," I said, pulling away. "I hate your shit."
I was wrong to be there. It was not good, it wasn't right. But I
went there because I was mad. I knew where to look and I was
right.

"Don't be mean to me, don't." She pulled me back.

"I'm not. I just don't wanna hear it."

"But I do like you. Can't you tell I like you?"

She had one lit and we took hits back and forth wordlessly.
Smoking it *meant* sex to me. It slowed quiet into numb. We took
swallows of the wine cooler she made too. It let me like her
touching me, her hand going down and pushing at the back of
my pants and, guiding me to the bedroom and bed, pulling them
off me, and her hands gripping my cheeks, putting her mouth
all over me there. The mota made me learn how to wait too,
taking her up to me and making her. My hands moving on her
were streaking sparks on a roller coaster's rails. She still was showing me things to do. At first I didn't think I would like my tongue
where she wanted it, but then I did, my hands holding onto her
nalgas, as soft and hard as her titties were. She moaned with me
in her mouth. When she did, it was sunlight and moonlight at
the same time, yellow and silver and too bright, too scary even,
to stare straight at. She tangled us up, but I liked her from above,

her nipples tickling my chest, or turned around, the dimples above her butt like thumb holds to keep her where her curve was the sharpest, her back arched, the lines of her body a broad marker white in my mind, my eyes not even imagining before the pleasure that they were getting to see, my mind taking on light from this other sun or moon.

She was laying there naked on the bed, eyes closed. My face turned up and saw the photo hanging crooked on a wall with a group of others. It was another of him in a white cowboy hat and black snap-button Western shirt, smiling—not happy smiling but smiling like Yeah, here, I'll smile. He was a man, a grown man, and he had a gun, I knew he had a gun. I'd seen it before. I saw it when she'd been in the bathroom too and I dug around. Now I felt like a big man, real bad, real chingón, while we were doing it. I don't know why I wanted to mess with him too, but I did, and that's why I was there, why I did it, why I came.

"You like what we smoked?"

"I guess."

"It had something else in it."

I was a little scared and it made me feel more fucked up too. I was too high. "I gotta go," I said. I was so stupid!

She looked at me like it never crossed her mind I might leave. "Please don't, Sonny. Not yet."

I was already getting my clothes back on, thinking smarter.

"It's still too early," she said. "He always works late now."

"I don't wanna get killed." He was death, because he would kill me. He had a gun and he would shoot me dead. I'm thinking, I'm him, I cap me, then I cap her. No French word for any of this could make me smile.

"But I want you to stay with me," she said.

"I'm gone." I had to make sure I didn't make any more mistakes. I was way past just taking some dollar bills here and there. This was dangerous.

"Just a little longer. Stay with me a little longer. I'm always alone. I'm lonely."

I was tying my shoelaces too tight.

"I don't even love him anymore. I don't really. I know what he really does. I don't want it to be like this every day. I'm too lonely here, Sonny. Please don't leave yet, please, Sonny?" She got up off the bed because I'd started walking. "We could eat dinner in the living room and watch TV together. I can get Chinese food delivered. If he came, he wouldn't think anything, I swear. He knows I like to have company. I have to have friends, and he would think we're friends. I know him. He wouldn't think anything was going on. Can't you trust me?"

She didn't even have her clothes on. "Yeah, I'm sure he wouldn't think nothing," I said.

"I don't know what to do," she said. "I don't know what I should do."

"I'm gone," I said.

Already, going by Cloyd's office whenever I came in wasn't freaking me so much. I was over being fidgety now and feeling like I could handle whatever came. It was like I didn't care or that the scare had worn off. It was going to play out however it played out, at whatever speed or loudness. I gave Cloyd a friendly *bonjour* when I passed and regretted it.

"Where's your mom?" he asked, squealing the chair as he spun it.

The dead eyes were lit up on me in his office. "Pues," I said, dragging the thought, "I don't really know."

"You don't really know." It wasn't a question.

"No sir," I said.

"You know what time she's getting back?"

"No sir."

"You don't know?"

"I really don't, man." That *man* took off out of me, but he didn't seem to notice.

"I wonder where the hell she is this time," he said.

"I don't know either," I said. "Sorry."

"Do you know about Pink?"

I didn't want to jump back, like a nervous twitch, but I might have. "What about him?"

"You hear about someone living with him?"

"No sir. Why would I?"

"Because you talk to him. Don't you talk to him?"

"Not that much."

"You take the trash out?" he said, swiveling so his back went to me.

"I'm gonna do that in just a second."

Sometimes the bedroom door shut gave me a safe and private sense, or at least an extra second or two if someone came to it. I started liking the boyscout book being a hiding place for that money. I'd thrown away the envelope and put the bills in the pages. It was smooth. I put some of my own money in the pages too, and then put the rest back under the rug, like before. I didn't care anymore that it was running out.

I was hearing Nica's dad upstairs. He wasn't even yelling. He was telling her about her ironing. Didn't she learn yet? Why couldn't she learn to do it how he told her? He wanted the starch. There was a can right there, she could put it on. Did she see this can? Did she know how to push the button? Didn't she know how to put the starch with the can? Was she a goat? Was pushing an iron too hard? She had to do something here, he worked many hours. Then he said he didn't want that her mom would have to make the lunches. She could make the lunches. Her mom worked and was tired. Every day she ached until she can barely work, and they both have to work. Couldn't she make the lunch

for them? Was it so difficult to do that for them? He left, and it
was silent, except I knew those were tears hitting the floor, the
dripping off the roof after a light rain. She made the steam of the
iron puff. Nica put the radio so low because he would've turned
it off if it was too high.

Bud's voice was at the edge of the kitchen at the door of Cloyd's
office. There were clinks of ice in a glass. I cracked the door to
hear better.

"Well, what if it's true?" Bud said.

Cloyd's voice came muffled. He was in the office, the swivel
chair squealing, Bud was standing at the door. Would I hear better
with the door closed because I would listen feeling safer? I didn't
close it.

"I'm telling you what I saw," Bud said.

Muffle.

"I can get him to leave. I can get both of them to leave."

Muffle. More muffle.

"Why don't we both go up there and knock and, then, if
nobody answers, you got the master key. See who and what the
hell is in there."

Cloyd was talking muffled, before he stopped talking. Bud
must have gone in the office too because I couldn't make him
out either.

Then I heard Bud's voice come in clearer because it got
louder. "It ain't right, it ain't right. I'm tired of these kind of
people."

Cloyd came into the kitchen and dropped in a fresh ice cube
from the freezer.

"You sure you don't wanna have supper with us?" Bud said.

"I got that under control," he said.

"Okay, but Mary, she can cook some beans. You like beans.
She's got a pot of them. Probably some chicken too."

"Real nice of you, but I got it under control."

"Maybe bring some down to you later?"

"Nah, when she gets here, me and Sil'll just go out to dinner tonight."

"She's awful late," Bud said. "I'd be worried too."

"She'll be here any minute, I'm sure of it."

"Okay then," said Bud, opening that back door. "You
change your mind. . . ."

Workboot steps came hard toward this bedroom I slept in. The
only thing I could grab when I jumped over to the bed was the
French textbook.

"What're you doing?" he said like I was doing something
wrong. He was in the grays, and they were not ironed anymore,
his hair stuck on his forehead, pointing every direction. He didn't
have on the stupid grin, but the eyes were drooling whiskey.

"Reading."

"What?"

"French."

"French?"

"Yeah," I said, avoiding the *oui* word that always made me
want to smile to say it. "It's French. *Français.*" I couldn't resist
smiling.

"What're *you* doing with that?"

"You mean studying the language? Why am I studying
français?"

"You know what the shit I'm asking," he said.

"Not really."

"You don't read fucking French!"

This was what I had wanted, though it was making me a
little tense. He was mad, which is what I wanted, but now I had
to deal with it.

"I'm learning to. It's one of those books, you know, that teach language."

"They don't talk French in Mexico."

Mexico. I was feeling smarter and richer.

"French," he said. He swirled the ice cube.

"They talk French in Paris," I said. "Didn't you say you were French?"

"My ass speaks French sometimes," he told me. He tipped all his whiskey into him, then laughed once all the swallowing was gone. He cracked himself up with that one. After a freaking long time, he stopped.

"Where's your mom?"

"I don't know. I didn't see her."

"She didn't tell you?"

"No sir. I didn't see her."

It was like he was trying to stare through a thick bourbon bottle to see.

"You ever see any black man in Pinkston's apartment?"

"In Number Six?"

"He sells them his used cars."

"Sure, I know about that."

"Bud says he's got a black man living in his apartment."

My mom came up behind him. Neither of us heard her come in.

"Bud says," she said, shaking her head and rolling her eyes. She wasn't near enough to shake Cloyd's hand hello, let alone kiss him hi, and she meant not to be.

"Where the hell you been?" He was too gone drunk to be taken by surprise.

"Shopping," she said like she'd told him a hundred times.

He stared at her too, squinting through a bottle that wasn't there.

"Bud says there's a black man living up in Pinkston's apartment."

She was looking at me, and I was looking back at her. I say she was thinking about the dead owl, and him, and this apartment we were living in. "And so what if there was?"

"What, a black man? What if there was a black living up there?"

"Yes. What if there was?"

"Damn it, Silvia. You know there'd be hell to pay! You know it! What're you saying? You see one up there?"

"No, I didn't say one thing about that." She put her fingers to that hole he put in the wall.

"Bud says he saw someone black in that apartment. That just wouldn't be right." He'd been looking at the hole too, then something jerked his head. "Better not be nothing happening."

"Even if it were true—"

"Goddamnit, I don't want no shit! I didn't rent to one of them! Wouldn't either! Goddamnit!"

"Slow down," she told him. She looked at me again, like I would agree with whatever she was going to say, or about what we talked about that other time, about living here. "I'm sure it's not true."

"Goddamn better not be! I own this goddamn building and it's my property and I do what I want."

"It's Bud," she told him. "Bud's a troublemaker."

"He's a stand-up man. Knew him before I met you."

If she'd been trying to be nice, no more. "Ay, que lindo." And she took off. He took off not more than a second after.

A dim yellow light stained the curtain in #6, probably not from the living room but the bedroom. It didn't seem possible that if any stranger was living there, nobody'd seen him. It didn't even seem like Pink lived there. I'd never seen him go in or out of the apartment either. I was afraid to knock on Nica's door. I was afraid that if I did, and her stepdad was there, that'd be it with us. Mr. Josep's chair was out, empty, by his apartment door. It never was before, it was never there without him. It meant he still wasn't around. I thought it'd be okay to sit on it. I wanted to listen sneaky into Nica's apartment because the window was slid open enough. But Mr. Josep's chair was so weak, I thought it would burst into splinters if I moved any part of my body too much. Every little joint in the chair wobbled and gave in, so it was hard to lean to the side, and to fidget—like moving my ear might bust it. How could that man sit here day after day and not move? Because he couldn't move in it, nobody could move and not break the thing. I thought about sitting as still as him and shut my eyes. I sat as lightweight as I could, and though I couldn't hear much out of the window, not even half as good as from that room I slept in, it was more that I could hear too much everywhere else. Like tires that were too hot and were being cooled by running through cold water on the boulevard. Loud. Too loud. Every defect in tire tread beat on the street like the bass was up too high. A turn left or right cried like it was squeezing the air out of a crow. Radio music broke off like from a metal grinder. People were driving home with groceries, wanting hot dogs or ice cream or bananas or peanut butter or cookies or cereal. People were driving with beer and quaaludes and whites and black beauties, wanting to have sex or watch it or talk about it, and people were snapping at kids in the backseat who were playing and happy, rolling the windows up and down and they were getting yelled at about food they ate or would eat or a toy they could have or lost, and people were driving alone and people were driving with their husbands and wives and they weren't talking to each other, and old people were driving scared, afraid of every turn and stop like they'd never been there before or maybe they'd seen so many things they didn't know what to expect next. People were driving happy, so happy because they were in love and kissing, and people were driving in hungry or out stuffed, leaving La Costera and the pescado or Adriana's and the steak tampiqueña or Elizabeth's Bakery and the tres leches cake. People were driving to the hospital because she was having a baby or he was accidentally shot and people were driving in from New Mexico or Arizona to find a job or driving out to Texas or Sinaloa or Chihuahua to visit the family. They were driving to the phamacy to get medicine, to Tony's El Mejor Que Hay to get huevos con chorizo and cafecito. She just bought a new dress. He just bought underwear and work socks. He was wearing glasses for the first time and felt dizzy and she was too scared to tell her mommy's new boyfriend to stop driving so fast and she was dizzy, dizzy. Maybe it was another black man who pulled into the World Motel right around the corner because he'd driven from Oakland and he was lost and he was tired and he had to stop and he wanted maybe to watch TV and fall asleep and he liked that there were Mexicans parked on the street next to it drinking and laughing and screaming over the norteña music and talking and drinking beer and they were talking, though he didn't know it, about life in Mexico and Califas and tortillas back home and chilangos and he didn't know that they were out there sharpening saw blades—how could he know that?—and then driving off really mad because he didn't believe when that clerk said there were no rooms and when the police stopped him he was still pissed off and he had been drinking, a little, yes, but not so much and he didn't need no ticket, he didn't need no DWI, no, don't be giving me that, officer, please officer, goddamn you.

Out of #7 was *Shut up!* and *You shut it down now!*, each word a sentence in Bud's voice, and then the apartment door opened, and that was when Mary came out and hung her legs on the stairs. She wasn't in her substitute teacher's dress, which she probably had more than one of but seemed like just one to me. The gray sweats made her seem a little fatter—women who wore them proved they thought it about themselves anyways. Right then I didn't think about that much, maybe because her face was in the palms of her hands.

"Are you okay?" I asked.

"I didn't see you there," she said.

"I was here. . . ."

She was sniffling, trying to hold back and make a happy face.

"Are you all right?" I was standing by her now, leaning on the railing.

She surrendered and nodded. "Just a bad day is all." She took a handkerchief to her nose and wiped the tears on her sleeve. She sat, elbows on knees, until she let out a sigh of breath. "Don't get married to a man." That made her laugh. She still didn't look at me. "Sit with me?"

I didn't really want to sit close. Once I was on the rocky step near her, she didn't seem to want to say anything, but I didn't know the polite way to leave or how long I would have to stay.

"Mr. Josep's chair is pretty sad," I said, pointing to it. "I don't know how he could ever sit in it."

"Oh," she said, getting her bearings about what I said. "Josep sits there a lot, doesn't he?"

"Lots."

"I think his wife didn't make it," she said.

"Really?"

"Poor man."

"I wonder where he is," I said.

She shook her head. It was like she was praying. She started to talk with her head down.

"When I was very little, my father would drive us across, to a colonia outside Juárez. I didn't like visiting my grandfather. Everything was filthy, and there was too much sun in the day and not enough electricity at night, and the smells hurt my nose. There were potholes so wide and deep my daddy would say they were shortcut tunnels to China, except they heard it was worse there than Mexico so everybody went around them carefully. Dust was bigger than dust and it was blowing everywhere, and everything, the biggest and the smallest things, seemed like they needed scrubbing. Everybody was so poor. The women walked around in hand-me-down housedresses with aprons and chanclas, and the men, the men all wore those baseball caps with sweat stains that made them have white streaks around the visor and band. I didn't want to feel poor, so I didn't like to visit there much. Our family lived in the newest housing development on the east side of El Paso, near the best mall. I refused to speak Spanish. If someone talked to me in Spanish, I answered in English. I didn't like it when Mommy or Daddy spoke it. It made me mad when they did, and I was ashamed of their accents in English too. I thought once you learned English, you learned how to be a good American citizen." She stopped. She acted like she'd forgotten what she came out of her apartment for. "I almost didn't remember what made me tell you this."

Even though I wasn't looking at her, I really was listening. I knew she wasn't talking about her grandfather or Josep. It was about Bud.

"Thank you for sitting with me."

I nodded. I meant it too. It was okay.

"It's really nice of you."

"Well, I saw you crying."

"My 'uelito, he would sit there and sit there too, calm and patient. He could only whisper at the end, and still you could tell he had been such a strong man. The pictures of him when he was young—he was very handsome, and even more so on horseback. He was a vaquero, a cowboy. He would never come to live with us. That's what my mother wanted. Abuelo wanted to be on his own, and he didn't want anyone taking care of him."

I didn't even hear the street.

"You know, my mom's from El Paso," I told Mary.

She either knew it or didn't care. "I met Bud in San Antonio when he was in the military. I was in college there."

"So both you guys are from Texas," I said. It was like saying they were from the old country. Texas was maybe more far away than Mexico to me. Mexico was lots of people, land everywhere, mountains and rivers and oceans. Texas was all dirt, it was hats, it was way far away, it was mean hardasses.

"Those are days past," she said.

"I didn't think about you being from there before."

"Everybody's from somewhere else," she said.

"I didn't grow up exactly here, but close. Not like from Texas or Arizona or Mexico."

"Some people think we're from one big nameless place, and we're invading."

"Invading?"

"You know," she said, like it was obvious. "Like what Bud thinks."

"Bud?"

She took a second. "My grandfather was such a good man. I don't know what I was thinking back then. I'm disappointed in how I was and what I believed. He worked hard and made his own way the best he could. I wanted to be considered American so much, to fit in, to be smart, to be . . . I don't even remember exactly now."

"My mom talks about stuff like that."

I heard her cat whining by the door.

"Your mom is lucky," Mary said, listening to the cat scratching. "Some women are just born with looks. My husband talks about her all the time."

"He talks about my mom to you?"

"I think men do that. Beautiful women can do no wrong."
Mary was getting up. She made a face that could have been
about her unbending her legs but also about what she was saying. "I probably should go back in. My baby wants to be wherever I am. It was so nice to get to talk to you."

The dark carried an ink in it, moving like a special liquid in the
wind, like a swirl you see in gas or oil in a puddle of water. A
wind that wasn't much, only you knew it was there when it
brushed by. When a car passed, all its noise and smell you could
touch, yellows came that crashed into the darkness. Little flecks
of silver and red light scattered everywhere, the littlest rainbow
worlds in them. Like mirrors or glass, if I could catch one and
see inside it, hold it, stare. Go there. I looked up, and as I passed
the World Motel I swore I saw Cindy across the street coming
out of La Copa de Oro, her blonde hair lit up like a sign, leaning
against the shadow and wall.

"Why are you here at this hour, muchachito? It's late for a young
boy. Aren't you in school by the morning?"

The bowling lane were lights off. Besides Mr. Zúniga, who
was counting money at his register, there was one other man,
with messy hair like he'd been wearing a hat though he wasn't,
and he was holding his glass of beer and looking at it like he was
watching maybe a baseball game in there.

"I'm hungry," I told her. I don't know why I always liked
to say the same thing. "It's that I love your food." I hated
talking in Spanish. I was mostly self-conscious if I said anything,
though, okay, a lot less when it was Mrs. Zúniga, who'd I'd been
talking to more in it. She used it with me without a thought,
whether I spoke in it or English. I wanted to answer with French
words to play around but I didn't think she'd get it.

She didn't ask what I wanted to eat. She made me a plate of enchiladas with hamburger meat and onion and chunks of green chile with white cheese all over it. Beans, rice. It was as good as food got! Home cooking. If only my mom cooked.

"No, she doesn't very often," I told her. "For a while she was. Not so much now." Mrs. Zúniga was wearing a black dress with roses that she wore, it seemed like, all the time. I don't know why I saw that this time.

"What does she do all day if she has no job then?"

"I don't know, you know?"

"She cleans the house?"

"Not my mom."

"Does she sit around and watch TV and get fat?"

"Not my mom, no. She goes out. Does things out."

"Maybe she does have a job in a manner then."

"She used to, but now she's married. We're living here because she married this man."

"That's why," she said. "That's why."

She gave me two more enchiladas while she was talking. They were the last ones in a glass casserole. I could've eaten more.

"And no brothers or sisters?"

"My sister's older. She's gone, already a long time ago."

"So you're alone."

"More or less."

"She doesn't have time for you either."

"It's okay," I said.

"He's a good man, the husband?"

"Who knows. She's married, not me."

"But he treats you well?"

"Oh sure. He works a lot of hours."

"That's good," she assured me.

I shrugged. I wanted to say something real funny in French

so bad. "*Qu'est que c'est,*" is all I could come up with. It came out funny enough to make me smile anyways.

She ignored me. "He loves her," she said.

I'd never thought about that. I shrugged again. "*Qu'est que c'est.*"

"He has to love her if she doesn't have to cook for him."

"I guess you're right. But she more or less makes food for him, a little."

"If he works hard, and she doesn't cook well for him, then he loves her very much."

"Maybe," I said. I didn't think so, or not exactly. I got to thinking of what Mary said. "Everybody loves her."

Mr. Zúniga was telling the man with his beer that he had to go now because they were closing. I'd eaten so fast I was already finished too.

"Thank you," I told her as she took the plate.

"Until tomorrow," she said.

Mr. Zúniga didn't look at me when I asked him how much I owed. He barely shook his head. "Thank you very much," he said.

I don't know why I was blowing around like I was an electric fan. I hopped straight sidewalk borders and jagging cracks, miniature rivers and cliffs, on my way to somewhere I'd never been. The song in my head was jukebox románticos, guitar and horns, a giant voice I didn't have except in my little head, and I was translating into French, laughing.

When I turned the corner toward Los Flores, I went over to the Bel Air to stop and breathe a minute. I sat behind the wheel and sank the key and it roared.

"Hey there, young blood."

I about peed from the surprise. Pink's face leaned sideways in the car window, his skin full-moon white. I wasn't close to thinking he'd be out here. He'd come from behind me. I must have locked my door when I sat down, though I didn't remember, because he was knocking on the glass too once he couldn't open it. He was already going around to the passenger's side before I could get my brains back. I reached over and pulled up the knob for him so he could get in.

"So you're liking this, you're liking it a lot. I knew you would too. Didn't I say?"

I nodded.

"I told you, I told you."

I nodded.

"It's good, it real good, this one. It's yours too, I knew it, knew it first thing." His voice might have been saying what it was, but it also was moving somewhere else. It was the same thing with his eyes. "So what's been up, what's been doing around here?"

"Nothing new," I said.

"Nothing new," he repeated. "Nothing new may be nothing, may be something." Then he looked straight at me. "You ain't heard nothing?"

"Nothing?"

"Any one thing, that be nothing. Nothing from your stepdaddy. About me."

"Oh," I said. "Well, I guess, yeah. They're worrying that you got a black man living in your apartment."

He started laughing. "Oh yeah, there you go, oh yeah." He started laughing more, like he was celebrating. Laughing so hard he was spitting. "There it is."

"So it's true," I said.

"Did I say that?" His voice was hooting. "Did I say that? You did not hear me say that."

"No."

"I did not say that." He was kind of laughing, but it shifted.

"Okay," I said.

"I did not say that, but I could," he said. "Listen, little brother, I'm gonna tell you something. I'm gonna tell you something because I know you and your momma ain't them, and you know it too."

"Okay," I said. I agreed and I didn't, I understood and I didn't.

"These people," he said, "these people are motherfuckers." He said that as simple as throwing a punch, and he said the word like it was in the Bible and he was being religious. "They is motherfuckers and they deserve to be got."

He took a lot of time. He laughed, he shook his head, he laughed. It was as though he were imagining a conversation with that junkyard man. When I turned off the engine, which I'd forgotten was running, he turned to me.

"You know what they say? They say they don't like black folk living here in their nice apartment complexes, like they got some kind of right black folk don't. But they ain't got no right. They are blue-eyed-devil motherfuckers and fuck 'em."

I was scared of him and I admired him.

"It all gonna change, little brother man, it all gonna change, no other way."

"So it's true then?"

He didn't even hear me. "Them dumb motherfuckers." He wasn't listening. I wasn't there, not even close by. But this time he used that word like everybody else who meant to be talking shit and cussing. "You keep that ear to listening," he told me as he got out, disappearing into the darkness at the back of the Bel Air.

"Don't say anything," my mom snapped at Cloyd. She was already coming toward me. They were sitting there like they were watching TV, but I didn't think it was on. Cloyd's eyes were so bloodshot that if he bent over on his favorite chair he'd stain the green rug red.

The magazine I stole the other day was on the maple table. I didn't know why I did that. It was real dumb, I know I know. It was that I was taking out the trash, like always, and I went to grab those grocery and drugstore and all those advertising flyers that pile up there, and the magazine was there too. That was how it happened every other time. In a way, it was like I had to take it again or else I would look guilty—after that Gina'd accused me, I couldn't just stop right then. This time I meant to give it to the twins right away, first thing, and I don't know why I didn't remember. Worse, I'd stuck it there in that bookcase, under the pile of dumb heavy old geographic magazines that were always there, right below the row of books. Right below the boyscout books.

"You better just go to your room," my mom said. She was dressed in something new.

I was relieved to do that. Well, only to not stand there and wait for what was going to happen. Mostly to go see if they knew about the money I stole. All of it was still there like I left it, even the money I kept stashed at the corner. After a couple of seconds, I knew if that'd been found—well, I wouldn't have gotten to go to this room. Still, I was scared and I was embarrassed. I was really embarrassed. Nica's radio was on upstairs but I couldn't concentrate on it or her. I didn't hear nothing in the walls or outside, no spiders, no cats, not even dogs, only the nervous chatter in my own head, its sparklers making crazy like I was driving wild with even faster cars going the other direction on either side of me. My real eyes were shut, but I was seeing too much light, so much I could see only white.

"It wouldn't have been as much if he weren't drunk," my mom said when she woke me.

I was blinking. She didn't even seem to notice that I was asleep when she sat on the bed.

"It's not good that you did that. I told you before."

I couldn't look at her, and not only because I wasn't focused yet.

"You were stealing, m'ijo."

I nodded. "I'm sorry." She smelled of perfume I liked.

"You have to stop it."

"Yeah."

"Yes?"

I nodded.

"Es que, I don't want you to get into trouble. I have con-
fidence in you. I want you to be a man. I want you to learn how
to be a man."

She was playing with her hair, pulling it behind her left ear
over and again. She still had on her jeweled earrings. "He laughed,
you know. He thought it was what any boy would do if he wasn't
afraid to. But he didn't want you to think it wasn't serious. He
said he thought he should punish you. I wouldn't let him and
we argued. I don't trust him, but then it didn't matter after a few
of his drinks."

"You guys got in a fight about it?"

"It's nothing new. Don't worry too much."

Joe said, "Hijole, man."

Mike said, "Ay, dude, I'd hate if *our* mom found that shit."

"Don't even talk like that," Joe said.

"It's what I'm saying!" said Mike.

"Pero, what your mom said, that is toda madre, güey," said
Joe. "She was all right, eh?"

Mike was nodding in agreement.

"Yeah," I said. "I guess." I was ready to think more about
it, but then some dudes, a couple with rags tied around their
foreheads, bounced by slowly, screaming *PUTOS!* laughing like
they were bad to come up with that word and chingones to shout
it out too. They drove a four-door wannabe lowrider—all they

had was suspension and shocks so fucked up that the ride sagged. The wheels were dirty hubcaps on baldies. They did have tinted windows, and the word *relámpago* was painted in glittered silver in all-electricized letters on the back side panel.

"I don't know why mamones like that gotta be like that," said Mike. "They're really embarrassing, really punkass payasos."

"And they're too afraid to stop, to say it to us," Joe said.

Mike shook his head at Joe like he'd lost his mind.

"They had guns, anyways," I started. "Shit, I don't even have my rock!"

"I didn't see a gun," said Joe. "You saw a gun?"

"I saw one for sure," I said, "and another probably."

"Hijole, man," said Joe.

Mike didn't want to talk facts. "I'm sick of having to hear them or hear about those pendejos y sus pendejadas."

After we walked some, Joe said, "Yeah, like because we're Mexicans we have to apologize for being as stupid as they are."

"I can't wait to go to college," said Mike.

Joe nodded. We walked quiet for a while.

"So did your mom throw that magazine out?" Mike asked.

"Look at how my brother is!" Joe said. "He's still angling to get it from you!"

We laughed.

"Your mom," Mike said. "I think she is all right."

"Simón, tu mamá es muy padre," said Joe, smiling. "We'd be in the shithouse."

"Worse!" said Mike. "We'd be outside the dog shithouse, sleeping next to piles and piles of poops."

"I'd die," said Joe. "If we got caught, I'd die."

"N'hombre! We'd get spit-roasted and chopped up como cabrito, dude!" said Mike. "I wouldn't wanna imagine how Dad would cook us."

★ ★ ★

"He wanted me to make a Mexican dinner," she told me. I think the apron she had on was new. It was a red-and-white checkerboard. I think it would be called cute. She wore a white dress under it, sandals, her hair—well, *muy* nice. "Can you believe that? He thought I should cook, and not only cook but cook *Mexican* food." She definitely wasn't doing that. She was making spaghetti, and she dropped a couple of jalapeños into the sauce. "There. Now it's Mexican."

"You're cooking, that counts for something."

"Things are kind of upset around here," she said. "I want to warn you."

"What?"

"You haven't seen someone going in or out of Mr. Pinkston's, have you?" she said.

"I haven't, like I said before."

"Bud keeps on saying that some man who is black is living there. He says that's how they're doing it now, by getting someone else to rent an apartment with a roommate nobody sees until later. He thinks that's what's going on."

"Can I tell you something? What I heard?" I wanted to tell her about me sitting with Mary, how Bud talked about her. I would tell her without telling her.

"Is he bothering you?" she asked. She heard me asking something else. "You're not going to tell me he's bothering you too, are you?"

"No," I said.

"Because Bud used to be a cop," she said. "I don't know if he quit or they got rid of him. Can you imagine him a cop?"

Maybe me telling her anything else about Bud talking about her wasn't necessary.

"Have you seen anyone else in that apartment? A white person?"

"Not me. I never even seen Pink in that apartment."

"They're talking about him too."

"Pink's okay. I like him. I think he's cool."

"He's an albino," she said. "I don't think Cloyd knew it before."

"Albino?" I didn't know it either.

"It's an idea I heard. Nely told me. It's right too, explains why he's like he is. He's not as obvious as most albinos. Nely says some don't look like albinos exactly."

"Nely?"

"Yeah," she said, not really wanting to get into that with me. "He's white but he's really black. It makes sense, it explains it. Cuando le dije a Cloyd, ay, he died de un infarto! I thought his heart would attack him out of his mouth, he was yelling so much."

We both liked so much the idea of Pink messing with Cloyd and Bud, him maybe having a black roommate, there was no room to say anything about Nely or not Nely. I was almost finished eating.

"M'ijo," she said. She sat down next to me, but she didn't look at me. "It's not so bad here for you. . . ." She stopped there too long. "I have to think," she said. "Did you get enough to eat?"

"Oh yeah," I said.

I was sweeping the lower walkways and Cindy had to lean hard over the upstairs railing. "Hey," she said. As always, she was practically naked, at least it seemed like you could see everything even if it was covered.

"Hey," I said.

"Hey," she said again, stretching the sound out, playful.

"Did I see you the other night?"

"What're you talking about?"

This time I didn't say nothing.

"Sonny," she said, all sweet, my name yellow and warm.

"No," I said. I didn't see what she did or where or how because I kept my head down and swept. I wanted to be good. I swept everything. Then I cleaned the laundry room. I'd dragged over a trash can from the back and while I was thinking of it, I went over to the mailboxes to grab the flyers that had to be thrown away too. That's when Bud's pickup wide-loaded the driveway, almost pinning me against the building.

"Looking for the titty magazines again, Sonny boy?"

I almost said I didn't do that shit, out of habit.

He'd rolled down the passenger's side window from a switch on the driver's side.

"Your age, it's the only action you get!"

I still didn't say nothing. Made me mad that Cloyd told him.

"Your mom getting things ready in there?"

I didn't say nothing to him still. I swore to myself I was gonna start pumping iron.

"You gone deaf? They say that's what happens after you keep whacking it so much! You keep at it, hear say you go blind too!" He was laughing and laughing like he was watching himself on TV.

I wanted to steal something from him. Put nails under his tires.

"You better watch yourself, kid," he said. "I'm telling you." He drove in.

Maybe it was the word *kid* that did it.

Nica came out of her apartment with Angel in her arms, rocking him fidgety and moving her feet—like being out of the apartment was dangerous. "Tonight," she said. She pointed to #7, Bud and Mary's apartment. She was grinning fifty smiles but showing it to me and me only. She made it seem like she was only talking to the baby, and then she turned back around. She had to answer her dad inside the apartment.

I wanted to run laps around The Flowers instead of spin in

the tight circles my brain took. I rushed over to the Bel Air and went in. I sat and waited. I saw anybody, I ducked and hid. Cloyd's butt-heavy truck, those huge toolboxes hanging on either side, squawked and squealed onto the driveway. Neighborhood people were walking from parking their cars way down the street. It was the time of night when some headlights were on, some still off. Waiting waiting. Gina's car, her perfect husband Ben's sporty car, Mary's plain car. People from the whole neighborhood coming home. I sat and sat and sat, waiting. I was happy! I dreamed in my Bel Air. I dreamed of what it would be with Nica and me cruising the boulevards, pulling in this place, parking there—a desert, the cactus and sand, or mountains, or a river, a lake, and there'd be a real sky, a real moon, stars falling all over us, and trees, and dew. The windows down would let in air, or be up to keep warmer—all about not being here, all about being with Nica, Nica being with me, everything I ever wanted to see all around us. Stopping. Sitting someplace pretty. Kissing. I only wanted to kiss her, I swear it's all I really imagined. No, I wanted her to kiss me. We could go to movies. I'd never been to those Spanish ones. She wouldn't want to either. She liked the same radio music I did. We could drive down to the beach. Probably she'd never seen the beach. She could watch and listen to the waves. I would kiss her lips! My fingers would touch her cheek, hold her chin. I'd kiss her on her neck, under her ear, and feel her goose bumps rise. She would be against me, warm. Her body. I imagined it, sure. I knew I would love her body, but I only saw her lips while I was holding her.

"Young blood," Pink said. His face was at the passenger's window this time.

"You did that again," I told him, shaking my head.

"What I do again?"

"Surprised me when you came up. I didn't see you."

"You better be watching yourself better then," he laughed. "You better always know what coming up behind you. At all times you better be knowing what coming up on you, my little brother." He got in and sat with me. "So everything cool?" His eyes were watching the front door and windows of Cloyd's apartment too. "Like they having a party. Good. That is nice, that is good. Good for them."

I looked at him.

"Give me some time," he said.

"Time?"

"Gotta be leaving here," he said. "I am gone."

"Really?"

"You don't say to nobody, you didn't hear that."

"Okay, sure."

"Don't want Longpre knowing till he knows."

"So, the car?" He knew what I meant.

"Little brother, I told you. I told you, this is your ride."

It didn't make any sense, I really didn't understand, but I didn't want to say no. If he really was out of here, if he was really leaving it to me, I'd even go ahead and learn to drive it. Not play in it like I did now, not pretend. "I guess you haven't had a lot of cars around lately, now that I think of it."

"There you are, you *have* been paying attention. This here is the last and only. But little brother, I am around. I come around time to time. You gonna see. I come around. You gonna be seeing me again, and we got a deal."

"Hard not to see you," I joked.

"You only just said you missed seeing me, didn't you say that?"

I laughed.

"So it ain't that easy unless you be watching careful. You don't be watching careful, you do not see."

I shook my head.

"Buncha shit I'm talking, ain't it? Ha! Buncha bull and shit, ain't it?" He laughed and laughed. "I better get on up. Hey-uh, they still talking?"

"About a black man living in your apartment?"

"That, yeah."

"No more than I said."

"Well then little brother man, I better get up on it."

The door of #7 opened fast. Nica had a finger over her lips. "He just went to sleep." Her eyes would barely to look at mine, but she was smiling. "He'd never seen a cat."

"You mean the baby," I said.

"A cat!" She said that loud for her. "The cat is the baby! Can you believe? The lady wanted me to take care of her little cat!"

"I told you already they didn't have a baby."

"No, you didn't tell me."

"I did too, I swear."

"Then I didn't hear you, or I didn't understand."

"It's that you didn't believe me."

"How can she call a cat her baby? He won't find out? Maybe he won't understand either. Who would call a cat a baby?"

"This world is a crazy, I don't understand nothing."

"I thought it was a baby, and that's why Margarito said he would permit it."

The cat was hiding under the couch, balled up, scared. I got down on my knees. "Come here, baby baby baby."

Nica laughed the laugh of ten hours of dopey Mexican TV skits, without me talking any French.

Angel was asleep on a small bed in the bedroom across from the master bedroom. She let me follow her to see, and then we both wanted to go into the big bedroom. I couldn't help but want to, neither of us could. I wanted to see the bed and clack the metal drawer knobs on their chest of drawers and untangle bobby pins and clips and earrings and scratch myself with the hairbrushes and open the face cream jars and smell and look inside jewelry boxes and a big wooden chest at the foot of the bed. I saw some

cash. But I already had so much now. I didn't want to scare Nica,
if she was watching, which she wasn't, because it was more like
she'd fallen asleep with her eyes open, so she wasn't sure whether
she was looking at the ceiling or through it. On their floor there
was nothing but apartment carpet. Not one corner of a shirt under
the bed, not a flip-flop, not a sock, no dirty chones balled up. I
say Mary cleaned it all up for Nica's babysitting. On the bedroom walls were a really not too great painting of a desert and
another of a snowy mountain with a gold cross at the top, Cristo
Rey, and one of baby Jesus with the Virgin Mother, a little like
Guadalupe from Mexico but not really. None of them were re-
alistic exactly, and though they didn't seem very good to me,
they did seem like they weren't from a store. I say they were
hers, that she painted them herself. That she was a substitute art
teacher. They had a couple photos of other family people, probably their moms and dads, that yellow-gray kind, and the others,
modern in color, were probably brothers and sisters. But there
were no pictures of the two of them.

"That's kind of fucked up, I think," I said in English,
until I went back to Spanish. "You don't think? That it's not
common?"

"What're you're talking about?"

"That they have no photos of themselves, like, together.
Not even at their wedding."

"Probably," she said, unsure, uncritical. Then she was on
the bed, on her back, watching the ceiling. "Maybe they don't
love each other. Maybe they don't love."

I didn't want her to think I was going to try anything if I
got on the bed where she was so I didn't get on it at first. Then
I sensed that she trusted me so it didn't cross her mind, and I fell
on my back and stared at the same ceiling she stared at. I swear
her happiness, which I couldn't see, was changing the air like
we were getting high. We could feel the earth under us and hear

the whish of it spinning us, even while our eyes saw only the ceiling and that cottage cheese sprayed on it. We both stared up like it was 3 A.M. and we were outside and the nightsky was far and close and it was real and there weren't any words for any of it. At first we were only squirmy, but that kind of changed, like months and months passed in minutes of not talking.

"Sometimes I forget," she said.

"What?"

"Everything. That people don't live like I live."

This was *exactly* what would happen to me when I used to sneak into other people's houses! I'd start thinking exactly like this. But never once had I imagined anyone else being next to me thinking it. I had never imagined Nica before, never imagined a Nica, never imagined a voice like hers, never imagined her so close to me.

"You won't have to live over there forever," I said. It came out of me like someone else talking. Because I didn't know what I was telling her. What did I know about her or her life, about mine, about life? Not shit. Not nothing, about anything. I guess it just seemed like the right thing to say, and besides being probably true, it had to be. It especially couldn't not be true, not now that we were here. We were changing everything because we were together, because me and her were on our backs on the big old soft bed and were staring up.

"What if I were named Carmen?" she asked.

"I thought you liked Cathy."

"I like that name too. You don't like the name Carmen?"

"I guess. I like yours already."

"It'd be so beautiful."

"Why are you thinking of this?"

"Oh, that little old man next door. He told that story about Russia. When I was a little girl I always wished I were from Spain. He made me think of that, of living in Spain. Then, I would have pretty white skin and straight black hair, and I'd listen to music and dance beautifully."

"I don't know," I said. "I think any of that's Mexican too. You have beautiful black hair. I like your skin. Your skin is beautiful, your color better than theirs. Those people sit in the sun on a beach forever to get their skin to look like yours."

"Think of how perfect it must be in Spain. I saw photos once. Of Sevilla and Córdova. Have you ever seen photos from there?"

"No, I only saw a Zorro movie. That's Spain, right?"

"You have to see the photos. Then you would want to go. I think the whole city is painted white. It's not like Mexico. I'm from Mexico."

"I don't know," I said. I didn't know how to say what I wanted to say. I didn't like what she was saying but not what it was. "I like your name," I said. "I think Nica's a beautiful name." I wanted to say so better, but saying I loved her name—well, I wasn't really talking about her name.

"It's not really Nica, you know."

"Veronica," I said.

"No," she said. "It's not Veronica."

"It's not?"

"My name's Guadalupe."

"Guadalupe?"

"Like my mother's, María, it is very common. I hate the name María. I also hate the name Guadalupe."

"I like it, I like that name. It's nice. I knew a Lupe once. I like the name."

"Wouldn't you want to go to Spain?"

"I never thought about it. I don't know, Spain seems so . . . I don't know. Spanish. I don't speak Spanish the right way. I almost can't. I almost can't talk to you."

"Where would you go?"

It was almost like I was set up to say it. "France. Remember, *je parle français*. I'm learning French, remember?"

"France?"

"*Oui, oui.*"

She giggled. It is what I loved about this learning French. It made me get a smile, it made everyone make a smile, and it always worked. Now it made my Nica giggle.

"*J'aime le pizza,*" I said. "*Qu'est-ce que aimez-vous? No avec le faim?*"

"Oh Sonny," she said. Smiling!

I was going to kiss her. Our eyes were still locked on the nothing ceiling that was our own world. I moved onto my side. She didn't.

"Do you think you'll go?" she asked.

"I don't know. I never really thought of it."

"You said you wanted to."

"Yeah, but I don't know, I haven't really thought about it, not seriously." It was only because of Cloyd and my mom. It was a game I was playing, not a want. I only pretended. "And you? Do you think you're going to Spain?"

That was the wrong thing to say. It changed the mood like someone walked in on us, like Angel cried. I wanted to take it back. "You're right. I ought to go to France," I told her, trying to go back to the subject of me. I wanted to say, *with you.* I wanted to say we could go together. It was dumb, but it was what I thought, what I wished. "You're right. I could go. If I saved and everything, maybe I could go."

"Yes," she said. "You ought to."

"Paris, France," I said. "Notre Dame."

"Sonny," she said.

"What?" I was watching her again.

She took a long time. "Nothing."

"What?" I said. Then, when she didn't answer "I want you to go with me. To France."

"Ay, Sonny. And what would we do?"

I was thinking, fast too, I wanted to answer fast. "Talk French. *Bonjour, Nica! Como t'allez-vous, ma Nica?* But that's not right. Because we talk in the *tu*."

"Monica?"

"*Ma Nica.*" I think she liked that name too. "I meant my Nica. I don't talk French that good either, you know."

We both were laughing. "*Je t'aime,*" I said.

"And that?"

"I love pizza!"

"Sonny," she said. She was watching the ceiling, her long hair under her like it was a shawl. Her dress covered her like a sheet I could see through. It could have been new, an old-is-new style, but it was probably from a used store, washed and pressed and beautiful on her. It could've been a hippie throwaway. Wanting to touch her, I touched the dress at the sleeve. The material was like dried-up crumpled paper, dyed swimming-pool blue. I was thinking of kissing her. I was going to.

She turned her head to me. Every other part of her body was relaxed. "I get scared," she said.

"Of what?"

"I don't know"—sounding more like she did know.

"Tell me. You can tell me what."

She didn't say. I was touching her arm, her skin, with my finger. The light of it came at me like a silver wind.

"You can't," she said.

"Can't what?" It was warmer than just blood moving through her, warm not like what people call a feeling, but warm like a liquid, like a juice inside, heating. This little touch of skin, it was too much for both of us.

"You know."

"What?"

"We can't kiss."

I didn't say anything for a long time. I wanted to say I'd take her to Spain. And couldn't we go to France together? I really thought I meant it too. I had that money, you know? She'd turned on her side, she put her hands under her head. My hand came off her.

"What if I want to?" I asked.

"No," she said. She said it nice, sad, not mean or angry.

"You don't want me to?"

"Please, we can't."

"Whatever you want."

"Híjola, man, I wouldn't know what to do," said Mike. It was that I just told them both about Nica. I told them how I wished I could do something, how I didn't see why she had to live like that.

"I would, vato," said Joe. "I know I would."

Mike shook his head so hard at his brother that his glasses almost dropped off. "Cállate, güey."

"What?"

"Que shut up, cabrón." He said the words loud but like he was saying them soft.

"Why're you saying that?"

"Por cause," Mike said, dragging out the *cause* part. His head and eyes bobbled toward me. Even though I was not looking at either of them, I could still see from the corners. I was starting to get sick to my stomach. I was feeling all messed up.

"What?" said Joe. He didn't have a clue.

I caught something in the corner of my eye and stopped walking. It was an ugly brown car parked in a lot with more than a few nothing, shitty cars in an apartment complex that didn't have a name, only the not very fancy number 2131. It was that perv's car in the oil-stained lot, near a set of dumped apartment doors and windows and a couch without cushions turned on its side. "Wait," I said. "Stop for a second."

"What?" one of the twins said.

"It's that sickie's car," I said. "See? See where the windshield's cracked?" It was a big spiderweb, a wide and pretty one.

"Híjola," said one of them. "He's right."

"Hijo de la chingada madre," said the other. "He has raisins, he's very right."

"Whadaya wanna do?" That was Mike talking to me. "Whadaya think we should do?" That was Mike talking to Joe.

"Nothing yet," I said. "Except give me a fucking second." I wasn't moving.

"Pues, I think we should take off," said Joe.

"Me too," Mike said. "I don't think it's a good idea to stay here."

"Véngase, Sonny," said Joe. "Come on."

"Yeah, Joe," said Mike. "What más hay to do?"

I wasn't ready to leave yet.

"I think we should take off," said Joe.

"Me too," said Mike.

"Let's take off," said Joe. "Come on, Mike, we're going."

"Bueno, simón, come with us, Sonny, vámonos, let's go."

They took off walking, fast, toward the railroad tracks, which were up another block or so. I saw them look back, even though I wasn't really looking at them.

"What's the matter, muchachito?" Mrs. Zúniga asked.

"It's only that I'm not hungry," I said.

"How can you say you're not hungry? You're always hungry."

"It's only that I'm not."

"I'm going to bring you a hamburger and chocolate shake."

"It's not necessary, seriously. I only want to bowl."

I found the ball I used in my spot on the wooden rack. Not
that I had to look hard. I was the only one who ever used it. As
far as I could tell, I was the only one who ever bowled any of
the lanes ever.

I needed to get some concentration. I rolled a few that were
off, as off as I felt. I concentrated, stretched my body to the ceiling. Held the ball and focused until the pins got closer to me. I
made a strike, but it still felt lucky. Then I got another strike,
and this time it didn't feel lucky, more that my body had it all
from the moment I released. "*Voilá!*" I said. Suddenly that French
made a smile take over my face.

"Here you are," Mrs. Zúniga said, leaving me a hamburger
on a plate and a thick chocolate shake in a big fountain glass. She'd
never brought food to the lanes before. I always ate at the bar.
"You feel better."

I wasn't sure if she meant I did, because she heard me say
the *Voilà,* or if she meant she hoped I would after I ate. "Mrs.
Zúniga," I said, "do you have any orange juice?" What I was
really wanting to say was *orangeade,* just because that French word
made me smile too, even if it wasn't even orange juice. I could
have already looked up the right word for orange juice, except I
liked that other word too much.

"No, muchachito, I'm sorry. You don't like the chocolate
shake?"

"Sure, yes," I said. I went over to the food. "Of course!
Thank you so much."

"You eat," she said as happy as if she were talking French
too.

As I came up the driveway of The Flowers, a black dude was
stepping off the last stair. He was wearing a wrinkled black suit
too big on him and a black tie and black shoes that weren't shined.
Like he was a businessman but not in any business.

"Good evening," he said to me.

"How's it going?" I said.

I looked through the window into the Cloyd's office. He wasn't there yet. My mom hung up the phone as I came through the back door. I was going to tell her who I just now saw coming down the stairs.

"I can't talk to you right now, m'ijo," she said. She was up inside her own world. She rushed into the other bedroom, where I heard her go to the phone in there, and then she shut that bedroom door.

I took off to sweep, to get out of that apartment I stayed in. I started at the upstairs middle, #4. I think I was sweeping especially fast because I was keeping up with my brain and my body was trying to keep pace. I wished I could talk to Nica, which I couldn't, or I wished I could at least see her inside the apartment. I got close enough to maybe hear her, but the curtains in #4 were closed. The TV was on to a screaming commercial, but I still heard her stepdad talking on the other side of it, probably in the bedroom not hers, though I couldn't make out what he said over that TV. And then I wondered why I never heard her mom's voice. Never. Then I forgot all that because I was near Cindy's curtains, which were drawn closed too but seemed to be more forgotten than pulled together. The windows were slid half open, but she wasn't inside. She was always there but she wasn't there. I pushed the broom past Nica's again, and it was like it was always the same screamy commercial and the same screamy voices. When I got to Mr. Josep's, the curtain was open some. I couldn't see nothing through the dark inside but his chair was the way it always was near the door, like the feet in the spots he always fit them in. So then I got the broom to #6, Pink's, and the curtains were yanked closed like to the last tug of the cord. I was about to turn the corner at #7, where lights were on inside Bud and Mary's and the cat named Baby, and go down the stairs, when Mr. Josep came out his door and waved me over, and he had another chair.

"Mr. Josep, I can't right now." I couldn't either. I couldn't sit on any chair anywhere.

He didn't say anything about that. "You working hard," he said.

I couldn't say nothing. My body was like popping all over the place, up and down and sideways. I couldn't hold still.

"You good boy. You working hard."

"Not so good," I said. I couldn't hold myself still. I kept hearing the TV shaking the walls at Nica's and his voice from a bedroom, and the strain almost hurt my ears.

"I'm sorry," I said, "about your wife."

I think he wanted to talk. I think he was looking to get words to say something. He didn't think he was being slow about it, but I wouldn't tell him he was and I couldn't wait.

I hung the push broom on the shed hooks and finally it turned into dark enough.

"Hi there."

It was Gina. She could've been there for who knows how long and I wouldn't have seen her until she said something because she was so into wearing black. She was standing to the side as strange looking as always, her skirt like a plastic sign, her hair plastic too, the same too-shiny blunt cut like you'd see on a cover of a women's magazine but never in front of you to talk. Maybe it was a French style? That almost made me smile and feel better, because I could look up a new word in French, and it almost made me smile straight at this Gina too, but then my brain was banging against my eyes and, French or no French, I didn't want to say nothing about anything.

"Can I talk to you a minute?"

"*Non,*" I said, and that made me come close to laughing out loud. I should've said something nicer to her. Or maybe less nice, or something else. I just didn't.

I was already turning the corner on the boulevard. I swore I heard the Cloyd's truck squeaking behind me but I wouldn't no way, güey, look back. I was making time so quick I was already near to Alley Cats where Mr. Zúniga was, outside his door with a few other people, really a bunch of people, not only the viejitos who'd be drinking inside his bar otherwise. It was that across the street over at Three B's—Best Burritos & Burgers—where black-and-whites were pulled over with lights kicked on, bouncing off everything and everybody, and the police were facing a black dude going fucking nuts, hopping up and down and so at the top of his lungs you could not understand what the fuck, and a couple police had their clubs out and a couple had their hands ready above their guns. There was this vato sitting on the side against a wall, not saying or doing nothing, with no shirt on and his blue tattoos on his arms and shoulders there to see, knees up, hands behind his back, probably cuffed. Another black-and-white sirened up and two more police got out and traffic was slowing and stopping and more people were on the sidewalks and one of the police started hollering at the people and cars to move, move on, move, keep moving, almost pushing a man who was too close, and he went into the street, waving finger and hand and arm, screaming to get on home, go, go on, go on home, go on, go, and some of the people across the boulevard obeyed, like Mr. Zúniga, who stepped halfway back inside, but not everybody, and more people were stopping and a couple of black dudes who got out of a lowered red Bonneville came up and weren't mov-ing except getting closer, watching more. The wild black man was still shouting puros locos as another police car pulled up and then the police jumped on the dude and slammed him to the ground and were all knees on him and cuffing him and a few more black people around started screaming mothers and fuck and fingering desmadres at them, but especially those black dudes from the lowered red Bonneville, they started saying shit real loud, and the police yelled sticks up while backing themselves away and as soon as the loco was slammed into one of theirs, they were off like a switch, and then the whole world flattened out again, like there was nothing and never been something.

Once I got to that 2131 building, I was sick to my stomach. Could be I was also scared I'd get caught. This was not gonna be like other things I did. It was can't-see dark, and though blocks of icy light passed through the window squares of each apartment in the building, they wouldn't shine on nobody outside or on me either. Still, I was thinking how maybe I should've come here later, when it was more dark, like if I got up in the middle of the night, or past that even. I wasn't sure what I was gonna do. I'd picked up my rock on the way, that good one I carried for something like this—yeah, it must be it was there to use it, a plan to throw my rock.

The sickie's car was still right where it was or where it stayed at night. At first I only stood near, burying myself into no light of the street, breathing. I leaned along a wall tight. Cars rolled up and down the road, headlights searching the asphalt ahead of them, and they didn't shine nothing on me. I put my rock in one hand, then the other, and while I was there I kept breathing. A plane passed overhead, way up. I swear I could hear its red lights blinking, I was so not breathing with my body. I could tell what channel the TV was on from a house behind me, on the other side of where I was. I caught a black cat—another baby—staring at me, its zombie eyes as bright and faraway as stars. It took off fast across the street when I tapped a foot like I might jump at it, and a dog attacked a fence as it went by. Cars from another boulevard up there were like hearing a TV river pushing its way through a TV forest. A top forty was playing in a garage, one still far enough away that its light was half as small as one of the apartment's windows.

I back-and-forthed the rock in my hands until there was nothing else but that slap—in one hand, then the other—finally the only sound. When I stopped, it got too quiet and slow, like you know how the bad is coming in a dream. Or real good: I saw myself sitting on the fuzzy gold couch with Nica, her hair warming me, her hair exciting me like it was more than hair.

Hey but what if I didn't want to throw my rock? I didn't know what to make of what was going on in me. It was like, why should I leave the rock *here?* I didn't want to leave my rock. Like that. Even though it was supposed to be thrown, what a rock is, if I got to throw it while sickie man was rolling, after it bounced off his car, I could go get it back like last time. And better in the daylight, right in his face. I wanted it, I liked it. It was my rock. I never thought I was gonna have to waste it before, and if I threw it here, it was gone to me. I dunno, man. It's that I walked with it every day. I carried it when I was with the twins now. But how could I say I came here and didn't fuck his shit up because I like loved my rock, like say I were to even explain to the twins?

I was messing it up and so I started running out of there. I ran the street alongside the railroad tracks and then I saw a car, and I don't know why I felt it was coming for me, slowing down up there and pulling over like it was waiting for me to get next to it. I stopped. It wasn't much of a car, not low or high, but I couldn't make it out as a Chevy or Ford or Olds except it had bubbly tinted windows. My mind caught a smell on it, you know, so I turned and I got running fast and then I heard the dudes coming behind me who were not gonna catch me even with the rock in my hand. And then I felt a sizzle of air brush my ear and saw a pipe sparking in front me against the sidewalk. I couldn't look back to see who it was—fucking culeros who could be white dudes, black dudes, or brown dudes. I was running full out and I crossed back over the tracks, and when that ride came around again I crossed the tracks again and ran straight toward an alley where I thought they wouldn't see me turn and I was halfway down it when that car peeled in. I hopped a backyard fence and landed on some hedges and dogs started barking, ones next door. Then I busted through a wooden gate—took it out, dropped it flat—to get to the front and the street, and once I was around the corner and I kept on, I knew that car lost me.

I stopped at the Bel Air because it was by itself, no car in front or behind it. Having all those empty spaces made it look like something bad had happened, and I was standing near it seeing if there was damage on the grille or tail or hood, something I couldn't see. Maybe it was sirens in the air too—they were everywhere, and even though my head was on everything else, my ears could hear like everyone else's.

"How it been riding?"

Like every time, Pink was in front of me out of nowheres, scaring the pee out of me.

"Man, you know, I don't ever see you!" I took a couple of seconds. He was not hearing what I said. "I can't drive it yet," I answered.

"What's that? You ain't riding in it?"

"I don't have a license. Like I told you."

"Oh yeah, a license, a driving license." He was nodding and shaking his head both, but looking at the big picture window of #1, which was lit up like a movie screen. Inside the Cloyd and my mom and Bud and Mary were standing around the TV set. "You told me about that license before, didn't you, little brother. You told me before."

I didn't know what I'd been thinking. A license? I just needed to drive it. I didn't need a license to drive it.

"So, they acting up a little in there, wouldn't you say?" he asked. He turned to smiling big enough it was almost laughing but also like he was gonna call them motherfuckers again. "It got their attention, ain't that the way it is, little brother?"

The way I saw them in the window was they were standing still. Only Bud was pacing, and he was doing it twice the size of everyone else.

"I don't know what they're doing," I said.

"They watching the TV. They watching what going on."

"What's going on?"

"You ain't been hearing?"

"Kind of. I saw your friend coming down the stairs."

He looked at me like that wasn't what he was asking about. "That so?"

I nodded.

"There you are, there it is." He laughed how he laughed.

He took a second like that wasn't it, then started nodding. "All right, all right," he said. "I'm getting my automobiles here, almost all turned on out."

"So that's why the spaces," I said.

"Oh yeah, moving 'em on."

"Then"—I nodded at the Bel Air—"you want the keys back?"

"Little brother," he said, his head disapproving. "Little brother, little brother." He put his hand on my shoulder. It was the closest he'd ever been to me. I saw how big it was. Huge! I don't think I realized what a big mother he was. And I saw that jagged scar too good. It was a nasty one, real serious ugly. "Now what'd I tell you? I told you how we got a deal here. You ain't in on the deal, that be a difference."

"To watch?"

"Eyes and ears, that is all you got to do, yes, yes. You can do that now. I know you can do that now."

The TV was booming and Bud too.

"I am so sick of these fuckin' jigs!"

"Bud," Mary said, his name dragging out as she shook her head, sad.

"Don't fuckin' tell me shit," he snarled at her.

That one even tripped up Cloyd's attention for one second. My mom was already making her way to me before he said that. Cloyd went right back to the TV screen on second two, barely swirling the ice cube in his whiskey glass, the whites of his eyes red as apples, the sirens inside the TV set way louder than the newsman's voice. Mary was taking her husband's advice.

"I don't know where we live no more," said Bud. "They think this is African jungle."

Mary rolled her eyes and sat down on Cloyd's favorite chair.

"No pase por ay," my mom said. There was so much noise, it was as if she were whispering. "Están pisteando, y ella, she can't get him to go home."

"What's going on?"

"Dice que, que there's un negrito living next to him—"

I interrupted her. "I mean on the news right now."

"The riot? Es que, there's a riot. You didn't know?"

"Take your baton and hit that nigger, then fuckin' kick 'em after that!" Bud hollered.

"You didn't hear?" she asked.

I shook my head.

"Where have you been?"

"Out."

"Why don't they just fuckin' shoot at 'em?" he shouted. "Aren't they throwing bottles? Isn't it them? That deserves shooting at!"

"Please," she said, making her breath closer to my ear. "Mary's trying. If she can't, me dijo que she's going to leave him. I don't want to be around him either. I feel bad for her, m'ijo."

Je lance la pierre. I loved this French so much! I was suddenly almost crazy happy. *Pierre!* Could it get any better? I'm thinking of poodles because the only Pierre I heard of was a tiny white poodle. I liked the *lance* verb too. I picked it out of a couple of possible verbs and it seemed right. It got me to see things and smile seeing them, me and a lance and my *pierre*. A dark brown horse with a black mane prancing on a dark dirt path, green grass and green trees and green green like I imagined France, and I had on a hat that I didn't even know how to describe. Like it wasn't even me no more. I kept saying it as good as I could. *La pierre. Je lance la pierre. Ma pierre, je lance!* It could have been that I repeated this so much that my smile got pushed away by a wild laugh, but I was also feeling como más confident and serious, as I tried to pronounce the words in a real dramatic French accent. It was working enough that I wasn't hearing them in there with the riot news no more either. When I stopped saying it over and over it might have been because of watching a twirling spider near the open window, and then I was hearing the old couple next door who talked whatever language to each other and their English to their perrito or gatito and then I started hearing blue-gray air in the room, swirling around, floating up or down like dust except it was sound, like when you hear a wall clock clicking somewhere, just barely, until it's bigger and bigger. The mixed air in the room got more important, blue here, gray there, and it was filling up everything until it went down into my ears soft, a music, and it became a pretty new color, not one, not the other, and a calm ocean wind.

When I was waking up it was maybe early, early morning or late night, and it was Nica's stepdad saying to her it was a cat, it was a cat, it was a cat, how could it be a cat? Did you know it was a cat? Why didn't you tell me? He was saying she was stupid and it was stupid to stay with a cat. Why would you stay with a cat? Why would that lady want you to stay with a cat? Why would she pay you to stay with a cat? What did she say to you? Why did she ask? Don't lie. Are you lying? Why are you lying? You have to stop lying. You are lying. What were you doing over there? What did that lady want you to be there for? Did you talk to her? What did you say to her? What did she say to you? What did you do when you were there? What did you really do? Don't lie. Don't lie. Don't lie to me. I don't like it, I don't like this, I don't like this, I won't have this.

It was so early morning I could taste tears like they were in a foggy morning. Maybe because she told me about Veracruz, when she was living near a beach, in a light blue house with palmas secas and floppy green banana leaves shading it, and that green, and that blue, and some red in maybe parakeets on its roof and a striped lizard looping its tail from above like a monkey and wind blowing inside and over her and we were on the soft fuzzy gold couch and she was crying. It was so early in the morning I could see closer through the tears, like in a spyglass. I saw a squealing, white-tooth little girl with a cotton Sunday dress pulled up to her chones and she was at a river with the primos and their feet and legs were slapping the mud at the river and splashing it into their eyes and mouths.

Joe said, "You probably saw that shit go down, dude, you probably saw!"

"He probably started it, ese," said Mike.

That made Joe laugh and nod.

"Verdad qué no?" Mike said. "Pues, and then he wants to go start up a riot con los sickies también!"

"Ay, how would it go in a riot con sickies? A caravan of dirty cars cruising the boulevards, those vatos all hunched down below the steering wheel, alone in their four-doors, all hyped up, whispering out the windows while they circle the elementary schools, that classical music station low on their radio."

They cracked up.

"How do they say it started?" I asked about the riot in the news.

"After some cops pulled this loco black man over and he got whipped on, it went out onto all the streets."

"So you think it was at the same time as what I saw?"

"Simón, vato," said Joe.

"He don't know," said Mike. "He don't know any more than you."

"It sounds like it," I said. "Like almost the same time too."

"My dad said nada más que some todo pedo mayate got pulled over y then, salieron los diablos, the whole city went crazy."

"Maybe it was right after," said Mike. "You know? But it wasn't just one place, one thing."

"Pues, entonces, no es the same!"

"The police drove away fast where I was," I said.

"Ay está," Mike said.

"Bueno," said Joe, "the one that supposedly started it, he was throwing chingazos with the cops, and a black lady in rollers got arrested too because she jumped on his back. Once it got dark, people started throwing chunks of cement and bricks and anything at cars that came by."

"It was dark when I saw what I saw."

"They're predicting it's gonna get worse," said Joe.

"Sabes que, we should do shit like that," said Mike. "I mean our peoples. Show them."

"And show them how short we are? N'hombre! Los blacks ain't shorty indios como nuestra gente!"

"We could throw balled-up tortillas at them, lots of them, because our hands can squeeze harder than anybody's and do that shit."

"Orale vato, come on, pero, porqué no las de harina, heavy con un buen chingo de manteca."

Throwing flour tortillas heavy with lard, that was funny to all of us.

"Pero even that'd be nada más like throwing spit wads, dude, and they'd just stick to them like they do on the school clocks."

"Little piedritas entonces. Throw handfuls. Maybe we wouldn't be no cannons, pero we'd be little shotguns, and then 'cause we're chiquitos we could split de volada and hide easy."

"Hey so what'd you do to the sickie's car with that chingona roca?" Mike asked.

Je lance la pierre. Right then I was going left to right hand, right to left with it. I started doing it faster. "Nothing."

"You went over there last night and nothing?"

"Yeah, dude," said Joe. "I swore you were gonna get us busted before, and then you went back for more, vato!"

"You said you went over there," Mike said.

"You can trust us, for real you can, ya sabes," Joe said.

Mike nodded to agree. They both waited for me. I didn't want to say, but the longer I took, the more they thought I did something.

"I didn't do nothing," I said. "I swear."

They didn't believe me. I stopped switching the rock from hand to hand. "*Je lance la pierre,*" I announced.

They each took a bunch of seconds going over it before they both cracked up. When they stopped, Mike said, "Did you? Did you throw it?"

"*Je ne lance pas la pierre,*" I said. I lobbed it in the air, caught it in the right, caught it in the left. "I should've. I want to."

That sort of stopped the laughing. It was that they weren't sure what I was going to do and got scared, for real, again.

Gina was over there talking to my mom. It seemed like my mom was probably headed somewhere and got stopped. My mom couldn't stay still. They both stared at me for a couple of seconds when they saw me coming from a distance. Then I saw my mom say something else and take off and Gina was mad too and slammed into #2. My mom went through the back door of #1 and was waiting for me. "I told her I wasn't going to do anything."

I stood still, didn't even close the door all the way. She was so mad, I didn't want to say anything because anything was going to be wrong.

"I am so mad!" She got down a shot glass, poured herself some of the Cloyd's whiskey, and put it away in two swallows. "I don't know what to do!"

"Are you okay?"

"You don't have them still, do you? Do you have them?"

"No." I hated having to talk about the nudie magazines, I was still embarrassed and ashamed. And to my mom. Maybe doing this was worse even than the money.

"I can't believe you would steal," she said.

It wasn't worse. I had the inside jitters.

"I want to leave."

"Okay," I said. I started to move away from the door I was still standing close to.

"I mean *leave*. Leave, me entiendes?"

That's when we heard the truck tires rumbling the whole entire earth under us and when we both saw Bud see us through the window as he passed and he braked his shitkicker troca in the driveway and flew out and right to the door like he was gonna start a fight.

"Where's Cloyd?"

Neither of us could think of what to say fast enough.

"This is important. Where's he at?"

"I don't know, Bud," my mom said.

"And you don't know what job either," he said. Even when it was supposed to be about something else, he looked her up and down in a screwed-up sex way.

"Bud, I only know he's out there."

"You don't even know what job."

"You probably know more which jobs better than me."

His smile was not a smile. "No doubt that."

"What's wrong with you?" she said.

He was nodding her way, nodding the other away. "Niggers, that's what."

My mom went *ay ay* just enough.

"Don't you say *nothing* to me!"

"Hey!" I screamed. "Don't yell at my mom, fuckass!"

"What?" He didn't even try to fake-smile at me.

"Stop, stop now!" my mom shouted.

"You got something to say to me?" he said to me. "You got the hair to say jack-fuckin'-shit to me?"

"Stop!" my mom yelled.

"Go jerk off," he told me.

I came at him and he tossed me into a maple chair and the table. My mom was punching on him, but he kept her at arm's length, and I came back at him, surprising him with a good one to his nose and eye. He almost swung back at me but stopped and instead grabbed me and flipped me around. His strength tore at my shoulder muscles as he forced my arm behind my back with one hand and locked under my neck with his other, lifting my entire body. My mom still screaming at him, Bud rotated both of us into the living room, where that owl was into one of my eyes and the fish in the other. "I'm gonna let go, you hear

me?" and just like that we were moving forward again. "Don't
nothing, don't nothing," he said into my ear. His palms popped
my chest and he shoved me onto the couch. It was the first time
I saw a shotgun leaning by the front door next to it. I jumped up
again, so I'd be standing. I didn't care, I didn't care how much
he could beat me, I was going to find out.

She was screaming at him as she came to me and held on.
"Get out! You get out of here now!" She was pushing me back
now, holding me. "No, no!"

"Sick of Mexicans too," we heard him say.

"*GO!*" It was more a sound that would come off the boulevard, so loud it didn't seem like it was in the room.

The back door slammed behind him.

"I'm gonna hurt him," I told her. I don't know why those
eyes were in my vision still. "Let me go now, let me go."

"No," she said, "no." She was not crying, not one tear. She
let loose of me.

"I can get that asshole, I swear I can. With a bat if I have
to. Make him fucked up." I was looking at that shotgun.

"I know you can, I know, but no no no." She was too calm.
"No," she said. "Please, Sonny."

We listened to his truck tires squealing.

"We have to be smart," she said.

"What're you talking about?"

"I don't want you to do anything. Promise me."

"What are you talking about?"

"I'll be right back. I have to go. I have to. But I'll be right
back, as soon as I can."

I didn't know what she was saying or what I should do.
"What?" That wasn't the right word.

"I know you're a man now," she said. "Please, Sonny," she
said, "I have to go, and you have to promise me."

"Mom, I don't understand."

"I have to go. I'll be right back. Don't do anything. Promise me! Please."

The glass windows at Alley Cats were busted out and plywood was already up. The glass front doors were cracked too. It was open for business still, but Mr. Zúniga was too much not talking and too much about cleaning up. And no customers, not the regulars either. Only one man, Mr. Cervantes, who wasn't saying nothing.

"I don't know, muchachito," Mrs. Zúniga said. "It is hard. If we don't get the people, I don't know what we going to do."

Mr. Zúniga hadn't turned on the alleys and she didn't know if he would, or when, and it wasn't like she was planning to ask him.

"Ay, maybe it is just another day or two, nothing else."

I ordered only what she said she had, which was a hamburger and beans. She couldn't even make french fries.

"Why did they come here?"

"I don't have not one idea," she said. "We didn't do nothing against them. They don't visit us here very often, you already know, but we don't say nothing when they do. The neighbor, who sells the liquors next door, he is a Greek who, you understand, maybe it was because of the way he speaks bad about them. But the black people, they never come here, you already know that."

"They did it driving by?"

"It seems, yes, because they live so close, right there."

"Last night, after that thing across the street?"

"When we weren't down here, after we already went to sleep. We found it like this. And now we are scared. He doesn't want to leave here, and he doesn't want to stay."

"He's afraid of tonight."

"It's what they say, it's what is on the news."

Mr. Zúniga didn't even want money from me. That was a good thing, because I didn't know I didn't have enough on me.

The Cloyd and my mom weren't in #1. Which meant something was up. Good for me though, for being alone, and I didn't want it to change for a while, a few minutes anyways. Maybe after I rested on the bed a little. I wanted . . . it wasn't that I wanted to go back home like I used to. That was before, candy and comics down the pants. Though this room with the bed wasn't mine and I didn't want it, maybe because I'd been having my sleep on it long enough anyways, it was mine enough, comfortable, like the rock was mine.

First I went to the corner and pulled it up and counted what I had. Even after I been putting more bucks in, almost all gone, too much. I was going through it. All I needed to do was lie about my age and maybe I could get a job. I reached for the scout book and pulled it off the shelf, and I fanned out the hundreds and counted them. I never looked at them before, not really. I counted because I wanted to touch them, even if it made them more like paper and not money and not worth what I did. But money was a paper that made colors even in the dark. It was like a mota high that passed straight in through my eyes and into the brain. But then also what it could do, what it was gonna do if I got popped for taking it. That was a poison. That part was getting me a little sick. Then I would go like, Fuck getting popped! Fuck getting sick about it! Fuck him, fuck them, I got it, I'm not gonna be fucked up.

It was more cash than I ever saw before, in my hands or anybody's or spread out in front of me anywhere, maybe even on TV. I liked playing with these bills because I wanted them to be mine and because I wished I knew what to do with them next. I kept staring like I would see something, or say when you're

listening to the radio and waiting for nothing and for something
at the same time and all you're really doing is listening and thinking outside the music.

Then I got an idea and looked it up. *Argent. L'argent.* It
worked, like it did every time, and I smiled!

It was dumb to have the bills out on the bed. It was dumb to be
touching them as much as I did. I stacked them and unstacked
them and fanned them out. I wanted to talk to them like they
had ears and talk about them in French. I moved them around
and poked at them on the checkered bedspread. And it was what
I was doing when I thought I heard someone close to the other
side of the door. I wasn't moving fast and that was stupid. I wasn't
even high and I was leaving the money there so long and I was
even telling myself I wasn't messing up, I didn't want to mess
up. I don't know how come I didn't get caught right then. I
couldn't even trust myself. Still, I guess I was quick enough because I dropped the French book over it all.

"I'm sorry I have to bother you," said Cloyd. His hair was
sweat-frazzled from being inside his work cap, flat here, stuck
out there, but he did take it off to talk to me. He was drunk, but
no glass in his hand. "I'm sorry. Can I come in? Are you busy?"
He looked at the French book.

He was already in and I wanted him to leave fast. He was
standing over the bed and I was afraid he would want to sit. I
had my hand on the French book, and under it my hands clutched
the bills except I also wasn't sure I had them all.

"I heard what happened. I heard and it wasn't right."

I nodded. "It's okay. I'm over it." Of course it wasn't and
I wasn't over it either. All I could think of was how to bust that
man up.

"Shouldn't of happened, shouldn't of." He shook his head
and then shook his head more.

But I swear he was wanting to pick up my French book. I wanted to see what he saw but I would not turn my head. I was feeling panicked, like one of the hundreds was flapping out.

"Is that that French?"

"Yeah."

He didn't shake his head, but he spent time wanting to. "Can I talk to you?" he said.

"Yes sir."

"We gotta talk. You don't have to call me sir."

"Sure, okay."

"It's about what's going on. Not just Bud. That was wrong. I'm sorry that happened."

"Like I said, I'll get over it," I said.

"Good. It's good you say that."

As he came closer to me, I got tighter. Though he wasn't looking at the French book, he was too close to it.

"That was bad, what happened. It was. He shouldn't of pushed you or hit you."

"He never hit me."

"Or threw you, because he could of really hurt you. You're all right, aren't you?"

I nodded, meaning, Hurry the fuck up. I wanted to stand up so bad. It was taking so long it ached.

"So you know what's going on out there, right? Outside? That's been a lot of it, for Bud. Not saying it excuses him. We're all just a little jumpy around here is all. And here's the thing. I don't want no trouble at my building. If it comes, I won't accept it. You understand, don't you?"

I nodded yes yes yes, every muscle in my body begging that this end. And now he was seeing the book again and he was going to say something but he stalled.

"Look, we gotta talk about protection. How we gotta protect our property." He started moving the other way.

I didn't jump up.

"You coming? Come with me. You can get back to that later, right? Can't you?"

"I'm coming." I checked out below with a glance faster than a fly's. No bills were showing. If the bed didn't move, I was okay. Much as I wanted to, I was more afraid to grab the money than leave it.

In the kitchen he got his glass of whiskey, and he swirled that cube. "We're in some dangerous times," he said out loud. I heard him say it from behind him. He pointed at the back door where a shotgun was leaning. It was not the one at the front door. I looked. That one was still over there too.

"Any of them come in, we're protected. You understand?" He gulped a swallow. He didn't look me in the eyes until he did. "You know how this weapon is?"

I didn't.

He picked it up. He made a couple moves and cracked it open and showed me red cartridges that slid in the barrels. "It's loaded. You get two shots. This here is the safety." He flicked it back and forth. "It's off now. This is on, this is off. I got one a these at each door. Probably we don't gotta use them. Probably we don't. If we do, I'll be here too."

I couldn't not take it when he gave it to me, and I was still feeling the money on my fingertips and seeing it in my mind, and all this weight was more like in somebody else's arms.

We both could hear police sirens—wasn't two, or three, or four passing on the boulevard, it was so many—and, after I gave it back, Cloyd leaned the shotgun back against the wall, close to the doorknob. It made us not want to talk anymore. It made me fidget. He downed the rest of the whiskey.

"I guess you don't know where your mom is either, do you?"

I didn't.

★   ★   ★

When I knew it was Mary's voice in the office I thought I could
get out of there, no talking, no seeing me. I opened the bedroom door so it was easier for me to hear. She was in there crying that Bud something, and that she was scared, and that the
riot out there, and money was missing. Which got me to hear
worse, you know? Cloyd was wasted by now 'cause he was already fucked up before she got there—he wasn't even talking to
her really, just like voice clearing. Once I heard him say he didn't
know where Sil was either. Mary was both in tears and kind of
screaming when a line of police cars made the glass of the front
window shake, and that killed those worries. They were burning rubber down the street outside, making for the boulevard
like shit was starting to blow out right on the nearest corner.
Cloyd screamed at me to get over there and turn on the TV like
he saw me standing and listening to them but he didn't, and
neither did she, so she went over and turned it on and then it
was TV news voices in the room too. I know he didn't see me.
He was all whiskeyed up. So right then I went to the back door
while he was there cuddling that shotgun and watching through
the front window, and she went back to crying into her hands
and sat saggy on his favorite couch.

I picked up my rock. The streets weren't wild, there was
nothing to see, but then there was the nothing, not even cars
cruising the boulevard, or just a few I could see going the other
way, and the police ones weren't there no more. A few people
were hanging at the World Motel, more like waiting, eyes
making loops looking, and more outside Copa de Oro, and then
I saw more people once I really looked around, leaning into
the shade of buildings, and then there were voices I could hear
that weren't nobody's I could see. Some voices were almost
yelling and like coming out of windows, and then I saw whites of
eyes squinting in shadows and like white teeth grinning at doors,

and when I got to Alley Cats—another window had been broken out, the glass with lines of surprise and pain—and the front door was locked with some yellowed lights on, dim and sad as Mr. Zúniga might be, in there near where the bar was and where Mrs. Zúniga should be cooking, but probably neither of them were around and I took off faster. It was a little run at first, on the wider sidewalk alongside the boulevard because there were no cars parked either. I was running okay, just running with an easy breathing, when the police car skidded and braked hard in front of me and the front wheels hopped up over the sidewalk. One of the police came on me so fast I couldn't see it happening yet, and when one policeman was going to take me down, I decided not to let him but my rock flew out of my hand right over there, I could see it. The other policeman was coming around the front end of their cruiser but behind him I saw people coming. He saw them in front of him too and he started screaming at them or maybe it was only to his partner, I couldn't say, I didn't hear really, because I was with this one who was pulling hard at my left arm and trying to kick my legs out from me to take me to the ground. I punched him hard in the face with my right hand, and then we dropped and were rolling at the curb, on the sidewalk and the street, and I saw that more people got around us now, mostly black people, and they weren't afraid and they were screaming at the policeman I was fighting and I felt the other one panting near me and they were both being loud but I didn't really hear nothing. In my eyes it was purple like in the morning sometimes when it's too early to be awake and too slow and I was mad *fuck you man fucking let me fucking go fuck off.* I was so not going to quit, and then some dude who to me was only black pants and a brown shoe that came inches to my face kicked the policeman hard in the neck and then there were more kicks and the police let up on me and as I jumped back up and everybody was cheering, I

saw the sticks and pipes too and they were drumming on the
police car and I let myself see over them too and I heard yelling but it wasn't in any language, though it probably was, but
I couldn't hear any words and I felt slow but went quick and I
got my rock and I ran.

"Ay, que puta madre, güey," said Joe.
    "Man," Mike said. "Man."
    I wasn't saying nothing else, just that I got away. I didn't
tell them that much in the first place. What I told them made
them not want to talk. I knew them enough to know how they
got. They weren't asking yet, though they really wanted to know,
and they'd ask non-stop later, like when, say, we were walking
home from school.
    "It's fucking crazy here," said Joe, making conversation out
of the uncomfortable.
    "I don't know what we're doing here," said Mike. "I'm
scared like a . . . I dunno, like—"
    "Like a girl," said Joe. "Like a girl in pink."
    "Well at least I'm not a girl," Mike said.
    "Well at least I'm not pink," Joe said.
    "You calling me a Commie?"
    "You're the one thinking this is good."
    "What are you guys doing here, man?" I asked.
    "Mom said we shouldn't," said Joe.
    "Our dad was like, if we don't go, we're more older than
him."
    "And we'd be maricones, don't forget."
    "He says like, get out and see if you daisies can pick some
daisies for your mom."
    "Can you believe that, Sonny? Our own dad, vato."
    "I didn't wanna go out, but yeah, it was like—well, it was
like having to get a job during summer."

"Like having to play football," said Joe. "He was like, are my sons male? If they don't want to go do any street violence, shouldn't they want to *see* it?"

"He thinks it's because of the glasses we wear, because of books and reading."

"I wanted to do what Mom wanted, myself."

"So we had to come," said Mike.

"Had to witness history," said Joe. "And now, que bueno que we can talk about getting our glasses all dirty."

"Yeah, reading can get you into tough, dangerous shit too, you know?"

"Viva la revolución!" Joe said.

"I dunno," Mike said. "So far only a few locos cussed out police cars."

"Revolt," Joe said to the two of us. "Fuck Whitey."

Mike shushed Joe and that started making a laugh.

"Mostly it's the black dudes we saw throwing bricks and bottles down the road, but we saw la chota chasing some brown vatos," said Mike. That made them both look at me for approval, wait a few seconds.

"Es buena onda, like a party, dude."

"You throwing any?" I asked.

"Cómo que no?" Mike said.

"Cómo que sí," Joe said. "We're too scared to throw a fart. I'm figuring we only gotta be here ten or fifteen minutes more so we can go back home and not get our butts kicked by our pops."

"Then we finally get to watch some TV."

"Watch this better on TV, verdad?"

"O mejor watch a sit-com."

"Revolt!"

"Yeah, tonight let's not even study, 'cause there's not gonna be any school tomorrow, right?"

They both cracked up over this.

★   ★   ★

I didn't see Pink hanging there across the street from Los Flores until I almost crashed into him. I was going over to what was the only car of his around, the Bel Air which he said was mine, so he couldn't have been there for it unless he changed his mind.

"My little brother. You doing any good?"

"I thought you moved out and . . . left your roommate in the suit to live there."

"Gotta be here, gotta wait." He rolled his head, frustrated. "Gotta goddamn wait."

We were both away from any streetlamps, close to the Bel Air. I was there to look into the picture window of #1 and Pink was too. The street was bigger than before, the building was smaller than before, so it was harder. We could see the TV set flicking on inside over at the right, and a stick of light, back there on the left, which was Cloyd's office, the door mostly closed, but we couldn't make out bodies inside.

"I don't want nobody to see me," I told him.

"They in there," he said. "They in there, little brother."

"Who?"

"They are. Your stepdaddy, he in there, don't you think?"

"Probably. You don't know?" I wanted him to tell me this so much I forgot I wondered what he was doing. "My mom? Did you see her?"

But he'd gone off into grumbling sounds, like he was fucked up. Not drunk messed up. High fucked up. And not mota either. And not only pissed-off messed up.

"You didn't see my mom in there?" I was seeing him but I don't think he was seeing me. He was saying something to himself. "You been here for a while, Pink?" I asked.

Like he'd been listening all along. "I been here, little brother.

I good goddamn been here and wanting not to. Motherfucker got me here waiting." He caught up with what he was saying and grabbed my shoulder, his big hand sweaty hot, making the blood rush up to it. "But it all be good, it's all good, we don't got nothing to worry, you know what I mean? It be all good, all of it gonna go good eventually."

I thought I saw someone in #1 at the window.

"You think they can see us? I don't want Cloyd to see me."

"They can't see us here," he said.

I backed up deeper anyways, toward a big tree with lots of leaves, and he did too.

"You see my mom in there?" I asked again.

"Can't see us," he said following me. "They don't see us."

When a light burst out from behind us and then against the glass across the street, we both dropped flat—it was flames jumping into the sky, maybe blocks away but so tall they hit up into the night above them and even reflected bright against the panes of #1. Voices went louder on the boulevard.

"Ain't this something? This is some fucking shit going on."

The door opened from #1 and we crouched more, stayed lower than the Bel Air's windows. By the time I let myself up to peek, the door was closed.

"Who was it?" I asked. "You see?"

Pink was talking to himself but not out loud.

"Cloyd's got shotguns in there next to the doors," I told him. "Took down his hunting rifles."

"That's just right," he whispered, shaking his head. "'Cause they just might wanna shoot at some black meat, like that."

I wanted to take off. Noisy as the street over there was, we seemed to be in a safe and quiet unseen darkness.

"Blue-eyed devil wanna kill him some niggerboys. Now you listen to me, you listen. He gonna use them guns. You understand? Might not be today or even next week. But he gonna. Now you listen to me. You be careful. You understand?"

Sirens were curling around from several directions; voices seemed to be dropping down onto us from the tree.

"I gotta get in there another way," I told him.

"You go on now. If I'm still here . . . well, goddamn, I better not still be here."

I probably wasn't making much sense either, so there was that. "Probably see you then."

"You keep them ears listening for me," he said. "You do that for me. Ears, brother, and you tell what they hear. We doing right, me and you. Ain't that right, little brother?"

When I saw I had the rock in my hand and that I'd been holding onto it like it was my doll, the words *ma chère* popped out of my head and, well, I started to smile and I wanted to laugh. And because of that, was that why I wanted to feel like it would all be good, like Pink was saying? That maybe he was right, whatever it was? *Peut-être. Peut-être* I understood what he said, *peut-être non. Vive la différence.* I was smiling so loud I should have been laughing with the twins.

The boulevard was working the air so fierce that landing screwy on the trash cans from the back fence didn't even make a dog bark, or I wasn't listening for one anyways. And it stunk like burning rubber everywhere, so that made it hard to hear too. Once I got my balance back, I kept sneaking in from the back of The Flowers, past Bud's truck. Even Tino's was there tonight, though not my mom's. I did not want to run into Cloyd, I did not want to. I tiptoed up the apartment stairs like I was in socks and for some reason fell over Josep's chair and it broke, I broke it, crumpled it like a toy. I stopped for only a second and felt sorry, but what could I do right then? It didn't seem to make no noise either, so then I went over and put my ear to Nica's window, lights on inside but no way with all the outside crazy could I even hear TV, so I just went on and knocked on it until I knocked on it harder and she bent the curtain and saw me and opened the door, already crying like she couldn't wait to see me or somebody.

"That I stole money," she said again.

I couldn't get it until she said it a couple more times.

"I didn't do that," she said. "I didn't do that."

I kept up asking because I couldn't believe it. I felt so bad. I never felt so bad.

"Sonny, I'm scared," she said, crying. "I didn't do that."

"You didn't do that," I said. "I know you didn't."

"But Margarito is very mad. He says that this man is going to make trouble for him and my mom. He doesn't have papers. My mom, she doesn't have the documents either."

"You gotta explain to me better what happened."

"Well he came over and told Margarito. He told him I stole money."

"From Number seven, that man?"

"The big man who is the husband of the woman with the cat. That one."

"That's not right," I told her. "You didn't do that."

"I don't know what I'm going to do. What can I do, Sonny?"

"It's that—well, I have to think of something," I told her.

"I want to leave here," she said, sobbing. "I want to go home, I want to go home. I am afraid of Margarito. That he is so mad at me and he will not stop. I am afraid. I am afraid of what he will do. Do you understand? I am afraid to stay here."

She was crying so fierce I was afraid she would wake up Angel.

"He's asleep." She didn't stop crying but she got up with me when I went to look in the bedroom. He was on the single bed he shared with her, naked except for a diaper. "I love him, it's not because of him, but I want to go home. I only want to go home now, Sonny."

We were back on the gold couch like I dreamed all the time, her body up against me, and I could see us in the mirror like I would always want to see us. I looked at us and I looked at us. Was the mirror real? Her tears wet me blue like a clean sky that never touched me before.

"Where could you go?" I asked her.

"Mexico," she said.

"But where? Do you have someplace to go there?"

"Xalapa," she said. "I can go there. It's Veracruz."

"Really?" I asked. "You have someone there? Family?"

She still sobbed, but without tears, nodding. She even looked at me straight into my guilty eyes, which she never ever did before. I flinched. I had to not look at her back, because that way maybe she would never know what she saw there. I wanted it to be as unclear to her as, like, English.

"But Angel," she said.

"He's not your baby," I said. "He has a mom, and it's not you."

She started crying and put her arms around me and she was crying even harder and I wasn't sure what else to do.

"Are you sure you want to go?"

She was nodding her head. "I don't like it here," she said. "I don't want to stay now."

I kissed her. She kissed me. We kissed. We kissed and kissed and there was almost nothing but me kissing her and her kissing me and kissing.

"I'll take you," I said.

She had no voice. Her breathing was more gasps, breaking in between sobs.

"If you want to go."

Her breathing was becoming air. She sat up. She breathed with her chest, sobs were fading.

"I have to come back. I have to take off. I'll be back though."

"Sonny?"

"You have to get ready. You have to bring everything you want."

I forgot about sirens and the streets and smoke too that made a taste in the mouth. Then there were shouts on the boulevard, so close they seemed close to the steps of The Flowers, though only silent ashes floated as much up as down, not even moths slapping any light on either side of Nica's, not Cindy's, not a creak from Mr. Josep's. No light on over in #7 or in #6 either, meaning, maybe, did Pink's roommate leave and did Pink leave too? If that was what he'd been waiting for. I went down wanting not to touch the steps—I probably could've stomped and nobody'd hear nothing. Dead lightbulbs kept it black inside Gina and Ben's so I pushed against the wall to the back door of #1 until I decided not to go in that way once I was at the edge of Cloyd's office—those lights were made of daylight. I turned back. I wanted to run but I only walked fast and I got to the other side of the building where the weeds were still jungle and itchy through my clothes and I made it over to the window where the bedroom I slept in was. Being expert with screens, I took this one off and started to climb in the open window when a lightbulb from the old people across clicked on and I heard their window opening, which scared the piss out of me so I pressed down onto the bedroom floor. I held still and grabbed the rock I'd thrown onto the bed. I kept myself there and I heard them talking from their window but there were sirens and other voices out there and now I could also hear voices in the living room of #1 too. I think they heard the noise I made but the TV volume was high. It was Bud getting closer, saying I don't know what, and Mary wasn't talking so I could hear. It was so much TV riot news. Under me from the floor I felt steps getting closer and then I could even sense his ugly eyes check out this bedroom, but since he wasn't looking for me he didn't see me clutching the rock. I had it ready. I peeked, and he was carrying a shotgun to the bathroom. He left the bathroom door open while he filled the bowl. I did not move except a little backward, more behind the bed in case he came in again. After he flushed, just like I guessed, he opened the bedroom door again, but he didn't see the window open or the screen off, maybe since the neighbor across already turned off the light. He left the door like it was and in the kitchen said *You're outta beers, Cloyd*. I stayed still I don't know how long until his voice went a couple times in the living room and then I took all the hundreds I'd put back in the boyscout book and folded them and put them in my front pocket and I lifted the carpet because I decided to get the other money too and I rolled that up for the other pocket and I went back to the window. I tossed the rock a little to the side, where it thudded into the grass. I hopped up and swung myself over and down until I had to drop. I didn't land perfectly. I had to catch myself with my hands and I hit sideways and on my shoulder and the rest of my body came behind that, and the tall grass made like bamboo crackled, not like some cat passing through but more some dude like me breaking in. As I fished around for my rock, that neighbor's light came on again and I heard the woman making those words of hers I didn't understand, but once I finally found my rock I just took off out of there because, though I didn't see her, I think she saw me or someone, because she was shouting out the window. I ran through the grass straight to the back of the complex, and when I got to that cinder-block fence I somehow climbed it and got over with that pinche rock in my hand! I ran through another apartment complex out that street and I kept running. At first I thought I would head away from the boulevard, but no, I turned that way instead.

I crossed over to the other side of the boulevard, wanting more distance between me and The Flowers, and I stopped where the ranchera music at La Copa de Oro made like clearer air because the rest of the boulevard was smoked. Only a few people and voices moved between buildings and the sirens looped close, for a fire you could smell: was it right over there or just a little down from that one, that one where the light seemed too hot? The money in my pocket was what was burning me, like it needed the water hoses.

At La Copa's doors it wasn't like there were people drinking inside, only a couple of dudes with bottles, more where they lived, not partied, and I was figuring my shit out near that door when Cindy, strapped in by a black halter top, was in my face. She was squeezed everywhere else too, like about to burst, and all of it at me, scooting and bouncing sideways and back, her hands and feet in pissed-off rhythm. It was almost like she'd come out of this Cadillac on the boulevard that'd been fucked over, not totally in a lane but not parked even close to the curb either and the tires on curbside were gone so it was sitting on its drums. The window glass on all sides was crashed out or smashed in and so were the headlights and taillights.

"Fucking ass!" she said.

It was like when you first wake up and you don't even want to open your eyes.

"I can't believe you would be an asshole," she said.

"Cindy?"

"And I told him."

"What?"

"I told him it was you. That's why. You asshole. Now I can't be there."

"You're fucking crazy."

"Yes!"

"Are you stupid?"

"We'll see who's stupid!"

Then she saw the rock in my hand—maybe I lifted it because I got fucking mad hearing her, or maybe I was protecting
my body and forgot it was in my hand—and she jammed across
the street over to the World Motel, where dudes started whis-
tling for her or at her or who knows what.

Ma chère, I whispered to the rock, *ma chère pierre.* It didn't make
me laugh doing that, didn't make me smile even, but almost was
good too. I was off the boulevard and was near the tracks and
trying to get my head back to Nica, even with the money straining
my pockets, so heavy I had to keep pulling up my pants. I rested
my butt on the tracks, which was like sitting in the middle of
nothing. Nothing nowhere and nobody. And soft too, kind of
like if it was soft lawn, even if my nalgas were on a steel rail. I
put *la pierre* down on the gravel and this time I did get a smile
out of me: My rock was like the biggest, baddest *pierre* there.

I was taking in some no-riot air from the sky, the best world
peace anywhere, what wasn't pushing on my sides but was straight
up there, where nothing messed up could be happening. My back
rested on the gravel, between the wooden ties, where I was wishing Nica . . . no, not here in this greasy shit with me staring up!
That's the best I had? She had to go, she had to go. When all I
got is space above, which I can't even hold, and that's only when
nobody's around? That's sorry. Nobody else who sat on the
tracks—which wasn't even like nobody anywhere because there
were suspicious dudes on the sidewalk on that side, shuffling way
fast like something was up, and over here a low car dragging along
like it was bobbing one shoulder, then the other, and another

pobre fucked-up one squeaking on this other side. Nobody and none of them saw me, even when I might be a dead body on the tracks. Or it didn't seem like they did or they didn't care if they did. Which was what I fucking wanted. At least the sky right above wasn't stinky gray even if gunky ashes were snowing. But watch: on top of the silhouette of a fat tree, watch, so pretty, see how really pretty! It was the color of orange juice, which she knew I loved. It was like a beautiful flower on a woman maybe in Sevilla where Nica wanted to go, like beautiful clothes on her too. She never once went out of #4, never, and once she left, you know, she wouldn't see an orange like this ever again, not tonight and not tomorrow and who knew how long this was going to go on. Nica could say to her family and her people, about when she left anyways, like when she got back to her pueblito, she'd be able to say how me and her were on these railroad tracks, me and her all by ourselves on a romantic night, our feet dug into the gravel like it was beach sand, the nightsky sweet like love and pure happiness, and above a silhouette tree there was the most beautiful orange sunset glow, which was really a building on fire during a riot. I was smiling again. It was like I was talking in French when I was thinking it, like I'd said *oui*. I meant yes though. It was yes!

Once I finally got all of it figured out—sure, every little cosita, dude—I was only giving my brains a little break when the sickie's car pulled up. I did not want to believe my eyes, could not believe my eyes that this freak was aiming his perv eyes at me and kind of showing his yellow teeth too. Until, I dunno, just like that I settled with it. Good with it even. So I stood. Like a dude, I stood up. I dusted pebbles off me and shook out some bigger ones stuck wherever and I crunched them with my shoes, fanning riot smoke that was clogging the air. The sickie was idling, saliva pooling up behind a quivering corner of his mouth.

He wasn't sure if he should hit the pedal or pull his body away or what when I got close. It was like he was shifting from the driver's side to the passenger's. He was twitchy, is what I'm saying. It was like, even though his windshield was already spider-webbed from that other time, he was thinking sickie. 'Course it had to be *ma chère* that freaked the dude some. And still he didn't take off. He let his head and neck muscles grip those parts of his body harder as he exposed the front of his teeth—that meant he was cool with what was happening.

"So," I said, "what is it with you?"

"What do you mean?"

"I mean what the fuck is wrong with you, mister?"

"Why are you asking this?" he said.

"Are you joking?"

"Why would I joke?"

"Marrano pig."

"What're you?" he said.

"Don't you know?"

"A little punk," he said. "A big punk."

He was grinning until he saw my rock going from my right hand to the left and back. He saw the rock good. It was a good rock, no doubt. The best. And I almost did it right then, and he thought I was gonna do it too, because he went to his shift stick to get in gear and the whole car jerked for him when it did but he stopped. He relaxed. He shifted back to PARK.

"What is it with you, mister?" I said.

He laughed, if that's what you would call it. I maybe'd call it a gurgle. I felt the rock on my palm and my fingers, light, heavy, just right. Sometimes when my bowling was off, I'd hold and weigh the bowling ball to make it more comfortable in my hand, get myself more connected. Make time slow up, smaller in space, get closer to the lane, more private. It'd be when I wanted to get a spare if I'd been missing them. Like once you get spares, then it's strikes again.

I don't know why I wanted to know, or what. It was more like the rock wanted to know. Right? Because here I was, for the very last time ever.

Every bit of color everywhere around was gone. The orange bloom was snuffed by smoke gone to the shadows now, which is nowhere, and it was only another fucked-up night.

"So what is it with you?" I asked him.

"What is it you want to know, son?"

"I don't know, man," I said.

"Just ask. We can talk about it."

"We can talk about it, huh?"

"Sure. Of course."

"Like you're just this good dude . . ."

"Absolutely."

". . . and we should talk."

"You understand."

"You say I understand."

"Yes. You do."

"And after we talk. . . ?"

"After we talk," he said, "we can take a ride."

"Eso es. Take a ride."

"If you want."

"So," I said, "you're only some old sick fuck, aren't you?"

"Why are you saying that?"

"Oh and you don't know."

"You're standing here. You're talking to me."

I nodded, I was nodding.

"So I must not be that bad."

"It's not that."

"It's not?"

"No, man. I just never get to ask. I never freaking understand people like you."

"What don't you understand?"

"Why you can't leave me alone."

He didn't say piss.

"You keep following me. You do, right?"

He nodded.

"Why won't you leave me alone?" I wasn't even looking
at him. He didn't have nothing, or I didn't hear nothing. "Why
do you do that? You know, follow me and shit. How can you
be you?"

"You want me to go away?"

I hesitated. Because I didn't know the answer. I wanted the
fuck to go, but I didn't want him to go. It wasn't good that I
didn't. I was kind of scaring myself. I knew this was it, this is
what I expected all along. What I wanted even. You know? But
it's that I didn't want to be scared of nothing.

"So you don't," he said.

He was so fucked up, man. Dude, the dude was fucked and
he was a sickie. He was way past fucked up. Fuck him. You
know?

"Yeah, that's it, I want you to stay."

He didn't believe me. The dude did not believe me. Or he
did. Or finally he did. Or it's that I'd been backing up. I didn't
realize I'd been taking steps backward. He was going for the shift
again and the engine was getting louder and so I threw the rock
hard, right at his head. He was rolling up the driver's window as
I threw the rock and it smacked at the glass but it took off inside
too and I didn't see how bad it got him or how much because
the engine got going, the car rolled forward fast and its wheels
even turned, and it was staying in the middle of the street until
it hit a parked car. Which meant, I threw the rock and it was
like everything went bright red.

* ★ *

I might have been walking now and I might have been running. White was coming out from the back of my head where the eyes saw and where the tongue tasted and the ears heard and white was inside my legs and in my feet and on my hands and the words and the shapes and lines in my mind and it pulsed my heart and was my blood. It wasn't like the soupy black that dreams played in, the black that everything pushed through and out of like Josep's river. This white was like a headlight before it hit on a street and what came at it dissolved. It was white but not the color white. It was inside me but there was no behind it, no where it came from, and it was coming through me. It shut down darkness and I didn't need to see. I was so far away on the street, in the night, I didn't need to hear or taste either. My legs were moving and they were in the white. My arms were moving and they were in the white, and when my hands rubbed my face, making sure, the white coated me like sweat.

At the driveway I turned without looking into the picture window of #1 and I went up the stairs. I was like way up there, not touched, not touching.

"You got all? That you need?"

I saw her blue tears in the gold-framed mirror.

"No," I said. "You can't, you can't. Not now."

She stopped herself. Like that. She bent away from the mirror and picked up two athletic bags. I got to their phone, where I called the emergency number—it's what I had figured out to do. I told the operator there was a baby alone at the address, in a building called Los Flores, apartment #4, and I hung up. As soon as I did that, it seemed like another wrong thing, but it was done too and this was all dreaming.

She followed me to my Bel Air. Out on the boulevard, voices were whooping and they were more than fire trucks or fires or police and they almost made us stop walking, Nica and me together, like first-date-close together, almost holding hands. I even opened her side of the car for her and then we were both inside it together—nothing like this had ever happened. I didn't even remember about apartment #1, I didn't look, I didn't remember it already. It wasn't there. It didn't exist. She wasn't crying and she kept watching me. Into the eyes, carefully. She looked and she saw me and then she looked out, at the boulevard, at the voices and fires and police. It was what she was leaving, what I was taking her from, where she wasn't going to live. She looked at me again. Like I was good. She made me feel like I was good too. Maybe she was talking and I couldn't hear her because the engine kicked right over and was under my foot. I had the Bel Air in first and I let out the clutch and it jerked up and down and bounced horrible. But there were no cars in front of me close and I steadied it and got into second and maybe I didn't go fast but I didn't want to go fast. I mean I did but I couldn't. At least we were moving, and that is what I wanted, and nothing like this had ever happened before, nobody like us, nobody but us, and nothing like this ever. I only knew one way to get to the bus depot and so that's how I was going, no matter, and I turned right. Thank God no cars were around because I couldn't make it stop and then I turned again, no cars around again, and then I was at the boulevard where I pushed the brake pedal and the clutch to the floor. The Bel Air stalled. The boulevard was empty of cars except the way we weren't going, where it was fire trucks and lots more people around them. Nica might have been talking and not only crying. I started the Bel Air right up again, and it jumped a little less this time when I let out the clutch, and on the boulevard I shifted to second. That's when something hit the side of the car and more started hitting it too. People were coming off the sidewalks as I drove and then the back side window got busted, and Nica screamed but very far away from my ears. I was afraid to shift and the engine was roaring like it would explode while lots of rocks and chunks were pounding the car on every side and black people came at us to beat it with sticks and fists as we passed them. Nica screamed when a bat splashed into the windshield and she held her head like the outside was dripping on her. I held on to the steering wheel and once we got past this, in front of us was a stack of police cars. No man, I just turned the wheel around them and let them yell at me too and didn't stop. I thought for sure they would follow me for real. I was driving steadier, straighter, waiting for them. This stretch of boulevard was empty: no one, no cars, every business closed, no police in front or behind. I kept the same speed. I was getting better even if I was driving slow, and I gripped the wheel hard, afraid to shift out of second gear. When I stopped at a light I left it in second gear and let the clutch out from there. Nica was sounding like she'd been hurt but she wasn't hurt. I could stop at the signals now. I could make the turns now too, and I'd learned the clutch and brakes.

And then I saw we were there, that I did it! I braked, I turned off the engine in a parking slot, and we could see inside the small lit-up depot. There were two older people with taped suitcases and cardboard boxes sitting in the waiting area. There was a uniformed clerk behind a counter. Nica was still sobbing but it was weak. I think I probably was shaking.

"I don't know what I'm going to do," she said after we sat there breathing again. "I don't know what I'm going to do."

"You're going back home."

"But you aren't going?"

"Me? With you?"

She slid over to me. She pushed against me, and her body made me ache.

"You want me to go with you?" I asked.

"I thought you were going too," she said.

I didn't think of it. I never thought of it before.

"Why aren't you going?" she asked.

I didn't know. I kissed her eyes, wetting my lips. She rubbed her head into me and that made a color I'd never seen before and I didn't know what to say for so long I think because of that. "Where do you go again?"

"Xico. Above Xalapa."

What did I know?

"Sonny, I don't have any money."

"No no, you have money. You don't have to worry. I have money, it's your money."

The people inside, the couple waiting for the bus too, they were Mexicanos.

"I don't know exactly how you get there," I said, "only that you can take a bus from here."

We were against each other for so long in quiet that didn't exist. It was quiet no one anywhere had ever heard before, this never existed before, this was the first time ever.

"No," she said. It was her who didn't want to stop. "Come with me."

I pulled out the hundreds. "We have to put this away." She didn't even look. Maybe she was crying but there was only the tears. "Please," I said. She stopped like before and got one of the bags. "Do you have pants in there?" She found some and I put the ten hundreds in a pocket and folded the pants. "Don't forget." She didn't ask what it was or why and it was that she didn't care. I opened the car door and she came out my side. I wanted this to go fast now, I wanted this part over.

Inside the depot, so many cities in Mexico listed on a handwritten board. I took her here, but I really didn't know anyone could really get to Veracruz on a bus.

"I can't believe we're still running the schedule," the clerk said, "but the driver's en route here now and then he goes to downtown where you gotta make a transfer. Guess the world ain't gonna just stop."

"Just one," I said, paying him.

"You get it right over there. Can't miss it. It's as big and noisy as a bus."

We went back to the car and I gave her the rest of the other money I had.

"I wish that you would go with me," she said, "because I love you, Sonny."

We were kissing and I felt sick with want, but as good as I felt, I didn't have anything else to tell her. I didn't know enough Spanish to say more, or anything really, but I didn't know the English now either.

"*Je t'aime*," I said. And it made me smile. 'Cause I didn't know what else to say or how, and that's what finally came to me. It didn't make me laugh but it did make me feel better, and it made her smile so much. It always worked, no matter what!

I asked her, "*Est-ce que tu m'aimes?*" and she laughed hard! "It means *Do you love me?*" I explained to her. "So, *Tu m'aimes?*" I asked her again, and she laughed and giggled all over me.

"*Te amo, Sonny*," she told me. "*Ya te quiero.*"

I loved kissing her and I wanted her and we kissed and, better than that, she kissed me on the lips, on the cheeks, on my neck. She wanted to kiss me and be next to me. She wanted me to touch her everywhere and in every way. I didn't want her like that, as much as I did, and anyways then there was the bus and its loud air blowing and sucking and its horn and squeaks and bells and stairs.

Once Nica stepped up, I rushed back to the Bel Air and watched the bus roar off, sunlight rising and its rays making little twisting rainbows, all the colors that ever were inside the broken lines of the cracked windows. Maybe if I drove better I could keep it close for a while. Instead it got smaller and turned, gone, was already not here—and that was it except that I could have told her I loved her better. I said it in French, it's that I only said it in French, you know, and I should have told her so she knew I meant it. I should have told her in Spanish. I just should have told her, no French smiling through me. No. *Non.* That made a smile. I liked that I smiled and that I wasn't scared. What I wanted was to feel like I could smile, just like that, anytime I ever wanted, especially when I went back there. *Je t'aime,* Nica!